IN TURKISH WATERS

A Common Smith V.C Story

Spring 1922. The Greek army is retreating from Turkey and Kemal Attaturk, the Turkish dictator, intends to have their convoy sunk. The resulting chaos will help a defeated Germany and Russia unless someone intervenes. 'C', the mysterious head of the British Secret Service knows that Britain is already far too stretched, the French have their own affairs and America has retreated into isolation. As always, in such situations, he turns to young Common Smith V.C and his gang on *Swordfish*. Against all odds, Smith and the *Swordfish* fight their way to Alexandria, where their real mission will begin...

IN TURKISH WATERS

IN TURKISH WATERS

by

Charles Whiting

Magna Large Print Books
Long Preston, North Yorkshire,
BD23 4ND, England.

British Library Cataloguing in Publication Data.

Whiting, Charles
    In Turkish waters.

    A catalogue record of this book is
    available from the British Library

    ISBN   0-7505-1818-9

First published in Great Britain 1994
by Severn House Publishers Ltd.

Copyright © 1994 by Charles Whiting

Cover illustration © G Haylock by arrangement with
Allied Artists

Published in Large Print 2002 by arrangement with
Eskdale Publishing

Magna Large Print is an imprint of Library Magna Books Ltd.

Printed and bound in Great Britain by
T.J. (International) Ltd., Cornwall, PL28 8RW

'Never trifle with Johnny Turk.
He's a dangerous beast.'

Winston Churchill, 1915

THE TURKISH SITUATION, 1922

Author's Note

'*Ethnic cleansing*' is the buzz word of the 1990s. Right across the world, from Asia, through the former Soviet Union, right up to Western Europe's doorstep in Jugoslavia, tribe massacres tribe, creed slaughters creed. Already, in the year in which I write, thousands of innocent men, women and children have been killed or forced ruthlessly out of their homelands.

But there is nothing new about ethnic cleansing. Over seventy years ago now, with the breakup of the German, Russian and Turkish empires, the same terrible thing was happening. Race murdered race, religion slaughtered religion. Hundreds of thousands of innocents were tortured, starved, forced from their homes at gunpoint. Chaos and cruelty reigned supreme in many parts of Southern Europe and Asia.

In his diary for February 1922, Lt de Vere Smith, known to the popular press of the time as 'Common Smith, V.C.' noted: '"C" [he meant the mysterious head of the British Secret Service] says if we don't succeed in this new mission, a terrible thing will happen. Thousands of Greek men, women and children will perish! We've got to go at it, the whole hog – *totus porcus.*'

Common Smith, V.C. was a typical product of his class and time. He was not given to expressing much emotion, and could even indulge in that awful public schoolboy's pun – *totus porcus* for the 'whole hog'. All the same he carried out his orders to the letter, saving the lives of countless Greek civilians in Turkey that spring.

Naturally nothing was ever publicized on the matter; it was too hush-hush. Not even the standard histories of the Turco-Greek War of those years mention the Common Smith mission. Even today when both Turkey and Greece are Britain and America's allies, it is exceedingly difficult to find out the details of that daring mission by a handful of bold young Englishmen – and one Scot – which saved the lives of so many Turkish Greeks.

But there is one small clue which still reveals the gratitude of those Greeks, whom Smith saved, and their descendants. That Greek shipping, once owned by a survivor of 1922 a certain Mr Aristotle Onassis, still regularly names one of its ships *Common Smith V.C.* Few today know why. Now for the first time *In Turkish Waters* tells the full tale of that daring rescue mission which saved the Greeks and perhaps prevented yet another great war in the Near East.

C. Whiting, Withernsea, Autumn 1993

PROLOGUE TO ACTION

'The Greeks must be cleared from Turkey, no matter how! We Turks must prove to the world that we are no longer "the sick man of Europe".'

Kemal Ataturk, the Turkish dictator, 1932

They raped the women prisoners first.

The Greek women were from the city, not peasants. They wore cotton drawers and the waiting soldiers had to pull them off. They did so, without too much violence. They were peasants from Anatolia and they took even their sexual pleasures stolidly and without apparent enjoyment. On command they began raping the women in the wet mud, standing patiently in line waiting their turn. Their officers watched, smoking moodily. The women were Christian, infidels. They would rather go to the disease-raddled whores in Istanbul than have anything to do with women who ate pork.

'*Lutfen?*' the German asked the Turkish colonel, who stood there in the thin bitter rain, smoking and staring at the bodies of the dead Greeks in the mud. He held up his camera so that the Turk would understand what he wanted.

The Colonel, his swarthy face set and intent, nodded wordlessly.

The German stepped over a body half-buried in mud and focused his camera. He wanted to get the expression on the Greek woman's face as the Turkish *askari*, his trousers around his ankles, gave it to her. He didn't particularly like what was happening. But the Chief wanted this sort of thing and it was his job to provide it.

The woman's face was contorted, her spine arched, mouth gaping open as she screamed and screamed. She must have known it was useless to scream, but they always did. She would continue to do so even when the fourth and fifth Turk had had her until she could scream no longer. Then she'd just lie there passively, perhaps crying a little in silence, letting it happen. The German had seen it all before. It was always the same. He wiped the raindrops off the lens and started taking his pictures, trying to get a shot of the cross around the Greek woman's neck before one of the *askaris* ripped it off and stole it. The Turkish dictator Ataturk hadn't paid them for months. This was the only reward they got for the dangerous lives they led, rape and loot.

After a while they finished with the women. They left them pressed into the mud, the semen trickling down the inside of their thighs, sobbing quietly. Now it was the turn of the men. Suddenly the dark faces of the *askaris* became animated for the first time. What was to be done now really appealed to them, the German photographer could see that. It was partly the ritual. They had been doing it all the time ever since the Greeks had started retreating down the

Karagatch road out of Adrianople as the Greeks called it. He'd got used to the daily rapes, even when the Greek women involved were big with child. But, he told himself, feeling a little sick at the thought of what was to come, he'd *never* become accustomed to this.

The first prisoner was brought up. He was a big strapping *Evizone*, the skirts the élite Greek regiment wore, dirty with mud, his white stockings torn and ripped. His face was black and blue with the blows the Turks had rained upon him after capture – one eye was almost closed – but still he was defiant. As he passed the silently smoking Turkish colonel, he spat in the mud at his feet. The Turk affected not to notice. *He* knew how quickly the Greek infidel's defiance would vanish in just a moment.

Five of the *askaris* got hold of the Greek. One put his foot behind him while another pushed from the front. He went down easily into the mud, helpless with his hands tied behind him. Still his handsome face blazed with defiance. Perhaps, the German told himself, as he raised the big, boxlike camera once again, he was an officer. Greek officers were usually very brave; their men, on the other hand, were normally rabble, who ran at the first sight of a Turk.

Up the road the guns were barking again. Obviously the Greeks were attempting to make yet another stand. The German told himself, they wouldn't have much luck. Their army, which had set out so confidently to conquer Turkey the year before, had been soundly beaten. Athens was just playing for time in the hope that Britain and France might intervene once again and save them.

'Pull his legs apart,' the *Iman* commanded in a thick voice.

Two of the *askaris* tugged at the Greek's legs. Another ripped off his skirt and stockings. He was naked underneath. Desperately the Greek twisted and turned in the mud, the raindrops beating down on his tortured, contorted face. He knew now what the Turks were going to do with him. To no avail! There were too many of them holding him.

The *Iman*, who led the company in prayers, but who was also the company butcher whenever they managed to loot some meat or killed a captured animal, advanced on the writhing *Evizone*, knife at the ready.

The German focused the camera, his weather-beaten face suddenly very pale, his stomach churning already with revulsion.

The Greek tried to kick out. The *Iman* dodged the kick easily. He bent and took hold of the Greek's penis with his left hand. There was a look of savage pleasure on his bearded face as he did so. The photographer wondered if he was some kind of pervert. Many of them were; it was common knowledge in the Turkish Army. He laid the sharp edge of the blade against the Greek's organ.

The Greek screamed in terror.

The *Iman* raised the blade and with one tremendous cut sliced off both penis and testicles. Blood gushed upwards in a scarlet arc, drenching the *Iman's* hand. Deliberately the Turk raised his hand to his mouth and tasted the Greek's blood, while the man writhed and howled on the ground, a great gory scarlet wound where his organ had been.

The *Iman* held up the organ for the grinning *askaris* to see. They clapped their hands with delight like children, their dark eyes sparkling. The *Iman* gave that cruel smile of his. Contemptuously, he tossed the organ between the spread legs of one of the raped Greek women, saying in Turkish, '*Cok gusel* – pretty eh, whore?'

The photographer took his shot, as the Greek died before his eyes, the hot bile welling up in his throat as he did so. Next to him, the Turkish commander threw away his cigarette. It hissed and then went out in the wet mud. He raised his cane and slashed down across the thin shoulders of the nearest *askari*. 'Enough!' he cried, raising his voice over the thunder of the guns. 'You've had your fun. Now we march.' He beckoned down the road with his cane. Tiny figures in white skirts were running across the road, followed by grey puffs of smoke. 'More *Evezoni*,' he snapped. 'More to be killed.'

Slowly – the peasants were always slow – the *askaris* formed up for the attack, kicked and lashed by their officers and NCOs, who knew that the *askaris* had hides as thick as the oxen they had once used to plough their fields back in their remote homeland.

While they did so, the German took his photograph. He nodded to the Colonel. This would make his last picture.

Wearily the Colonel sighed. He drew his big pistol out of its wooden holster and clicked off the 'safety'. The German raised his camera. The Colonel bent. He said something to the dying *Evizone* in Greek. The Greek stopped writhing and moaning. It was as if he accepted his fate.

The Colonel grunted and placed the muzzle of the big Mauser at the Greek's left temple. The Colonel's right knuckle whitened as he took first pressure. The German focused on the execution. He could see the Turkish colonel didn't like doing this. On the ground, the Greek closed his eyes. The raindrops trailed down his cheeks like cold tears.

A dry click. A sharp bang. A whiff of white smoke. The sudden stink of burnt cordite. Startlingly the top of the Greek's head flew off. A pool of red jellied gore through which the shattered skull bones gleamed like polished ivory. The Greek women began to wail and shriek.

With another sigh, the Colonel placed the smoking pistol back in its holster. The German went over to the wet-gleaming bushes, retched horribly and began to vomit. His chief back in Germany had yet another atrocity to stir up the world. But at the moment all he could think of was bringing up the hot rasping vomit.

Slowly, ponderously, the infantry began ploughing through the mud once more, heading for the sound of the guns. Behind them the dead started to stiffen in the cold…

ONE

A MISSION IS PROPOSED

'America will send neither ships nor men to help the Greeks. They are on their own and the Turks will show them no mercy ... unless *we* do something.'

C to Lt Smith, V.C.

1

C's square hard face flushed hard and the monocle popped out of his left eye. 'All right, Common Smith, just you look at 'em,' he snapped in that gruff, no-nonsense manner of his, as if he were still back on the quarterdeck of the dreadnought he had once commanded before the war.

Common Smith, V.C. took the first photograph in his hand and looked at it. Next moment he wished he hadn't. It showed a naked woman – at least the bottom half of her was naked – lying in a field of what appeared to be corn, with a bottle thrust deep into the dark patch between her legs.

C, the head of the British Secret Service, watched Smith's face for his reaction as he sat there behind the desk which had once belonged to Nelson. To his right in that rooftop London office which could only be entered by secret staircases and disguised lifts, there was a smaller table. It was littered with maps, models of aeroplanes and a row of bottles and test-tubes, which suggested chemical experiments. The evidence of scientific investigation always seemed to the young officer, studying those horrifying photographs, to heighten the overpowering atmosphere of strangeness and mystery that he always associated with C's headquarters.

Reluctantly Smith looked at the second photograph. It showed a grinning Turkish soldier with what appeared to be a naked baby speared at the end of his bayonet – and the baby was still wriggling. Hastily he dropped the photograph and felt he was going to be sick.

C nodded. 'Yes, I know,' he said, 'the abominable Turk – at his worst, what?'

'But, but,' the young officer stuttered miserably. 'What's going on? Why…'

'Why have I asked you to come here again after eighteen months since I last saw you in this place, eh?' C's voice was hard and incisive.

'You mean, sir, you have a show for us?' Despite his wretched feeling, Common Smith's voice was suddenly full of hope. He had been on the beach now ever since 1920 and the business with the Poles.* He was bored as was the rest of the crew of his beloved *Swordfish*. 'The chaps would find that absolutely ripping, sir. I can assure you of that.'

C smiled coldly at the young officer's use of the word 'ripping'. He told himself that despite his Victoria Cross and a chestful of

*See C. Whiting: *The Baltic Run* for further details.

28

other decorations for gallantry, Common Smith was really only a boy. The war had forced him to become a man – *quickly!*

'Ripping isn't quite the word for it, Smith,' C said thoughtfully, and tapped the bowl of his pipe on his wooden leg which was his habit when he had something difficult to explain. 'Now Johnny Turk isn't all that bad. He's a damned good soldier as we learned to our cost back in '15 at Gallipoli, eh.'

The handsome young soldier with the clear blue eyes nodded his agreement but said nothing.

'At the moment Johnny Turk's main concern is to get the rest of the Greek Army out of his country. Those photographs are just propaganda, aimed I suppose at stirring up the world against the Turks. Who takes 'em and who sends them to newspapers all over the West, I don't know. No matter.' He tapped the pipe against his wooden leg again. It was said that he had amputated the leg himself with a penknife after a bad car crash behind German lines in the recent war. Smith thought it was possible. He could imagine the Empire's greatest spy-master being capable of anything – and everything. 'Soon the Turk will have run the Greek Army – it's a mere rabble now – out of his country. Then, and there can be no doubt of that, Johnny Turk'll clear all remaining Greek civilians out of Turkey. In his eyes they are infidels, Christian dogs, as I believe the Turks call them in his own language.'

C rose to his feet and walked across to the big wall map that decorated the back of the office. 'Come over here and look at this.'

Obediently Smith followed and looked at the map.

C poked the stem at the section depicting Turkey. 'There's Istanbul. Over there is Smyrna. Now Smyrna has the main concentration of Turkish Greeks in the whole of the country. They're mainly engaged in the tobacco and dried fruits trades. Some of them have been there for generations, perhaps hundreds of years, ever since Turkey conquered Greece. Mostly they're pretty rich and control the country's main exports. As a result they are very envied by the local populace and detested by the country's dictator, Ataturk, although he was born in Greece himself.'

Smith nodded. He had heard of Kemal Ataturk, who had helped depose the Turkish Sultan and was now in process of introducing all sorts of weird and wonderful reforms in that backward country. He had already forced the local women to remove the veil, and the men to shave off their beards and wear cloth caps instead of the fez so that they could not touch their foreheads to the ground when worshipping Allah. It was said he was going to abolish religion altogether soon. All the same he wondered what kind of mission C could have for him and his crew in that remote country.

'Now,' C continued, 'it's pretty common knowledge that once Ataturk has kicked out the rest of the Greek Army, he'll start on the Greek civvies at Smyrna. They have the money he needs to replenish his empty coffers and the business his chaps want to control. So what will he do?'

'Terrorize them into fleeing the country and return to Greece, sir?' Smith ventured.

C shook his head, smiling slightly. 'I'm afraid you don't know Johnny Turk, Smith. There's nothing Johnny Turk loves more than a good massacre. Don't you know what they did to Armenians a couple of years back?'

Smith looked blank.

'Well, I'll tell you. The Turks slaughtered them by the thousand and hundred thousand – women and children, too. They did the same with their Kurds as well.' C's face hardened, and Smith whistled softly. 'Yes,' C said, iron in his voice, 'there's a massacre in the making, if we don't do something to stop it.'

'But what can *we* do, sir?' Smith objected. 'We tried to get through the Dardanelles and capture Istanbul back in '15 and the operation turned out to be a total failure. If

I recollect correctly, we lost several battle-ships in the attempt.'

'You do. We lost the *Implacable* and the French lost the battleship, *Bouvet*. At one point the Dardanelles are no more than three or four miles wide. The fleet was a sitting duck for the Turkish batteries on both sides, as they tried to get through. The battleships didn't have a chance in hell.' C suddenly looked very bitter and Smith thought he caught the glimpse of tears in his eyes when he said, 'My oldest boy went down with the *Implacable*.'

'Sorry, sir.'

C brushed his knuckles across his eyes and said gruffly, 'No matter, Smith ... no matter. It's long done with.' He sniffed and when he spoke again, his voice was normal once more. 'So, there is going to be a blood bath at Smyrna, if nothing is done in time. But his majesty's government's hands are tied. We've enough trouble on our hands at home, in Ireland, the Middle East and India.' He sighed a little wearily. 'It seems as if everywhere there are traitors and turn-coats out to destroy the British Empire.'

Smith nodded. Crossing London to the headquarters of the Secret Service in this discreet house in Queen Anne's Gate, he'd seen the alarmist headlines on the news-paper boys' placards – *'Further heavy fight-ing in Southern Ireland... India demands*

Home Rule... Egyptian mobs stones British Consul in Alexandria'. 'Yes, I know, sir,' he said stoutly. 'But no one and nobody can ever bring down the British Empire.'

'Well said, Smith!' C responded heartily. 'Thank God, our public schools are still turning out stout fellahs like you who are prepared to go over there and lay down their lives for the Empire if necessary.'

Smith nodded his head in agreement, face set and determined. That was what it was all about, he told himself, the Empire. All that red on the map.

'So *officially,* we can do nothing to help those poor souls. *Unofficially,*' he tapped the side of his big nose, a sudden cunning look in his eyes, 'we can do a lot.'

He paused to let his words sink in and Smith had a quick feeling that this was going to be his 'show'. He waited expectantly. Through the window the clip-clop of a horsedrawn cab penetrated, followed by the metallic clatter of a tramcar.

C broke his silence again. 'The leaders of the Greek community are planning to evacuate all their people who are prepared to go. One of their leaders, a chap named Onassis – a cunning devil by all accounts, but immensely wealthy – has chartered a fleet of freighters and the like to take his people to Greece. He has also convinced the US President, who, as you know is in his dotage, to promise his support for this evacuation–'

'You mean the Yanks are going to give the evacuation naval and military protection?' Smith asked in surprise.

'Of course not!' C snorted. 'Ever since they pulled out of Siberia and Baku in 1920, they have washed their hands of Europe. It's just a silly promise made by a silly man. America will send neither ships nor men to help the Greeks. They are on their own and the Turks will show them no mercy. Johnny Turk will slaughter the Greeks wholesale, unless *we* do something about it and after all the Greeks were our allies in the last show.'

'What, sir?' Smith asked boldly, for he was longing to know what his role was to be.

But instead of answering his question, C said, 'We've wondered how the Turks would carry out the Smyrna massacre, as it will undoubtedly be called *if* it takes place. Our guess here is that Turkey will take some notice of the American promise so they won't massacre them on land for every newspaper correspondent to see – and there are scores of them there already, waiting for the massacre to happen. No, the Turks will do it safely from prying eyes. They'll do it out to sea. Out in the Aegean probably, well away from the coast.'

'But the Turks don't have a fleet, sir,' Smith objected. 'After they lost the war on the side of the Huns, we took their remaining ships off them, just like we did with the Hun High Sea Fleet in 1919, sir.'

C peered at Smith's eager, handsome face through his 'window-pane', as his staff called C's monocle behind his back, and said softly, 'But they have a little fleet. Two battleships, in fact.'

Smith whistled softly. 'But where did they get them, sir? Who sold them to the Turks?'

'No one. They had them in storage, you might say.'

'*In storage?*' Smith echoed, completely bewildered now. He knew C of old. He dearly loved the oblique approach, always trying to startle, bewilder his operatives.

'Yes,' C said, 'at the bottom of the Dardanelles.'

'You mean the *Implacable* and the *Bouvet?*' Smith cried.

C looked pleased with the effect he had had on the young officer. 'Exactly. Last winter the Huns raised them for the Turks in secret, or so they thought. They are currently re-fitting them in Istanbul. You are going to sink them before that refit is completed, Smith.' He paused and licked his lips, as if they were suddenly parched. There was no sound for a moment, save the grave one of the grandfather clock in the corner ticking away the seconds of their lives with solemn metallic inexorability.

Finally C spoke. 'Smith, my dear boy, you are going to do – for me – another Kronstadt...'

2

They had gone in just after dark, cruising softly down the narrows which led into the great Russian naval harbour at Kronstadt. The fog had been wet and dripping, muffling the sound of the torpedo boats' motors. Suddenly the fog had parted. Dramatically the whole of the Red Fleet had been revealed, silhouetted stark and black against the lights of Petrogard. Like sheep in their pens, waiting to be slaughtered, the great dreadnoughts and cruisers lay motionless and silent in their berths. Like savage hunting dogs, suddenly let off the leash, the four tiny torpedo boats leapt forward, heading straight for their objectives.

One of the dreadnoughts came abruptly to life. Sirens howled. An Aldis lamp began to clack urgently. Somewhere a red flare, signalling the alarm, sailed into the night sky. A moment later the first star shell burst over the narrows. The four little craft were instantly bathed in its icy, glowing light. Tracer started to speed towards them.

Twisting and turning crazily, going all out at thirty knots, the torpedo boats raced through the maelstrom of fire, escaping disaster time and time again – just by inches.

De Vere Smith, standing at the helm of the *Swordfish* had watched as the first boat had shuddered violently. For one dread moment he thought it had been hit. Then he gasped with relief. Two white splashes at either side of the knifelike prow indicated she had just fired her torpedoes. Automatically he counted off the seconds as his own bucking, twisting, heaving craft hurtled towards its target. Five! He blinked as the night sky was lit abruptly by a great searing flash of violet flame. Next to him CPO 'Nobby' Clarke yelled, *'Hell's teeth, sir,... They've got a hit!'* The first boat had. One moment later and the whole sky was full of flying metal as the Soviet cruiser exploded and started sinking immediately.

The second craft raced in. Pluckily it made its attack. Rattled and nervous the Red gunners turned their weapons on the vessel as it appeared to skim across the harbour. In a lethal morse, red, white and green tracer sped towards it. Pom-poms chattered frantically. Bigger guns thundered. All around the flying craft the water erupted as shell after shell just missed the torpedo boat.

Still the young skipper pressed home his attack. Time and time again, the little craft disappeared behind huge fountains of flying white water. Desperately Smith prayed his comrade would make it. Surely they hadn't come all this way, across the North Sea and through the Baltic, to fail now?

Suddenly the number two craft swung round in a great wild curve. White spray spurted up high into the air. She had just launched her deadly fish. Two tons of high explosive were surging through the water at her target.

Again Smith started to count. '*One ... two ... three ... four ... five...!*' Abruptly he stopped. His face was slapped by the blast. He gasped and momentarily closed his eyes. A great crimson jet of flame seared the length of one of the Red cruiser's deck. Like a giant blowtorch it swept all before it. The paintwork bubbled and popped obscenely. Screaming, frantic men, already aflame, jumped over the sides. For already the huge ship was beginning to keel over to port.

Abruptly her boilers burst. A huge cloud of hissing steam ascended to the night sky. Mushrooms of brown smoke like gigantic smoke-rings erupted from her funnels. Then with dramatic suddenness, the cruiser was gone altogether, sliding below the fuming water, creaking and groaning as if protesting against her fate.

'Did yer see that, sir?' CPO Clarke yelled above the racket the engines kicked up. 'If I hadn't seen it with me own eyes, I wouldn't have believed it possible. Crikey, 20,000 tons of steel gone before yer could say Bob's yer uncle! Cor stone the ferking crows!'

Smith did not respond. He was too busy concentrating on his own attack now. There was one more boat to go in and then it would be his turn. And he knew that the Red gunners had already overcome their initial surprise. On all sides searchlights had clicked on, parting the darkness with icy-white fingers. Suddenly they coned on the third craft.

Desperately the skipper at the helm flung his craft from side to side, making erratic zig-zags in an attempt to escape that blinding cruel light. To no avail! He was trapped in it. With a terrific crash the enemy gunners opened up. All around the little boat the water heaved and boiled. To Smith, praying desperately, it seemed that nothing could survive that deadly bombardment. Still the young skipper pressed on, heading for his target – fleet oiler, a huge vessel obviously packed with oil.

The third attacker staggered. Smith groaned. Had it been hit? No. There was a sudden flurry of bubbles. The first torpedo was on its way. Clarke roared into Smith's ear, 'He's launched his first fish, sir!' Smith nodded, as he steered to starboard, trying to keep the *Swordfish* in the shadows and away from the searchlights as long as possible.

Relentlessly the two torpedoes sped towards the unsuspecting oiler. At that range they couldn't miss. In two gigantic hammer blows they struck home. The oiler's aft tanks went up immediately. A great frightening hiss. Flame, tinged with oily smoke, shot to the sky. Almost at once the burning tanker started to sink. Next instant a great all-searing, all-consuming torch hissed and roared terrifyingly across the harbour.

Clarke, old salt that he was and veteran of two wars at sea, turned his head away momentarily. He simply couldn't watch as the Russian sailors were literally flayed of their flesh by that enormous flame-thrower to reveal the bare gleaming white bones beneath.

Smith forced himself to watch as he had done as a seventeen-year-old snotty at the Battle of Jutland in 1916 when he had watched the *Iron Duke* go down and all the other ships he had seen sunk thereafter during the terrible battles fought between the 'Dover Patrol' and the German light craft from across the North Sea.

'Clarke,' he said in a voice he hardly recognized as his own, 'we're going in – *now!*'

'Ay ay, sir,' Clarke said smartly, turning to

look ahead again, as Smith opened the throttle wide. 'I can see her now, sir ... the *Spartak*. To port.'

'Me, too,' Smith said, throwing his white silk muffler over his right shoulder and tensing his shoulder muscles, ready for what was to come. He thrust the throttle to its fullest extent. The engines roared. The prow came out of the water at a steep angle. Suddenly the boat was hitting each separate wave as if striking a solid brick wall. Smith felt his stomach being forced back against his ribs. He had that old familiar sick feeling. He forced himself to forget it.

Almost immediately two searchlights coned in on the flying vessel. The sirens on the *Spartak* shrieked their urgent warning. Tiny dark figures pelted to their posts. The pom-poms and the heavy machine guns on the side of the deck facing the British craft started to spit fire. Scarlet flame slashed the night. Tracer hissed towards the *Swordfish*, growing larger and faster by the instant, hurtling at them like great glowing golf balls.

But they seemed to bear a charmed life. With all his strength, his shoulder muscles ablaze with red-hot pain, Smith swung the vessel from left to right, drenching those on deck with cold seawater. Time and time again the *Swordfish* escaped destruction by inches.

Now, his eyes narrowed to slits against the

41

glare of the searchlights, Smith forgot all fear. His whole being was concentrated on the Red battleship. It seemed to fill the whole horizon. Next to him Clarke shouted off the range. *'Eight hundred ... seven-fifty ... six hundred ... five-fifty...'*

That was it.

'Fire one ... fire two!' Smith cried at the top of his voice, his face wild with excitement and lathered in sweat, as if it had been greased.

The *Swordfish* shivered violently. A flash of yellow smoke. The two one-ton torpedoes smacked into the water. A flurry of bubbles and they were speeding away. 'Running true, sir,' Clarke sang out. Smith waited no longer. He wrenched the boat round and raced for the exit to the harbour. Behind them the two torpedoes headed for their prey like vicious steel sharks.

Now as Smith fought his way out, shells dropping to either side of the racing craft, Clarke watched eagerly to their flying rear. He counted off the seconds at the top of his voice like a man suddenly gone mad.

As one two torpedoes exploded. A flash of vivid orange flame. A great creaking and rending of metal. The towering super-structure began to shake and tremble alarmingly. The wireless mast came down in a shower of angry blue sparks. Panic-stricken sailors started flinging themselves overboard. One man dived straight from the crow's nest, misjudged the distance and hit the deck by mistake. He crumpled there like a sack of wet cement. Others fought desperately to wriggle their way through the tiny portholes. For all knew the *Spartak* had broken her back. There were only minutes, perhaps seconds left, before she went under.

Smith had no eyes for the *Spartak*. That was over and done with now. He concentrated on getting *Swordfish* out past the boom, before the Red torpedo boats came speeding in from Kronstadt, just across the water. His little craft, torpedoes gone, armed only with two Lewis guns, stood no chance against the Russian cannon. He *had* to get out before the Reds tracked him!

The little craft hushed across the surface of the sea, weaving from side to side so that at times its wireless mast seemed to touch the water. Time and time again the men on the heaving deck were soaked by huge torrents of water. Shrapnel ripped the length of the *Swordfish*. Great ragged holes were being torn in her woodwork. Somewhere something was burning, but Smith had no time to find out where. He prayed it wasn't in the engine room.

The dark outline of the boom loomed up with startling suddenness. Men were running along it. They fired from the hip as they did so. Clarke grabbed hold of the Lewis gun. He pressed the trigger. 'Try that on for size ye red boogers!' he cried. He ripped off a whole drum at the running figures. They were swotted off the boom like flies being cupped by a giant hand.

Smith flung his head back and forth urgently. Beads of sweat were threatening to blind him. Which way out should he take? Close to the boom or on the far side where it was darker? He decided to steer *Swordfish* on to the far side. It was almost a fatal decision. As he swung the boat to port, the twin searchlights coned on him. He was trapped by that blinding white light. Desperately, he yelled, 'CPO … knock them out … at the double!'

Clarke rammed another drum of ammunition on top of the Lewis gun. He swung it round. Too late! The cannon sited next to the searchlights fired first. The shell slammed into the bow of the *Swordfish*. It reared up violently. Smith felt something like a red-hot poker plunge into his left shoulder. His arm dropped to his side, useless.

A thick red fog threatened to engulf him. Aft, the engines started to splutter and spit. Black smoke drifted by. The *Swordfish* lost speed immediately. Grimly Smith held on to the throttle with his one good hand, willing the *Swordfish* not to sink, to keep on going. Next to him Clarke lay on the shattered deck, coughing blood and dying. Somewhere else a rating, lying tangled in the wires of the radio mast and pinned down, moaned piteously, 'Lord help me, please … please … I can't see a thing.' No one came to aid him. The crew of the *Swordfish* were either dead or dying now.

Smith fought that terrible drowsiness. Dimly he felt that the firing was dying away; that the searchlight had gone out. 'Keep … keep going,' he commanded himself. 'For God's sake – *keep going!*'

Thus it was that the anxious lookouts on the *HMS Vindictive* first spotted the seriously wounded youngster in a bloodstained tunic, hunched over the wheel of a sinking Thorneycroft, surrounded by dead or dying rating. As one of them breathed in awe at the sight. 'Gawd Almighty, that young snotty's dying on his frigging plates o' meat.'

3

'Forgive me for asking, sir,' the voice broke into Smith's reverie about the attack on Kronstadt, 'but aren't you Common Smith, Victoria Cross?' The voice was refined, polite, that of a gentleman, obviously, but the accent was not altogether English.

Smith, lulled almost to sleep by the motion of the train bearing him north from London, opened his eyes with a start.

Seated opposite in the compartment, which had been empty when they had left King's Cross, was a small, smiling man of middle age dressed in a conservative business suit, with above his head on the rack a leather briefcase of the kind carried by solicitors.

'I'm sorry to have disturbed you, sir, but I'm afraid my curiosity got the better of me. You are he, I take it?'

'Yes,' Smith admitted ruefully, 'I'm Common Smith, V.C. for my sins.'

'Yes, I remember reading about you in the – hm – *Daily Sketch* a couple of years ago it was now. One of their lady journalists smuggled her way into Hasler Hospital at Portsmouth where you were recovering from your wounds from Kronstadt–'

'Say no more,' Smith interrupted him swiftly, colouring at the memory. That particular day was etched on his memory for all time. The reporter had come into his ward dressed as a VAD nurse, all prim and proper. After making a poor attempt to take his temperature, she had gushed about his 'beautiful medal', the V.C. which had been awarded him for his exploits at Kronstadt. She had been too pretty with her green eyes and delightful bust for him to have been suspicious. He had answered he couldn't talk about his 'beautiful medal' because he was bound not to speak about it and how he had won it by the Official Secrets Act. Thereupon, she had asked with seeming innocence, 'I believe you are the fourth son of the Earl of Beverley, Lieutenant?'

He had nodded and she had continued, 'Well, how do you call yourself? An Honourable? Or a hyphenated de Vere-Smith?' She had spelled it out for him.

He had laughed easily and replied with smiling eyes, 'Pater hasn't got a bean. Reggie, my eldest brother, will inherit the title and I must live off my naval pay. No miss, I am just *common* Smith, as in Smith's Yorkshire Ales.'

There had been a minor sensation when the *Daily Sketch* for which the bogus nurse worked, broke the story. Suddenly Smith had been transformed from the 'Secret V.C.' to 'Common Smith, V.C.'. The name had caught on at once. Ivor Novello, the playwright had inserted a little song entitled, 'I'm only Common Smith' into one of his shows running at London's Gaiety Theatre. George Robey, the great vaudeville comedian, had used the name as the basis for one of his monologues and some fool had petitioned the Prime Minister Lloyd George for an 'immediate knighthood for this jolly fine decent chap with no airs and graces'.

But the 'Welsh Wizard', who was very busy at the time selling off knighthoods at £1500 a time, had declined. Wisely. For Smith's superiors had been furious at the leak. Their Lordships at the Admiralty had banished Smith to the obscurity of the tiny Yorkshire coastal town of Withernsea, to which he was returning now – 'Devil's Island in Deepest Yorkshire', as he and the crew of the *Swordfish* called it at times when the winter rains and fogs set in.

'I suppose,' the middle-aged man opposite said, 'you have left the service by now? I don't suppose there is much call for dashing motor torpedo boat skippers in our post-war world.' He smiled winningly. 'The war to end all wars has been fought, hasn't it?'

'Yes, I suppose it has,' Smith in a non-committal manner. In these last few years ever since he had begun working for C he had become wary of strangers asking too many questions. He looked out of the window at the darkening countryside whizzing by as if the conversation were over for him.

But the other man persisted. 'We have something in common, you know, sir.'

Smith grunted.

'Yes, we are namesakes. Please allow me to tender you my card.' He reached into the pocket of his waistcoat just underneath the massive gold chain which stretched across his ample stomach and brought out a visiting card. He thrust at an unwilling Smith.

He glanced down at it idly and read: 'Hermann D. Smith, M.D. Specialist for Nervous Diseases'. Did that 'Hermann' explain the underlying accent, he wondered. He offered to hand the card back, but the doctor resisted, staying his hand with his own which felt soft and moist. 'Keep it my dear fellow, not that I think that a chap of your calibre will ever need my professional services, what. Oh, I say,' he exclaimed, as the express started to slow down. 'We're coming into Grantham. What about – er tot of grog, as I think you naval chaps – call it at my expense.' He chuckled and his fat jowls wobbled unpleasantly. 'I would deem it a great honour if Common Smith, V.C. would accept a drink from me.' He looked winningly at the young officer.

Smith's first instinct was to refuse. But then he remembered that by the time he reached Withernsea the pubs would be closed. Suddenly he felt in need of a drink. It had been a long and tiring day in London. 'Thank you, Dr Smith. That's very kind of you. I accept.'

'Capital, my dear fellow, capital,' Dr Smith said as if delighted. 'But we must hurry. There is only a ten minutes' stop here. Just in time for a quick one, as the younger people say these days.' Seizing Smith's arm, as if they were very old friends, he steered him outside to the cold platform, lit by flickering gas lamps, and urged him towards the saloon bar.

The platform bar, a cheerless place, was deserted save for an elderly LNER porter dozing close to a dying fire and the barmaid, a middle-aged woman, busy polishing glasses and stacking them on the rack behind her, as if she were in a hurry to close up the place. 'We're closing in five minutes,' she snapped without looking up.

The doctor laughed, showing several gold teeth. 'Ah, the famed English hospitality.'

The barmaid looked at them for the first time. She had hard suspicious eyes. 'None of yer cheek,' she snapped. 'Now what do you want?' Her jaw worked, as if on steel springs.

Smith shook his head. 'Only LNER personnel could be that rude,' he told himself.

'Whisky – no make it a double,' the doctor said and put a ten shilling note on the counter.

She poured the drinks, looked at the note as if it might be forged, then rang up the change.

The doctor took up the soda, 'Say when,' he commanded and squirted some into Smith's glass, then into his own. 'Here's to your very good health,' he boomed, raising his glass.

Automatically Smith did the same. The fat middle-aged doctor seemed the epitome of the hail-fellow-well-met middle-class English-man, but there was that accent, the un-English gold teeth and a slight watchfulness in his eyes behind the spectacles. Smith couldn't analyse it, but there was something about the man which made him uneasy.

'Night express – direct Newcastle-King's Cross,' the disembodied voice crackled through the loudspeaker set over the door to the bar. At the fire the porter gave a start and shuffled out, seeming to creak as he did so, *'The Hull train now standing at platform six will depart in exactly two minutes...'*

The doctor finished his drink with a flourish. He wiped his mouth and said, 'We must be off, my dear boy.' Over his shoulder he called to the barmaid. 'There is a three-penny bit for you on the counter.'

She sniffed haughtily and didn't even look up.

They went outside again. It had grown even darker. Smith glanced to his right. Up the track he could see the scarlet flashes of light from the oncoming train's firebox, as the fireman opened it and thrust in more coal. Steam drifted into the darkening sky. The tracks rattled and up in the signal box, there was the lack of the telegraph. A few travellers stepped back from the edge of the platform warily. The thunder of the approaching train grew ever louder.

'May I offer you a gasper?' Dr Smith said, 'or don't you indulge in the filthy weed?' He clicked open his gold cigarette case, took one out for himself and inserted it into his lips, holding the case for the other man to select his cigarette. 'I have them made for me by a little man in Bond Street.'

Behind them the signals clicked into position. An official shouted, 'Stand back please… Mind your backs there everybody!' The train was almost upon them now. The whole station echoed and re-echoed with the racket it made. Steam rolled in thick grey-brown clouds under the glass roof.

Smith reached out his hand to take a cigarette.

The doctor grinned at him, showing those gold teeth of his again, glinting in the flickering gas jet. 'That's a good chap,' he said coaxingly, as if he were attempting to get Smith to take some sort of unpleasant medicine.

Something made Smith look into the doctor's eyes – later he never could explain what. But what he didn't see there alerted him to his danger. They were full of evil intent. He had never seen such evil in a man's eyes before. He dropped the cigarette, as if it was red-hot. 'What the devil–'

Instinct made him spring to one side. With a shrill scream of absolute fear, the doctor went stumbling by him – right into the path of the speeding express.

At sixty miles an hour, it slammed into him. A thud, a spurt of blood and there the train was gone, a clatter of carriage after carriage trundling over the thing which lay on the tracks, broken and minced, with what looked like an abandoned football, but which was in reality a severed head, lying in the dirty pool of oil to the side…

'Funny sort of a doctor, if you ask me,' the inspector said in the flat slow tones of rural Lincolnshire. He pointed to the case which they had forced, while he had taken another drink in the bar which had been reopened despite the barmaid's protests that 'I've got to get home and cook me old man's tea. He'll knock me about someat rotten if he don't get his bangers and mash tonight!'

Smith, still a little shaken, looked at it. It contained an automatic pistol, spare magazine and a thick wad of notes.

'Dutch guilders, German marks and what looks like Belgian francs,' the inspector said, following the direction of his gaze. 'Probably nigh on a thousand quid.' He took a pull at his cold briar pipe. 'Where does a doctor get that kind of money these days, I ask you, sir?'

Smith took another sip of his second

whisky and said, 'Frankly, I don't know, Inspector. What do you make of it?'

The inspector hesitated. He tugged the end of his big red nose. 'Well, sir, he was no doctor. He was carrying a gun and all that foreign money. It seems to me that he was sent here–' he looked directly at the handsome pale-faced young man opposite him, whom he vaguely remembered from some place or other, 'to do away with you. The gasper he gave you I suspect was drugged, too.' He hesitated before posing his question. 'You don't have any deadly enemies, sir, do you?'

Smith didn't have to think. He knew he had. But who was this particular enemy and how had he got on to him so soon after seeing C? He shook his head slowly. 'I don't think I have, Inspector,' he lied.

The inspector nodded and taking out his notebook, licked a stub of pencil and posing it over the book said, 'Could I have your full name and address, sir?'

'I don't think that will be necessary, Inspector,' Smith said hurriedly. 'If you will be so kind as to call this number, which I'm sure you will recognize, that will explain everything.' Hurriedly he reached in his wallet and took out the Special Branch telephone number which C had given him for emergencies in the United Kingdom, handing it to the puzzled policeman.

He took one look at it and put his note-book away hurriedly. He touched his hand to his trilby as if in salute and said kindly, 'If I was you, sir, I'd watch my back. Good night, sir.' He went out leaving Smith alone with his thoughts. They weren't pleasant.

4

'So,' de Vere Smith concluded his account of what had happened at Grantham Station, 'Special Branch has lookouts now on the three roads into Withernsea, and they've also got their people patrolling Paragon Street Station, Hull doing the same job.' He looked at the grey-green sea off the promenade. As usual a sea fret was beginning to roll in. Another hour or so and the remote Yorkshire seaside resort would be swathed in fog, as it always seemed to be.

His Number One, Sub-Lieutenant 'Dickie' Bird broke the heavy, brooding silence. 'Now then Smithie,' he drawled in that languid fashion he cultivated, 'what was the dashed fellah up to, I mean?' He dabbed the fog dampness off his long face with a lace handkerchief, well soaked in an expensive eau-de-cologne. 'Surely he couldn't have been working for Johnny Turk, could he? Not many Turks in this neck of the woods, eh?'

Smith shrugged, 'I'm as mystified as you are, Dickie,' he said, while CPO 'Sandy' Ferguson, standing ramrod-straight on the dripping pavement barked, 'Bad bastards yon Turks, I dinna like 'em one bit, not after the Dardanelles in '15.'

'Chiefie, you continue to amaze me,' Dickie said. 'You've been everywhere and seen everything. I swear that you were with Nelson on the *Victory* at Trafalgar.' He laughed, but Ferguson's hard-face, which looked as if it had been hewn out of his native Scottish granite, remained unchanged.

Smith smiled too. He knew Dickie's affected, casual manner of old. Underneath it, all was steel-hard purpose. It was not everyone, after all, who could win the DSC as a seventeen-year-old midshipman. They had served together during the war, he knew he could rely on Dickie one hundred per cent; just as he could on the rest of the *Swordfish's* crew, such as the Leading Hands 'Ginger' Kerrigan and rolypoly 'Billy' Bennett, now rowing up in the dinghy to take them out to the *Swordfish*.

Smith nodded to the other two and they clattered down the wet steps from the Promenade in their nailed seaboots to where 'Ginger' was holding the little craft steady. 'All aboard the Skylark,' he said cheerfully, as 'Billy', nicknamed after the fat and very popular vaudeville comedian, brought up his hand, as if to salute.

Smith shot him a warning look and he dropped it hastily. 'We're not in the Royal Navy now, Billy,' he reminded the leading hand. 'Now we're just a bunch of down-at-heel merchant seamen.'

'Yessir,' Billy said and Smith groaned. Bennett would never learn.

Ten minutes later they were all standing on the deck of the *Swordfish*, its long lean shape already shrouded in fog, which was all to the good. For Smith did not want any prying eyes to note their departure this evening when they sailed for the Humber estuary and the start of their dangerous mission.

'All right, lads,' Smith commenced as the seagulls dived and cried like abandoned infants, as they gathered the slops the cook had just cast into the sea. 'Let me tell you what yer in for.'

Ginger Kerrigan raised his head and closed his hands together, as if deep in prayer, 'Thank you, Good Lord, for what we are about to receive, amen.'

Some of the men laughed, but only weakly. They knew they were going on another show and shows were always damned dangerous.

'We're to force the Dardanelles.' He paused and waited for the reaction.

It came all right. Ginger cried, 'Cor ferk a duck!' The others echoed that dread name, for all of them knew how back in '15 thousands of British and Australian servicemen had been slaughtered on the rocky heights of the channel which leads into the Turkish Sea of Marmara. Even CPO Ferguson's slablike face showed some little emotion.

'And if that's not all,' he continued, after giving the crew a moment to digest the startling news, 'once we're through we are to sink two Turkish battleships for reasons which you will find out in due course. Now,' he went on, not giving them any time to react, 'as soon as it's dark we sail for the Humber. Just off Sunk Island, we shall be provisioned, take on water and five thousand Horsemen of St George.'

'I say, Smithie, what the deuce are the Horsemen of St George?' Dickie Bird exclaimed, taking his cigarette holder, another of his affectations, out of his mouth.

Smith grinned. 'I thought you'd be puzzled. It's an idea of C's. He says if we need to bribe anybody we can use the Horsemen to do so.'

'But what are they?'

'Sovereigns. You know, they've got a portrait of St George killing the dragon on their sides.'

'I say,' Dickie said. 'One could have a jolly good time in Mayfair with that kind of money. Think of all the fillies and champers.' His long face grew suddenly very animated.

Smith sniffed. 'Forget the fillies and champers, Dickie. They're not on. Now as soon as we've got that little lot on board, we're off. My aim is to be in and out of the Humber under the cover of darkness. There are too many foreign ships sailing in and out of Hull on the tide these days, ever since trade with the Continent has started again. The few of them that see us, the better.'

There was a murmur of agreement from his listeners. 'Fine thinking, sur,' Kerrigan said in that cheeky Liverpuddlian manner of his. 'Couldn't have done it better mesen.'

'Thank you, Ginger,' Smith said, but irony was always wasted on the cocky youth with his ginger hair and spotty complexion. 'From Hull we sail down the coast till we reach Harwich. From there we sail for France.'

'For France, Smithie?' Dickie Bird said in surprise.

'Yes. C thinks it would be too dangerous to try to slip through the Straits of Gibraltar. We would be spotted, he feels. So we are to take the French canal system till we reach the mouth of the Rhône and enter the Med.'

Dickie Bird suddenly looked very pleased. 'Oh, I say, Smithie, that sounds absolutely ripping,' he exclaimed. *'La Belle France,* what! All that red wine and mamselles with bags of *"voulez-vous coucher avec moi?"* I think I'm going to like this.'

'A dirty unpleasant lot,' CPO Ferguson said dourly, 'yon Froggies. I ken when I was in Marseilles afore the war–'

'I say, Chiefie,' Dickie Bird interrupted him, 'do put a sock in it, there's a good chap. All that calvanistic moralizing does put the moppers on a chap's ardour, you know.'

'Let's get on with it!' Smith said firmly. 'There are things to be done before we sail. Now once we're in the Med we head straight for Alexandria.' He looked hard at Ferguson, half expecting the old salt to have some damning comment on the Egyptian port, but the CPO kept silent, and Smith continued. 'There we arm. Eight torpedoes – that's about all the *Swordfish* can manage. We'll be given a couple of Lewis guns. Those – together with our personal weapons – will be about it.'

'Crikey, in '15 we couldn't do it with half the Grand Fleet, plus the Frogs and we're supposed to force the Dardanelles with two machine guns and a couple of dozen rifles.

Cor stone the frigging crows!'

'We're not going to attack the Dardanelles, Ginger,' Smith reminded him firmly. 'We're just trying to sneak through it.'

'I see that,' Ginger counted. 'We might do it going *in*. But what about coming *out* when we've done the job, sir? What about then, sir – the Turks'll be waiting for us.'

'Leave it to the skipper, Ginger,' Billy Bennett said easily, jerking at his big belly, which always seemed to threaten to slip over his leather belt, perhaps to his knees. 'The skipper knows best.'

'I take your point, Ginger,' Smith said quietly. 'But we'll have to meet that one when we get that far.'

Ginger grinned at him. 'Just trying to have me say, sir,' he said quite happily. 'Thought I'd bring it up, like.' He lapsed into silence, as they all did, listening to the mournful croak of the siren at Withernsea's lighthouse, now totally shrouded in the sea fret.

Finally Smith said, 'I suggest that we all have a spot of tiffin before we sail. Cook tells me there's kippers for those who want them.' He looked at CPO Ferguson. 'And I don't suppose there'd be any objection to a tot of rum, Chiefie, would there? We're not in the Navy now so that there's no need for us to wait the time to splice the mainbrace, eh?'

Ferguson's crafty old face cracked into a

wintry smile. 'Och, none at all, sir,' he said eagerly, for Ferguson was a true Scot. 'A wee dram'd cheer us all up.'

Ten minutes later Smith and Bird were seated in the tiny wardroom tucking into two kippers apiece, washed down with scalding hot tea, well laced with rum. Ever since they had both left Harrow just before the war this was the kind of life they had both led: simple and dangerous, enlivened by such elementary treats as these – kippers and hot tea.

'Well,' Dickie Bird said, finishing off the last of his kipper and running a piece of bread in the smoky-tasting juice, 'what do you think, Smithie?'

Smith reached for his pipe, which he had just taken to smoking, because he felt it made him look older and more serious. He scraped the match, made a great fuss of lighting the tobacco, before saying, 'Think of what?'

'Come off it, Smithie,' Dickie snapped. 'You know what I mean – the damned Turkish business!'

'Well, we pulled it off at Kronstadt, didn't we?'

'Totally different kettle of fish, old bean,' Bird answered.

'There it was a matter of only a couple of miles before we got out of the harbour after the attack on the Reds. The Dardanelles is forty miles long with whacking great forts and gun batteries along its whole length on both sides. We'll be ruddy sitting ducks.'

Smith sucked in a great deal of tobacco smoke and wished next moment he hadn't. He felt distinctly queasy. He told himself that perhaps he wasn't up to pipe-smoking. 'It's a chance we've got to take, Dickie,' he said and coughed, hard.

'I say, Smithie,' Dickie said, as if in alarm. 'You're turning a ghastly shade of puce, you know.'

Smith ignored the comment. Instead he said with a wheeze, 'C told me that the successful massacre of the Greeks in Turkey might trigger off a massive reaction of Muslims in the whole of the Middle East and in India. Our Empire could be seriously threatened by Muslims triumphant over Christians. Not only that there would be one hell to pay in countries like Jugoslavia, Bulgaria, even Italy. There'd be calls to punish the Turks and that could precipitate another round of Balkan wars and you know who would benefit from that, don't you?'

'The Reds?'

'Of course, the Russians would dearly love to have that access through the Dardanelles to the Med. If everyone was against Turkey, who do you think Johnny Turk would appeal to for help?'

'The Russians.'

'Exactly. Our mission is basically to stop the whole of the Med. and the Middle East, plus India, getting into such a mess that the final outcome would be all-out war.'

'Oh, my sainted aunt,' Dickie Bird exclaimed, looking very worried. 'Not another damned world war! One was quite enough, thank you very kindly. I–' He stopped short, cocked his head to one side and asked, 'I say, didn't you hear that?'

'Hear what?' Smith put down his pipe. He, too, turned his head to one side. But all he heard was the lap-lap of the waves on the *Swordfish*'s hull and the mournful hoarse grunt of the Withernsea foghorn. 'Can't say I–'

He fell silent. 'You're right. There is some sort of craft out there. I can hear the engines.'

'And damned powerful ones at that,' Dickie snorted. 'I wonder who's larking around there on a filthy day like this? The locals haven't got anything as powerful as that. Most of their cobbles,' he meant local fishing boats, 'are still powered by coal.'

Smith was suddenly very businesslike. He grabbed his naval warmth off the peg behind the wardroom door. 'Come on, Dickie. Get the lead out of it. Let's go and have a look-see.' They hurried up on deck.

Now they could hear the throbbing purr of large engines quite clearly. It was obviously some powerful craft going quite slowly, not because of the fog, but because the vessel was going around in circles; they could hear how the sound of its engines grew louder and then softer as it circled away. Once a searchlight flicked on. They could see its dim reflection on a wall of grey fog. But it was switched off after a few moments, as if those on board the craft didn't want to draw attention to themselves.

Smith shot Dickie an enquiring look. The latter nodded his agreement. Hastily the former turned off the riding lights. Now there was no light to indicate the *Swordfish*'s presence. It was illegal and dangerous. But both the young officers knew they didn't want to attract the other craft's presence.

How long they stood there in the damp dripping fog, the two of them never knew afterwards. It could have been five minutes – or fifty. Then finally the mysterious craft drew away and they heard the roar as the big engines were given full power. Moments later it was drawing away north in the direction of Hornsea. They relaxed and Dickie said, 'They were looking for us, weren't they?'

Smith nodded, his face set and thoughtful.

'But who were they and why?' Dickie asked a little angrily.

But Common Smith, V.C. had no answer for that overwhelming question.

5

It was a week later.

Progress had been slow along France's elaborate canal-river waterway system. But Smith had kept in touch with London by telephone each evening and had been informed that the Turkish drive on Smyrna had not yet started; the Turks had not yet succeeded in driving the beaten Greek Army out of their wartorn country.

So they had sailed steadily southwards, the weather improving all the time. Soon the attempted murder at the railway station and the strange craft searching for them off Withernsea were virtually forgotten, as they relaxed and enjoyed the scenery and the balmy air of *Midi* in winter. Of an evening they would anchor at one of the many *auberges de port* or *auberges des pecheurs* which lined the waterways' banks, eat huge meals at ridiculously low prices, washed down by plentiful red wine or fizzy French beer to return half drunk to the *Swordfish*. All save CPO Ferguson, who detested all foreigners and their ways.

He preferred to remain on board at all times. 'I'll have none of yon froggie muck,' he was wont to declare. 'Ye ken the heathens scoff snails and the like.' Here he would shudder dramatically. 'Gimme me a bit o' decent fried corned beef and a wee dram to wash it doon and I'm a contented man.'

At the end of that first week they had reached the Sâone, where it would soon flow into the River Rhône and take them south another 400 kilometres to the sea. Now there were barges put-putting up, heading north to Nancy and Thonville and south to the great city of Lyon and beyond. Burly, red-faced men in red striped jerseys with battered naval caps stuck at the back of their cropped heads waved to them and called *'vive les rostbifs'* when they recognized from the *Swordfish*'s lines that it had once been some sort of naval craft. Fishermen held up their catches proudly and once or twice peasant girls, with their skirt tucked up into the elastic waistbands of their white bloomers, working in the fields on both sides, made obvious suggestions to them, which caused Ferguson to comment sourly. 'Ay, ay, now just go and touch one of yon hussies and see what it'll get ye. The pox doctors'll nae save ye!'

But even Ferguson's stern-faced aura of Scottish gloom and doom could not spoil what most of the crew of the *Swordfish* regarded as a foreign holiday – at government expense. What few duties the men had, they did cheerfully, while Smith and Bird locked inside the tiny wardroom spent most of the day studying the secret Admiralty charts of the Dardanelles' defences and what lay beyond in the Sea of Marmara. What they discovered was not very promising, but even the fact that the narrow straits seemed to be guarded not only by forts on both sides, but also by artillery batteries, underwater obstacles and mines could not spoil their good moods. Indeed of an evening they were as jolly as the rest of the crew who weren't in the know, tucking in heartily to huge plates of *potage,* mounds of *bifsteck avec pommes frites* and mountains of cheese, which the ratings wouldn't touch. As Ginger said, wrinkling up his nose in apparent disgust, 'Gawd Almighty, can't eat that stuff. Stinks to high heaven. Worse than Billy Bennett's unwashed socks.' To which the latter made no reply, for his mouth was too full of *pommes frites.*

It was on the Saturday at the end of that first week in France that they tied up on Sâone just outside the small town of Pont de Vaux. The nearest inn was the usual *Auberge des Pecheurs,* a small tumbledown place directly on the river bank. It was already growing dark and the anglers were going home and along the towpath a peasant came plodding, shotgun over his shoulder, two rabbits hanging from his belt. He nodded to the men of the *Swordfish* coming ashore now and mumbled something, Gauloise seemingly glued to his bottom lip.

All was peaceful and happy, save for CPO Ferguson, who as usual was staying on board; mumbling something grumpily about 'not eating none of yon garlic muck. Stinks up the heads!' They were in a good mood. Smith had just issued them with their week's pay and told them they could go into the little town for an hour after their communal meal. That put Ginger, in particular, in a high good mood. He chortled, 'Out on the razzle tonight, Billy boy. Lovely grub!' He smacked his lips as if in anticipation.

His shipmate, however, was more interested in food than going out 'on the razzle'. His big belly rumbling noisily, he said, 'Let's get some grub inside of us first before we start thinking o' that sort of thing. Besides I can't speak the lingo to them French tarts, Ginger.'

'Yer don't need to, matey,' Ginger chortled, clapping the big leading hand on the shoulder. 'As long as you've got these.' He held up a fistful of greasy French notes. 'Money counts more than words.'

Thus they passed into the *auberge,* a dingy sort of place that smelled of stale food and blocked drains, which even the smell of cooking could not quite overcome.

69

The *patron* came shuffling to meet them, feet in slippers, black beret at the back of his bald head, rubbing his hands, a look of fake hospitality in his shifty eyes, *'Bon soir la compagnie,'* he rasped, counting their number and probably already calculating how much money they would bring him if they all ate there.

Smith and Bird nodded coolly, taking an instinctive dislike to the shifty-looking innkeeper. *'Nous voulons ma-manger,'* Smith said in his best schoolboy French.

'Ah bien sûr, m'sieur' the innkeeper beamed up at him and rubbed his hands even more. *'Pas ici.'* He went in front of them, beckoning over his shoulder at them the whole while, as if he were afraid they might change their minds and walk out. Busily he pushed two bare tables together and slapped the dust off them with a dirty cloth. Then he hurried off to the kitchen and started shouting excitedly to someone inside in a dialect that Smith could not comprehend, while Billy Bennett's stomach rumbled even louder at the odours coming from the open door.

They were well into a mountain of *terrine*, accompanied by heaps of baguettes when the other guests came in. First came two very large men with sulky faces, dressed in city suits. They grunted in the direction of the hungry sailors wolfing down the good food. But it was the third man who caught Smith's attention. His yellow hair was cropped to his narrow skull so that it looked as if he were wearing a yellow skull cap. He was obviously some kind of albino, for he possessed no eyebrows and it looked as if he had no need to shave. But it was the eyes which struck Smith most. They were the pale icy-blue of a glacier. Smith was not a fanciful man, but to him they were the eyes of a murderer.

The albino bowed slightly in their direction, whispered *'Bon appetit'* in a curious kind of lisp and sat down. It was only then that the two burly men took their seats, one on either side of him, their hard gazes not flickering for a second. The albino was obviously the boss, Smith told himself.

Fawning, smiling that fake smile of his, the *patron* took the strangers' order, though in fact it was the albino who did the talking, not even consulting the two others about the food. When the food came the three of them ate in silence, with pauses when the albino would light a thin black cheroot, holding it in an affected, slightly effeminate manner, Smith couldn't help thinking, as he watched the three of them out of the corner of his eyes.

'Nasty piece of work,' Dickie said, confirming Smith's own thoughts on the albino, 'wouldn't like to meet him down some dark alley, what.' He took a drink of harsh country *vin rouge* 'Don't look French, though.'

'Exactly my thinking, too,' Smith agreed in a whisper, moving back as the sweating *patron* came staggering in bearing a large tray heavy with steaming piles of *entrecote*, exuding a heavy odour of garlic. Smith grinned. 'Old Chiefie Ferguson's not going to like us all this particular Saturday night,' he commented, then forgetting the three strangers, concentrated on the meat, though at the back of his mind he had a feeling that the three of them were watching the hungry young sailors with more than normal curiosity...

Fifty yards away inside the *Swordfish*, CPO Ferguson was enjoying himself in his own small way, if it could be said that dour Scot ever enjoyed himself. He had warmed up a great slab of greasy corned-beef, fried an egg on top of it, and sprinkled the whole lot with generous dollops of HP sauce. Now he was wolfing down the fatty mess, grease running down his chin, helping it along with generous dots of whisky from the waterglass at his side. Later he would wind up the gramophone and place on it his faithful, much scratched Will Fyfe record. Then he'd be off on his own drunken rendition of 'Ay belong to Glaskie, dear old Glaskie tuin'. It would be a perfect Saturday night – good scoff, a wee dram and dear old Glaskie, without any ribald comments from the Sassenachs who didn't know good music when they heard it.

He beamed pleasurably into his water-glass. 'Ay, it's gonna be a braw neecht toneecht.' He took another drink and felt even happier.

The blackjack exploded at the side of his head with such force that his false teeth bulged out of his mouth somewhat stupidly. CPO Ferguson had a particularly hard head. A normal man would have gone out like a light. Not the Scot. Indeed he started to rise to his feet, turning his bleeding head as he did so. 'What in heaven's name,' he commenced, catching a glimpse of a scarred runtish face and greedy dark eyes, when the blackjack struck him another vicious blow. This time he went down on his knees, scattered the tin plate and waterglass to the floor. The other man took deliberate aim. The blackjack slammed down at the nape of the old Scot's neck. He pitched forward, unconscious before he hit the deck.

Now the runtish man went to work systematically. He slipped a full bottle of whisky into his copious jacket pocket, doubled into the tiny wardroom, pulled the gold watch hanging there off the nail and it, too, followed the drink into his pocket. Now he began to go through the drawers, pulling them out, rummaging through their contents, stealing anything of value.

After a minute or two, chest heaving as if he had run a great race, he cocked his head to one side and listened attentively. There was no sound save the gurgle of the river and the muted voices coming from the restaurant. He nodded as if in approval. He opened the door and keeping to the shadows cast by the *Swordfish's* superstructure, hushed softly on tiptoe to the entrance to the tiny engine room.

There he remained longer than he had done on the deck, just long enough to do what he had really come to do here; then he was up and over the side nimbly. A moment later he had disappeared into the glowing darkness.

Smith and Bird were lingering over yet another cup of bitter French coffee, listening to the croaking of the frogs in the marshy ground near the Sâone, chatting idly in a relaxed manner like men do after a good meal. The others had had no time for coffee, even Billy Bennett who could never stop eating and drinking. The *patron* had told the crew through Smith that there was some sort of *fête* in the little town and every now and again when the wind was in the right direction, the two of them could hear a faint snatch of *bal musette* music, all tinny accordion and rapid beating on the drums.

They had gone straight after the meal, saying, as Ginger Kerrigan had put it cheekily, expectant grin on his thin, spotty face. 'Never knows yer luck, gents, on a night like this.' He had winked hugely and departed.

The three strangers who had hardly spoken a word and then in whispers throughout the meal had gone too. Now the two officers were alone save for the *patron* who pretended to be reading a paper at the bar, but who in reality was watching to ensure they didn't slip away without paying.

It was thus, sitting contended and replete, that the two of them were shocked first by a deep moan followed an instant later by a round curse in Gaelic. Next moment CPO Ferguson staggered through the open door, cloth pressed to his bleeding head, face ashen, crying, *'Sir, they've robbed the bluidy boat...' 'They have an' all!'*

6

Kapitanleutnant zur See von Horn counted out the greasy French francs directly into the scar-faced man's dirty hand. *'Ca va?'* he asked when he was finished.

'Ca va,' the man agreed happily and

touched his cap. He had been paid well. Not only had he the money, but he'd got the gold watch and other of the *rostbifs'* trinkets which would sell well in the *marche auxpouces* in the Arab quarter of Lyon.

Von Horn dismissed him with a wave of his manicured, lacquered nails. He clambered up the ladder to the deck of the barge, watched by von Horn's hard-eyed bodyguards. The bigger of the two said, '*Ja?*'

Von Horn nodded. The big man slipped after the petty French crook, pulling the length of very thin wire out of his pocket as he did so.

The other two waited. Von Horn smoked, no emotion apparent in his icy-blue eyes. There was a stifled scream. A sudden gasp. Then nothing until a splash on the far side of the barge indicated that it was all over.

'Dead men tell no tales, *Herr Kapitanleutnant,*' the other bodyguard said softly.

Von Horn said nothing. Instead he took up his pen and dipped the point in the special ink which he had brought with him from that secret headquarters of his in Northern Germany. He had already written a perfectly innocent letter to 'Dearest Auntie Luise' in normal ink. Now between the lines he began to make his report to his chief, Captain Canaris, head of Naval Intelligence, forbidden by the allies after Germany's defeat,

76

but still functioning secretly.

Even as he wrote, he thought again of Canaris's words to him before he had left for France. 'I think, Hanno,' Canaris had said in that quiet, reasoned manner of his, 'if we can – er deal – with this English party, it will be too late for those gentlemen in London to launch another party to stop the Turks.'

Hanno von Horn had nodded his agreement. Canaris' deceptive quietness hid the ruthless drive that lay below the surface. Anyone watching him at that moment gently stroking one of the little dogs he loved, his hair already beginning to whiten, would have taken him for some harmless old gent on the verge of a slippered retirement. In fact, he was a hardened killer, who had stabbed a priest to escape allied captivity and who had been part of the gang which had 'liquidated' the radical socialists in Berlin just after the war. No, he had told him, Captain Canaris was a force to be reckoned with.

'You see, Hanno,' Canaris had continued, 'if we are to save our poor Germany and begin the march back to power, getting rid of those socialist swine,' he had smiled apologetically and had added, 'forgive the word, please, well, if we are going to start managing our own affairs, we must rid ourselves of British and French interference in post-war Germany. How?' He had answered his own question. 'By setting the Middle East and Mediterranean, including North Africa, aflame. When their empires and spheres of influence are endangered, the British and French will forget Europe, and in particular, our beloved Germany.'

He had looked at von Horn with those dark secretive eyes of his for what seemed to the albino a long time before saying in a kind of hoarse whisper, 'Imperial Germany is dead. We can never go back to that. We were stabbed in the back by the socialists, the Jews, and the freemasons. But one day there will be a newer, a stronger, a better Germany, a country of which we can be proud again. Hanno, you are to play a vital part in the creation of that new Germany. I rely upon you.' With that he had bent his white head and Hanno von Horn knew he was dismissed.

Now he penned his report to 'Father Christmas', as Canaris was known behind his back on account of his white hair and seemingly benign manner. Swiftly he wrote in the secret ink what he had done and how he and his men would stay in France 'until this matter is concluded,' ending with the words, 'However, I think I can safely assure you, sir, that the problem will have been solved within the next twelve hours.' He signed the secret letter with a flourish, 'H v.H.'

He looked up at the waiting bodyguard, 'Another missive for – er Auntie Luise,' he said with a wintry smile on his narrow lips.

The thug, whose broken nose proclaimed he had once been a prize-fighter, grinned: 'Shall I post it now, *Herr Kapitanleutnant?*'

'Yes, but registered. I know it's after hours, long after, but you know these French? Ring the bell and offer them,' he made a gesture with this thumb and forefinger, as if he were counting money. 'It is the only language that filthy decadent race under-stands.'

'*Jawohl, Herr Kapitanleutnant,*' the thug snapped, sprang momentarily to attention and then departed swiftly, telling himself von Horn knew all about decadence all right. How often had he seen him in civilian clothes in Kiel and Hamburg, looking for those svelte young boys, with their pansy walk, plucked eyebrows and too tight trousers stretched across their skinny rumps. He grinned as he clattered up the ladder, 'Oh yes, the Chief knew all about that kind of piggery!'

Alone in the cabin under the wheelhouse, von Horn felt pleased with himself. He doubted if the English would ever suspect what was going to happen to them – and then it would be too late. He ran his pink tongue over his narrow cruel lips. He would wait till it happened, then he would go to Paris before he returned to the *Reich*. He had not enjoyed the *gamins* of France since the war and German money and power had bought any and every kind of delightful pleasure. The French were a deeply decadent people, but they knew how to give sexual pleasure with style.

He leaned back in the battered old leather horsehair chair and warmed himself on the thoughts of the delights to come. Above him on the deck, the other thug dug his face deeper into his thick collar, because the night was now becoming cold, and stared hard up the river where the Tommies were anchored. He didn't suppose it would happen yet, but he'd better keep a weather eye peeled – just in case. The minutes began to tick by tensely.

'But was it a simple robbery?' Dickie Bird blurted out, as on the tiny wardroom sofa, Ginger completed bandaging CPO Ferguson's battered head, while the latter sipped on a waterglass of wardroom pink gin.

'What do you mean?' Smith snapped, eyeing the disorder everywhere. 'He must have been some kind of sneak thief – an opportunist – who knocked poor old Chiefie over there about and then did a quick bunk with what he could lay his hands on – my gold watch, for example.'

'So why didn't he take me gold cigarette case, staring him – right over there – in the face?' Dickie Bird countered. 'And why when he went below—'

'How do you know he went below?'

'Because you can see the mud from his feet on the companion way. Must have got it on his boots on the towpath.'

Ginger whistled softly and whispered to his 'patient', 'Just hark at him, Chiefie, a regular Sherlock frigging Holmes.'

'Hold yer wish,' Ferguson growled, 'and get on with yer doctoring.'

'And,' Dickie Bird continued, raising his right forefinger like some lawyer making a point to a jury, 'why didn't he have a go at your celebrated Horsemen of St George?'

'Of course,' Smith breathed. 'They were down there. He should have spotted them if he was looking for money and the like. You're a bright chap, Dickie.'

'Brilliant actually,' Dickie corrected him, breathing on his nails in mock modesty.

'Silly ass,' Smith commented, face grim and not a little worried. 'So what was he doing down below?' he asked slowly.

'Let's go and have look-see,' Dickie suggested.

Ferguson drained the last of his pink gin and tugged the bandage away from Ginger. 'And I'm coming with ye, sir. If he's been interfering with ma engines,' he spluttered with rage and didn't finish his threat, but his granite face looked very fierce.

Together they trooped below, crouched

low because the space was very tight, for the *Swordfish's* mighty Thorneycroft engines which gave the craft such a tremendous speed took up most of the space, and stared around. For a moment or two they were puzzled, wondering what to do next until Dickie said excitedly, 'Look he must have stood on that stanchion. Can you see the dirty footprint on the rail?'

They could. Someone had balanced himself on one foot between the twin engines. The impression of a muddy sole was clearly visible.

Smith swung himself up on the framework of the first engine and, pulling out a little pocket torch, focused its beam between the two, down into the dark well, where patches of oil glistened in the bright light. He played the beam around, while Dickie asked anxiously, 'See anything, Smithie?'

'No, there's nothing–' Smith stopped short. 'Yes there is.' Balancing himself as best he could on the rail, he bent forward and plucked something metallic, which dripped dirty waste oil from the well. Next moment, breathing a little hard, he landed on the deck next to Bird.

Eagerly the others craned their heads forward to look at what he had found.

It looked like a small, rather plump cigar made of metal, some eight inches long, which gave off a strange odour of chemicals.

There seemed to be no opening anywhere on it, as Smith turned it about and up and down curiously, trying to establish what it was, handsome young face set in a puzzled frown.

Not for long.

Ferguson broke the heavy silence with a curt, 'Gimme yon devilish thing, sir – *quick!*'

Smith was not used to being talked to in that tone, even by chief petty officers. All the same, he obeyed instantly, handing the object to Ferguson.

The latter didn't hesitate. He took his big, all-purpose knife from his pocket. Swiftly he selected a small saw blade from the many different types of blade the knife contained and began sawing urgently at the metal, while the others watched in intense, mystified silence.

In a matter of minutes, grunting a little hard, the CPO had cut through the thin metal. He exerted pressure, cursing a little under his breath, face suddenly redder than ever, and broke the cylinder clean in half.

The onlookers stared even more.

Ferguson obviously enjoyed the moment of triumph. He poured a lot of yellowish-looking powder on to his horny palm, announcing 'picric acid crystals'.

'They're used for making explosives,' Dickie Bird explained, still puzzled.

Ferguson repeated the performance with

the other batch of crystals. 'Sulphuric acid – also high explosive.'

'But what is it, Chiefie?' Bird demanded urgently.

'I mind I'd seen something like yon thing afore,' Ferguson said doggedly, not wanting to be cheated for one moment of being the centre of attraction. 'It was on the China Station at the time of the Boxer Rebellion back in 1900–'

'What is it?' They all demanded at once in exasperation.

'A fire bomb. Ye ken that little copper disc – there – separates the two acids. The thicker the copper plate, the longer it takes for yon acids to burn through it and–'

'When they do,' Dickie Bird interrupted him urgently, 'they combine and start a fire.'

'Aye,' the CPO answered dourly, 'and it could have burned for hours.'

'Hell's fire!' Ginger exploded excitedly. *'We've been ruddy sabotaged, mates!'*

7

As the four of them walked to the *Auberge des Pecheurs* most of the lights had already been doused. But where the kitchen was located, they could still see the yellow glow of an oil-lamp. 'The *patron* still seems to be up,' Smith said, whispering for some reason he himself couldn't quite make out.

'And singing as well, sir,' Ginger just behind him on the towpath added, 'if you can call that singing. But perhaps that's the way the froggies sing.'

'Come on,' Smith said and moved on. 'At least we won't have to knock them out of bed.'

Ten minutes before, after the discovery of the firebomb, he had decided that they might find out something of the mysterious albino and his two thuglike companions from the innkeeper. The three of them had been the only strangers in the area, as far as Smith could make out. Were they the ones who planted the bomb? After the attempted murder, the mysterious boat searching for them in the sea fret off Withernsea, and now this, Smith was determined to find out what was going on. As he had told the others grimly before they had set out, 'I've got to make some sense of this deuced business. We cannot go on like this ... and on, yes, we'd all better take a revolver.' Ginger had looked significantly at Billy, but had said nothing. He had simply taken the .38 from the arms locker.

Now as they came closer to the flickering yellow light of the kitchen, they could hear the singing more clearly. It was drunken and certainly not in French.

'*Du, du habe ich im Herzen… Du, duc, habe ich im Sinn…*' the singer, who was obviously the *patron* sang happily, '*Weiss nicht wie–*'

'Well, I'll be blessed,' Dickie Bird exclaimed. 'That's German. I remember we tried to learn it in Harrow.'

Smith frowned. 'What the devil is a Frenchman in the heart of France doing, singing in German?' he asked.

'Well, there's only one way to find out, Smithie,' Dickie said. 'Come on.' He gripped the handle of the curtained french window that led into the kitchen and turned it. The door opened and Dickie gasped – an enormously fat woman, with her pendulous breasts hanging out of the front of her shabby gown with the slit open at the bottom to reveal fat legs encased in sheer black silk stockings complete with red garters.

At her feet, clad in a collarless shirt and dirty white underpants which came down to his skinny yellow shanks, was the *patron*, singing away mightily.

Dickie's mouth dropped open stupidly and he gasped, 'Good God, a love nest!'

The *patron* stopped singing. Hastily the woman tugged the gown to her ample body and cried, '*Que tu veux?*'

Smith pulled himself together. Under other circumstances the scene would have been laughable, the stuff of farce: the tiny little innkeeper, singing love songs to this huge woman. But not now. 'You were singing German,' he said in French to the *patron*.

'Naturally,' he answered. 'I was born in the Saar – in Germany.'

'Then what are you doing here?' Smith demanded.

The *patron* rose with stiff dignity, *'J'ai battu pour la France. Je suis mutilé.'* To show just how 'mutilated' he had been during his fight for France, he inserted the thumb of one hand just above his left eye, holding his outspread hand underneath carefully. Slowly, as they stared in open-mouthed wonder, his eye rolled out and dropped on to his palm.

'Cripes,' Ginger exclaimed, breaking the awed silence, 'he's got a glass eye.'

The *patron* nodded as if he understood English and said. *'Qui. À Verdun.'*

Smith recovered quickly. 'All right, I understand. Please put – er – it back. Now tell me. Those three men who ate here earlier, what do you know of them – *please?'*

The *patron* replaced his eye. With his dignity and credentials established now, he said quite coldly, no longer afraid of the four Englishmen, 'They were just three guests sailing the river like you. Of course, they were German and as Germans – understandably – are not particularly liked around here since the war, they kept to themselves–'

'Did you say Germans?' Smith interrupted the flow of words.

'Yes, I heard them talk among themselves quietly a couple of times. Naturally,' he beamed at his own cleverness, 'they did not know that German was my native tongue.'

'*Dites-moi,*' Smith said, feeling his heart begin to race with excitement at his discovery, 'what did you learn from their conversation?'

The *patron* shrugged his skinny shoulders. Behind him on the couch, the ladyfriend had begun to relax once more. Unknown to her her gown slipped open once more to reveal those enormous breasts and Billy Bennett, seeing those huge white melons emerging, licked his lips, as if he didn't know whether to eat or play with them.

'Not much,' he answered. 'They were Prussians from the far north. I could tell that from the accent.'

'Hm,' Smith muttered and considered the statement. North Germans coming all this way deep into a France which was still hostile to the Germans. France still occupied the German Rhineland with an army of occupation. Didn't seem a wise thing for a German to do, he told himself. 'Go on,' he urged after a moment. 'Nothing much in that.'

Again the *patron* shrugged. 'They said they were going as far as Lyon. Then they would go back.'

'So they have a boat, too?' Smith said urgently.

'*Mais oui!*'

'*Où?*'

The *patron* threw out his skinny arm. 'Up there, I suppose. They'll want to be where they can get water and food, just like you. They will not anchor in the wilderness.'

Smith didn't wait to hear any more. He peeled off a ten franc note and tossed it on the littered kitchen table. 'Here. Keep your mouth shut.' He jerked his head at the others. 'Come on, lads.'

They filed out, with Billy Bennett bringing up the rear. As he went out, the fat woman winked her eye and pursed her lips in a wet kiss. Billy Bennett fled.

A minute later they were on their way once along the dark towpath. Behind them the springs of the battered old sofa started to squeak mightily and Ginger whispered hoarsely, 'Fancy doing it to her, Billy?'

Billy shuddered dramatically and whispered, 'Don't even think things like that, Ginger! Gives me the ruddy creeps...'

They had been walking along the darkened towpath for nearly twenty minutes now. To their right *Pont à Vaux* had settled down for the night. Hardly a light was visible from the little eighteenth-century riverside town and there was no sound. Not even a dog barked. There were few craft tied up on the 'downstream' side of the river. They were mostly little fishing boats owned probably by the locals, a pleasure cruiser, covered with a tarpaulin, securely lashed down and anchored for the winter, and one ancient barge listing badly and obviously long abandoned by its owner.

Smith stopped and scratched his head. 'We're almost out of *Pont à Vaux* now,' he said to the others, keeping his voice down and remaining in the shadows, for now a sickle moon was sliding through the clouds to shine its cold spectral light on below. 'I wonder if they've already done a bunk, if those Huns really did plant that firebomb?'

'Hardly likely,' Dickie retorted. 'Would they not want to see the result of their work … if they'd brought it off or not?'

'Yes, I suppose you're right, Dickie,' Smith agreed slowly, as he wondered what he should do next. 'They would. The question is – where?'

'Sir.' It was Billy Bennett.

'Yes.'

'You remember I was on the Zeebrugge Raid in '18.' He meant the famous raid to bottle up the German submarine pens located in the Belgian port. It was an episode which Bennett was always recalling with pleasure, because it was there that he had earned his Distinguished Conduct Medal for bravery under fire.

'Yes, I remember, Billy,' Smith said a little wearily. 'But what's the Zeebrugge Raid got to do with our present problem?'

'This sir. Me and the lads did a bit of scrounging around afterwards, looking for souvenirs and the like.'

'Looting, yer mean,' Ginger Kerrigan hissed scornfully. 'You've always had an eye for winning gear–'

'Ginger,' Smith said threateningly.

'Well, sir,' Billy continued, 'I – er – found a box of Hun cigars, and when we got back to Harwich, I smoked some of them–'

Smith groaned and hissed, 'Get on with it, Billy.'

'It's the smell, sir – the smell of them Hun cigars. I can smell that now, sir.'

'*What?*' Smith and Bird exclaimed in unison.

'Yessir. And it's coming from round the bend there,' Billy Bennett held up his nose like the two Bisto kids smelling the fragrance of the famous gravy powder. 'Very definitely ... round that bend.'

'What? Are you sure?' Smith asked urgently.

'I am, sir.'

Smith thought quickly. Someone was smoking a German cigar – if big fat leading hand was correct – round that corner up there. Could it be the Huns they were looking for and were those Huns the same ones, if indeed the saboteurs were Huns, who had planted the firebomb on the dear old *Swordfish?* He made a quick decision. 'All right, we're going to have a look at 'em,' he hissed. 'If they are people we are looking for, they'll probably be armed. We're taking no chances. Take off your safety catches, and have your .38s at the ready. They could be desperate men ... and keep your eyes skinned.'

'Like tinned tomatoes, sir,' Ginger said cheekily and pulled out his revolver. Then they were off.

A couple of minutes later they saw it. A small barge, no single light showing, tied fast to the river bank, but moving back and forth slightly in the current. Now they advanced cautiously, hardly daring to breathe, nerve-endings tingling electrically. Smith knew there had to be someone on guard or lookout because the smell of rich cigar smoke was very strong now. He stopped and whispered in Dickie's ear, 'See if you can spot him, you've got the best eyesight of us all, Dickie.'

Dickie said nothing, but nodded his understanding. For a tense moment or two they crouched there in the bushes while Dickie surveyed the dark silent barge. The silver light of the moon slid across the craft's bows and Smith could just manage to read, *'Grube III, Saarbrucken'*. He remembered from his school German that *'Grube'* meant a coalpit. Presumably this barge carried coal from the Saar mining region.

'There he is,' Dickie hissed suddenly. 'Can you see the red glimmer of that filthy weed he's smoking... Just below forrard.'

'Got it, Dickie,' Smith hissed back. He tugged the end of his nose. From what he knew of barges the crew usually slept forrard – normally on a barge of this size there'd only be one of them – while the owner or skipper with his wife commonly had their sleeping and living quarters below the deck house. Thus if they could nobble the lookout, they could easily trap the rest of them, even if they were outnumbered, below deck.

He made up his mind. Swiftly he rapped out his orders, while the others listened intently. 'Understood?' he hissed finally.

'Understood,' they replied as one.

'All right, what are we waiting for? Let's go and have a look at these chaps.' They needed no urging. On tiptoe they stole forward...

8

'*Now,*' Dickie hissed.

With surprising quietness for such a large heavy man, Billy Bennett heaved himself over the rail, while Dickie Bird crouched there in the shadows on the towpath covering the man leaning against the rail smoking. If anything went wrong, he'd fire. For what did a barge need a lookout or sentry at this time of night? Obviously there was something fishy going on.

Billy Bennett came in, ducked low, his feet almost noiseless on the deck, for he had resorted to the old trick; he had pulled a pair of spare socks over his boots. Now the lookout was about ten yards away, leaning over the rail, smoking moodily as lonely men do late at night. He licked lips which were suddenly dry, feeling his heart thumping like a trip-hammer.

It had been like this those last few moments before the balloon had gone up at Zeebrugge back in '18. Everybody on board had known that they would have one hell of a scrap in front of them. But when it did, with a devil of a racket, they'd been surprised all the same. He clenched the pistol more firmly in his big right hand. Peering through the glowing darkness, he could just make out that the lookout was not wearing a hat. Good, he told himself. A hat might have softened the blow he was going to land at the base of the squarehead's skull. The aim was to knock him out first time so that he didn't have chance to raise the alarm.

Five yards. Now he could see the man in silhouette quite clearly. 'Big bugger,' he told himself. 'Shoulders on him like a prize fighter.' He tightened the grip on the muzzle of his revolver even more.

Suddenly the man stirred. The red arc of the burning cigar stump soared through the darkness and landed with a slight hiss in the water below. 'Christ,' Billy cursed, 'he's off.'

But the big rating was wrong. He heard another hiss and a sigh of relief. Billy smiled to himself as he identified the sound. The man was taking a leak into the river. 'Just the job,' he said and lunged forward.

The lookout didn't have a chance. Both his hands were occupied elsewhere, as Billy's pistol butt slammed into the base of his skull. He gave a soft moan. Still spraying urine, he started to collapse. Hurriedly, Billy grabbed hold of him. Just in time. Billy grunted, as he took hold of the dead weight with his one free hand. Teeth gritted, he lowered the unconscious man to the deck as quietly as he could.

Now Dickie Bird clambered over the rail. He nodded his approval when he saw the lookout stretched out on the deck. Hastily he reached inside the unconscious man's jacket. He pulled out his wallet. It was stuffed with franc notes, which he ignored. He was looking for something else. He tugged out the little green passport, opened it and flicked through the pages, holding them up to the fitful light of the sickle moon. 'German all right, Billy... Ah, here we have it.'

'What,' Billy whispered, revolver still clasped menacingly in his big ham of a hand.

'Hard to read in this light and my German is decidedly ropey. But it says *"Sonderausweis."*'

'What's that when it's at home, sir?'

'Sort of "special identification document",' Dickie Bird answered, 'and who would be carrying a special identification document on a boating holiday in France, eh?'

'Some sort of agent, perhaps, sir?'

'Exactly. It would be useful for crossing the frontiers in and out of Germany without any awkward questions being asked. Yes, I think we're on to something here, Billy.'

He hesitated no longer. Sticking both fingers between his lips like some street urchin whistling for his mongrel dog, he whistled softly. It was the signal for Smith and Ginger Kerrigan hiding in the bushes next to the wheelhouse to go into action. 'All right,' he hissed, 'come on Billy, we'll have a look at the forrard hold and watch your step. You never know. Come on now.'

Von Horn awoke with a start. He had been indulging himself in his favourite. It dated back to the days when he had been a cadet in the German Imperial Navy. They had been swimming naked in the fiord at Kiel, a great gang of cadets, none of them older than seventeen. Suddenly as he had seen those lean muscular bodies cleaving the seawater, he had forgotten just how freezingly cold it was. He had been overcome by a powerful sense of longing, desire. So much so that he had stopped swimming and had almost gone down choking on the salty water. He had known at that particular moment that he was different. It had been the turning point of his life.

Now he banished that delightful moment of awakening, instantly. 'Georg,' he hissed to the bodyguard snoring in the bunk opposite. He reached out a hand and shook the big petty officer. 'Georg.'

Georg sat up suddenly. '*Was ... was ist los?*' he asked grumpily and scratched his tousled hair. Then he saw von Horn sitting up, pulling on his shoes and said. '*Herr Kapitan-*

leutnant?' Drilled in the harsh discipline of the Imperial Navy he actually sat to attention.

'I think there's someone on the deck,' von Horn hissed, reaching for his jacket. 'Take your pistol and have a look.'

'*Jawohl, Herr Kapitanleutnant.*'

'And don't put on your boots,' von Horn whispered urgently, pulling the big automatic out of the pocket of his jacket and clicking off the safety.

As Georg moved to the ladder which led to the wheelhouse and the deck, von Horn's mind raced madly. He knew instinctively that the intruders up top had to be the English. They had found the firebomb and somehow they had linked him with it. Now they were seeking revenge or something. He knew the English. They were a cruel, violent people. They could possibly kill him, but he didn't think they were going to do that. Once they discovered who he was, their well-known cunning and perfidity would overcome their bloodlust. He and his identity would be used for diplomatic purposes. By the Versailles Treaty, Germany was not supposed to have an intelligence service. In his person, they would discover that the defeated *Reich* still possessed one. Those damned treacherous socialists and Jews who now ruled Germany would be outraged. The whole plan for the future of a

New Germany would be endangered.

But how was he going to get out?

Now he could hear Georg clambering into the wheelhouse. There the door opposite the wheel led onto the deck; and it would be that the damned Tommies would be waiting for him. And he knew Georg. He wouldn't make a fight for it, if they beat him to the draw. He was just another time-server. He wasn't in this business because he believed in the Holy Cause. No, he served because the Intelligence Bureau fed him, paid him, allowed him to believe that he was of some importance. These days life outside the Navy meant misery, even starvation. The docks at Hamburg and Kiel were swarming with ex-regular naval sailors begging for jobs from the straw bosses, even paying those exploiters who could pick and choose their workers. No, Georg wouldn't be of any help.

He made his decision. There was a chance he could get off in the confusion. He had to take it now. He raised the automatic. Above he could hear a rusty creak as Georg started to open the little doors. He waited no longer. He fired once, twice, three times. The noise in the confines of the little room was ear-splitting. He paid no attention to it. Already the alarm had gone up outside.

Someone shouted angrily. He heard Georg curse. He began firing now. Von

Horn smirked cynically. He had no other option now, he told himself. Then he was clattering up the stairs. The cold air of the open door hit him in the face. He ducked almost double. He sneaked out of the door. Georg was on his right knee pumping bullets at someone further up the deck. From below the hull someone, probably the English, was returning the fire. Scarlet flame stabbed the silver darkness. He could hear the howl and whine of slugs striking off the metal stanchions.

He could hear more fire coming from forrard. So that's where they were – forrard and aft, but on the side closest to the towpath. A slug shattered the woodwork, just above his bent head. It made him realize that he hadn't much time left. It would have to be the Sâone. His mind made up, he rose from his hiding place. They spotted him immediately. He heard a shout in English. An instant later flame stabbed the darkness again. A bullet missed him by millimetres. Then he was pelting desperately for the far side of the barge.

Slugs chipped the woodwork at his flying feet with bursts of angry blue sparks. He zig-zagged crazily. Behind him Georg screamed in mortal agony and crumpled to the deck. Even as he raced for his life, von Horn told himself that he, at least, would now no longer be able to talk to the English.

Now he was almost there. He knew his luck wouldn't hold much longer. He took a deep breath and dived blind, praying there were no obstructions in his way. There weren't. He gasped with shock as he hit the icy water in a great splash. For a moment he panicked as the breath fled from his lungs. He was going to drown. But only for a moment. Next instant he was striking out with all his strength, blind to everything save that he was fighting for his life.

The bank of the other side loomed up out of the darkness. On the deck the firing had ceased and he guessed they were unable to spot him in the water. Still he was taking no chances. He kept going all-out. He raised his head out of the water. He could see the other bank pretty clearly. There was a straggle of houses lining it above the towpath, all in darkness and what looked like one of the shiny, tiled steeples, typical of that area. He made one final spurt. Next instant he was lying in the mud at the bottom of the bank, gasping like a stranded fish. He had done it!

On the barge Dickie Bird turned over the dead German with the toe of his boot. 'Nothing much here, I'm afraid,' he said.

'Makes a handsome corpse though, sir,' Ginger said unfeelingly.

'Search him,' Smith ordered, 'while we look around. We've got to be damned sharpish. Someone will have heard the firing. We don't want anything to do with the local bobbies. Come on, Dickie.' He raised his voice. 'Billy, bring the other one over here. We'll see if we can wake him up and get something out of him, at least.'

'I'll wake him all right,' Billy said grimly, as he grunted and lifted the big German as easily as if he were a child.

Hurriedly Smith and Bird went below. They lit the paraffin lamp and started to search the little cabin. There wasn't much. The three 'sailors' had obviously been travelling light. But they were German all right. There was no doubt about that. Their clothes all bore German labels and there was a German newspaper crumpled in one of the cases.

Smith sniffed. 'It had to be them,' he declared. 'They had weapons and all. But why?' He stared at the little cabin in bewilderment.

Dickie nodded his agreement. 'Yes, I understand, what have the Huns got to do with this Johnny Turk business? I know they were allies in the last show. But now Germany's finished. They've no navy, no air force and a tiny army – the Versailles Treaty has seen to that.'

'Yes, what did Churchill say recently? The word has gone out – kiss the Hun and kill the Bolshie.'

Bird laughed. 'Yes, I suppose that about sums it up, Smithie.' He yawned. 'God, I'm tired.'

'What about the one Billy knocked out?' Smith asked, knowing that Dickie was about worn out; they all were. They ought now to get underway and be a long way down the river before the French police arrived and started asking awkward questions.

'Well, what can we find out from him?' Dickie countered. 'We know they are Germans. We know they are the obvious suspects – the ones who planted the fire-bomb on the *Swordfish*. Why – can we afford to hang about, old bean, and grill the old Hun.'

'No I don't suppose we can. Right, you're on. Let's get back to the *Swordfish* and be underway before the forces of law-and-order arrive.'

Minutes later they were gone, leaving the unconscious German lying on the deck. Shivering and trembling in the reeds, von Horn gave them another ten minutes, willing himself to stay in his hiding place. Then for a second time he swam across the River Sâone, his heart burning with rage. The English wouldn't escape him, he swore, as he kicked the unconscious bodyguard back to life, declaring, *'Come on, you damned hero, do you want to live for ever?'*

9

'We have made some enquiries, very discreet enquiries,' the Passport Control Officer said carefully. He was C's man in Marseilles, working in the office of the British consul as the official who dealt with British passports. 'That barge of yours has vanished from the face of the earth. Nowhere to be found. I can only assume that it has been sunk in the Sâone.'

Smith and Bird nodded their understanding. Outside in the street the place was thronged with people of every possible race and colour. There were huge Sengalese soldiers in fezes, their broad black faces covered in tribal scars. There were Berber peddlers, hawking their carpets and silver coffee cans. Legionnaires, already drunk and swaggering, their brilliant white *kepis* tilted on their cropped heads. Faintly the cries of the mob in half a dozen languages came up to them on the second-floor of C's man's office.

The official followed the direction of their gaze. 'A dangerous place, Marseilles. You can get everything here – at a price – from little boys to hashish. But never turn your back on anyone. You could find a knife sticking out of it, if you do.' He smiled a little wearily at his own joke, as if he had cracked it often and was becoming bored with it.

His smile vanished and he was business-like once more. 'I did learn one thing from *a friend–*' he made the gesture of counting money 'in the Lyons police. Two Germans left the airport there yesterday bound for Paris and then booked from there to Cologne. One was very blond and an albino. The other had a heavily bandaged head under his hat.'

'One of my chaps has a rather heavy hand, especially when it is wielding a revolver,' Smith chipped in.

'Apparently.'

'So that's the couple. Can we find out anything else about them?' Dickie Bird asked.

'Unfortunately no. As you know our Army of the Rhine occupies the Cologne area up to the left bank of the Rhine. The local airport is on the other side and therefore not under our control. However I will contact one of our chaps in the Old Firm,' he meant C's secret service, 'in Cologne and see what he can find out. One thing is sure, however, this albino chap seems to have given up on you and has returned home with his tail between his legs.'

Smith sucked his bottom lip thoughtfully for a moment. 'Well, that's a relief anyway,' he said after a moment. 'Now we'll concentrate on the next leg of the journey to Alexandria.'

'Well, I don't know if you're in the clear yet,' the Passport Control Officer said carefully, telling himself that C had probably sent these brave young officers to their death. He had fought in the Dardanelles in '15 and knew how damned dangerous that forty-mile narrow stretch of water was. 'One thing I would suggest is that you keep a tight control on your chaps, while your craft is anchored here and that as soon as you have taken aboard what you need to cross the Med, you leave Marseilles.'

Dickie Bird grinned and said boldly, 'Sir, if you could see the crew of the *Swordfish* you'd realize that the locals are more likely to be afraid of them than the other way round. Sometimes they even frighten me.'

C's man returned his grin and then turning went to the big green safe in the corner. He twisted the dials and with a grunt opened it. It was stuffed full of papers and blank British passports. Over his shoulder he said, 'I could retire to South America with a fortune if I sold this little lot at the next street corner here. Half the world, it seems to me, is clamouring for a

British passport. They are worth their weight in gold.' He took out a thick bundle of dirty, used French franc notes. 'Here,' he said to Smith, 'this should pay for all you'll need while you're here in Marseilles. The French franc is also legal tender in Egypt. Use them there and not pounds.'

'Thank you, sir,' Smith said accepting the money and stowing it away inside his shirt for safety. He had heard all about Marseilles' notorious pickpockets.

'Just one more thing,' C's man said carefully. 'Have a look at this, please.'

The photograph was gritty and had obviously been taken secretly, for the edges were blurred. But it was good enough for identification purposes. It showed a tall blond man, a fur hat of the kind worn by the Russians tilted at a rakish angle on the yellow thatch. Below there was a handsome confident face. The man smiled, but the eyes did not match the warm smile. They were hard, wary and very clever.

'The man you are looking at is the head of the Petrograd *cheka,* the Russian secret police and espionage service. His name is supposed to be Aronson, but I doubt if that is his real name,' C's man continued. 'They say he bears a Jewish-sounding name because a lot of the Reds' top people are Jewish. Others say he is really a German, one of those Baltic Germans, who inhabit that coastline all along the Baltic. They maintain his real name is Ahrenstein. But one thing is certain.' He looked at the two young officers who might well be dead before this month was out. 'Aronson is the most dangerous man in Russia.'

They both looked at him puzzled.

'Oh yes,' he insisted. 'Aronson has his finger in every pie. We are certain of that.' He looked down at the crowded street below, his face very serious. 'For all I know he – or his agents – are down there at this very moment.'

'But why, Russia, sir?' Smith asked puzzled.

'The Russkis have always wanted to get into the Med through the Dardanelles so that they have an outlet for their Black Sea. Anything which weakens Turkey means that they'll be able to put pressure on the Turks in order to give them access to the Dardanelles.' C's man tugged the end of his long nose and smiled a little cynically. 'The old Czars might be dead, but the Reds are continuing the same old expanionist imperial policies, believe you me.'

Dickie vented a frustrated sigh. 'Oh, my sainted aunt, what a confused mess! First Huns, now the Russkis. A chap could end up in the looney bin, trying to understand it all, sir.'

C's man looked at him a little indulgently.

'Young man, this is the real world of 1922. Europe and the Near East is in total disarray. The old empires and the old certainties have vanished. In their place we've got a lot of little states, where religion fights religion, race fights race and people go to war at the drop of a hat, with none of the great powers prepared to do anything about it, except ourselves – and then only unofficially.' He looked very grave suddenly. 'The Americans are ditherers or isolationist. The French are selfish, concerned only with their own affairs and interests. That new man in Italy, Mussolini, might be of some use in the future, but not at the moment. He's too bothered with internal affairs, consolidating his new power.' He paused and then said, 'Ah well, the Empire will come through it all, I don't doubt. It always does. Now then,' he stretched out his hand, 'the best of luck to you, Smith.' His grip was weak and tired, Smith thought, as he took the proffered hand. 'Good luck to you, Bird, as well.'

'Thank you, sir,' they both said as one.

C's man forced a weary grin, as he searched their keen young faces, as if he were trying to etch them on his mind's eye for good. 'If I'm not here when you come back, I'll probably be sitting on some South American beach, contemplating my navel and surrounded by dusky nubile maidens, thanks to the sale of several score of British passports. Goodbye.'

'Goodbye, sir,' they said and went out into the misty morning sunshine, pushing their way through the throng, chattering and calling out their wares in half a dozen languages.

'This is the drill,' Smith said, as they attempted to avoid the peddlars and pimps and seedy looking men, with dark bags under their eyes, offering them dirty postcards in several languages, *'Schmutzige Bilder ... beaucoups de cons ... naughty ladies'* etc. 'We tank up the old *Swordfish* with as much juice as she'll take. I intend to go right across Med, with no stops at Cyprus, Crete or the like.'

'She should just make it to Alex,' Dickie Bird agreed. 'Go on.'

'I'll see to the supplies. There are plenty of ships' chandlers and the like in the *Vieux Port*. Gosh I wonder how to ask for Bass' Pale Ale in French – the chaps do like their ale.'

'They like something else, Smithie,' Dickie said cheekily, neatly fielding an Arab in a fez and dirty robe who was trying to hand him a grubby little boy, rasping, *'Seulement quarante franc, M'sieur ... très, très bon.'*

Smith gave a mock moan. 'Must you bring *that* up, Dickie?'

'A sailor's lot is a hard one,' Dickie replied

with a mischievous twinkle in his eyes. 'All work and no play makes Jack a dull boy.'

'They all get filthy diseases, I'll be bound. But they're good chaps,' he conceded. 'They need a bit of fun before the balloon really goes up. But we're going to do this thing properly.'

'What do you mean?' Dickie asked, as they turned the corner and saw the packed harbour stretched out in front of them, the water dirty, oil-scummed and full of floating trash.

'I'll put CPO Ferguson in charge. He'll march to a – er – house of ill-fame and supervise what's going on there.'

'Rather like a church parade,' Dickie said cheekily. 'What about calling it the knocking-shop parade?' he chortled.

'I'll be *knocking* your blinking block if you say another word,' Smith threatened and then in a high good mood, he linked his arm under Dickie's crying, 'Now let's get on with it.'

That afternoon they worked flat out. While CPO Ferguson took charge of filling the *Swordfish's* tanks, eyeing the pumps' meters with an eagle eye in case the Frenchman attempted to cheat him, Smith went shopping, accompanied by Ginger Kerrigan and Billy Bennett. Two hours later they were on their way back to the Old Port, followed by a procession of barefoot Arab boys bearing crates of beer, sacks of potatoes, paper bags full of French bread on their heads.

'Feel like a frigging slave trader with this little lot behind us,' Ginger complained as the rest of the crew broke out laughing and cat-calling when they saw the little procession. 'Don't whip me massah, sir... I's only poor black fellah,' they mocked in what they thought was a foreign accent.

By that time the ship was almost ready for sea. Bird had carried out a thorough inspection of the hold and engines and told Smith, 'We're ready to sail on the midnight tide, Smithie. Everything's ship-shape and Bristol fashion.'

'Thanks Dickie,' he replied. 'What's the met forecast?' He flashed a look around the bridge, as if to reassure himself that all the instruments were in place and functioning.

'Pretty good, if I understood the French harbourmaster's chap correctly. Wind Force three, visibility at dawn two miles and no storms in the offing.'

'Excellent.' Smith looked down to where CPO Ferguson was counting out the tips for the excited Arab urchins, turning over every *sou* in his horny palm, as if it were his own money he was giving away instead of the government's. 'All right, I suppose the men deserve a little – er – entertainment if they fancy it, Dickie. But ensure that they're all equipped with french letters.'

'I say, Smithie,' Dickie Bird protested. 'You'll be ordering me to put them on next.' But dutifully he trotted off to tell CPO Ferguson that he was in charge of the men who wanted to visit the whores.

Ferguson didn't like it; he didn't like it one bit. 'I've never disobeyed an order in thirty years in the Royal Navy,' he protested, face an angry red. 'But it's asking a lot from a petty officer to command a party o' dirty lustful men to take them to yon harlots.' He indicated the nearest waterfront brothel with the bored whores hanging out of the windows, smoking sulkily or making offers to the passing sailors. 'It's no right, I'm telling yer, sir.' He shook his grizzled head in indignation.

'You don't have to look, Chiefie,' Dickie said cheerfully. 'Just get them in and out – in one piece – that's all.'

Five minutes later those who wanted to visit the whores were being mustered by an angry, red-faced Ferguson to cheerful cries from the others, *'Get fall in, knocking shop party'* and *'Don't forget, lads – whip it in, whip it out and then wipe it.'* Moments after that they stepped out excitedly, while the whores at the windows waved excitedly, *'Par ici … venez vite!* … come quick, *Rostbif!'*

'Which undoubtedly they will,' a smiling Dickie Bird commented.

Up the cobbled quay, the little runt of a man in the black beret who had been lounging, watching all the time, spat out his Gauloise. Slowly, casually, he walked over to the phone box in the *Bar du Port* and changed a franc piece for a *jetton*, which he inserted in the box. With one hand over the mouthpiece, he dialled the number they had given him swiftly. The voice at the other end asked, *'Stoi?'*

'Alexis, gavorit...'

At the bar, the bored owner heard the words in the unfamiliar language. He shrugged. Why couldn't any normal person speak French like everyone else? he asked himself. He shrugged again. But then these White Russians who were everywhere now since the Revolution were a funny lot, even at the best of times. He spat drily into the water he used to wash the glasses.

10

'Now hear this,' CPO Ferguson said grimly, trying not to see the half-naked whores in their black stockings and garters and precious little else, who thronged the main hall waiting for the sailors. 'You've got an hour in this house o'shame – nair maer.

You'll all wear one of them french letters and ye'll all wash that filthy – *carefully* – afterwards, Ye ken what I'm talking about?' he demanded.

Cheekily, Ginger Kerrigan quipped. 'We ken an' all and all, Chiefie. But do we really have to do it to numbers, one, two, three, one, two, three, Chiefie?' He grinned wickedly.

'Hold ye blether, man,' Ferguson snapped. 'Ye've got yer orders. Now get on with the filthy business. I'm gonna post myself on yon chair and no one leaves without reporting to me. Get on with it!'

The sailors needed no urging. They burst ranks and hurried to the waiting whores, who were rubbing their crotches and making obscene gestures with their tongues as if they simply couldn't wait for the excited young Englishmen to take them.

Grumpily Ferguson took up his seat, back ramrod straight as he sat there, glowering at the madam in her black silk as she crouched behind her cash register, busily engaged in doing her sums with a pencil and a scrap of paper.

Ferguson had frequented brothels all over the world. 'White, black, yeller and mixed, I've had 'em all,' he had once boasted to his shipmates in the petty officers' mess in the old days. Now he considered himself too old. 'At fifty,' he had confided in another old petty officer, 'it's not dignified for a chief petty officer to be seen in one o' yon places. The ratings lose respect for a CPO if they see him in such a place, rollicking and spending his bawbees on loose women.'

So it was that Chief Petty Officer Ferguson, who had suppressed all carnal thoughts since he had got drunk after the Battle of Jutland and had found himself in bed with a Hull housewife, whose husband had gone down with the *Black Prince* during the battle, felt a surprising stirring of his loins. He looked down and the bulge in his dark blue trousers confirmed it. 'Good God,' he muttered to himself, 'yon thing's a-moving.'

The cause of this earth-shaking movement was a dark lithe creature in see-through pyjamas, her brown body naked from the waist upwards, revealing splendid little breasts, the nipples of which had been painted a bright carmine-red. And she was looking invitingly directly at the old sea-salt, sucking her middle finger with all the innocence of a depraved nine year old.

She seemed to slither across to Ferguson under the watchful gaze of the black-clad madam, who was probably already working out what it would cost for her to pleasure the ancient *Rostbif*. Now an agog, slightly panting Ferguson could see that she wore nothing below the transparent harem trousers – and that her genital hair had been shaven off. He had seen some things during his time at the China Station back at the turn of the century, but never anything like that. He began to pant even more.

'*Gavoritu-vi pa russki? … hable Espagnol … können Sie deutsch … parla Italinao … Speak you English?*' she rattled off the question in the parrot-fashion of someone who had been used to doing it many times before, inserting her middle finger between her scarlet lips with a knowing look in every pause.

CPO Ferguson swallowed hard. As if from a long distance away, he heard himself say, 'I'm a Scot, but I do speak English.'

Her dark face lit up, as if this were very important to know. 'A Scot!' she exclaimed. 'Those are de English who wear de skirts–'

'Kilts,' he corrected her.

She didn't seem to hear. She placed her hand on his crotch and breathed. 'How I want you wear de skirt. I could put fingers under here and do ze naughty tings to you.'

Up above on the landing, Ginger, already naked to his underpants, chortled, 'Put it in crutches, Chiefie, and bring it upstairs – *smartish!*'

Five minutes later CPO Ferguson was lying spreadeagled on a rickety bed protesting, 'I've na done it for a long while, Miss,' while Tanja, as the whore said she was

117

called, ripped off his trousers to reveal the skinny white legs below and that monument to youth and enterprise which stood again after so many years of lying dormant.

'*Grossartig* … *magnifique* … *molto bene* … *tremendous*,' she cried, eyeing it as if it were the first time that she had ever seen it. 'You naughty boy, hiding zat from Tanja all ze time.' She pouted. 'You give Tanja … if you love her. Tanja want him – *now!*'

So saying she squatted on top of the old Scot and before he knew what he was doing he was back to the joys of his youth, when young sailors used to declare fervently, 'There's three things that keep Jack Tar happy – *baccy, booze and a bit o' the other!*' He was getting a 'bit of the other' once again.

Afterwards, she lay in his hands, playing with the grey hairs on his white skinny chest, proclaiming that nobody had 'loved me like this' and 'I am ze happiest girl in ze world', which under normal circumstances, CPO Ferguson would have doubted very strongly. But these weren't normal circumstances, not for him. A well-content CPO Ferguson was prepared at this moment to believe the dusky little whore's most blatant and transparent lies.

'Och,' he said generously, 'it's no much to write home about. But ye ken I have been doing it a long time.' He shook his head in fond self-admiration.

She said. 'You are a wonderful sailorman. You have been many places.'

'Ay, that I have, missie.' He beamed. Her cunning little hand was beginning to slip down to his loins once more. Could he do it another time he wondered. At his age!

'Where you go now?' she asked and stuck her tongue in his ear wetly, while her fingers clutched what they sought.

Ferguson felt his breath coming more quickly. By God, he told himself excitedly, he was really going to do it again! 'Go?' he echoed, hardly recognizing his own voice. 'We go ... I mean,' he corrected himself, 'to Alexandria. That's in Egypt ... on the night's tide.'

She burrowed her tongue even deeper in his ear, her hand moving very busily now so that he was already panting for breath, as if he were running a great race. 'And from Egypt where then?'

'What?' he cried, skinny old body lathered in sweat, as his spine arched with the almost unbearable pleasure of it all.

'Where do you go from Egypt, darling?'

'To Turk–' He could stand it no longer. Face crimson, mouth gaping open, to show his yellowing false teeth, CPO Ferguson cried, *I'm coming... Oh, God, I'm coming...*' And he was.

A moment later Ginger Kerrigan was hammering on the door, crying, 'Come on,

Chiefie, we've got to get back to the *Swordfish*. Or do you want me to come in there and give yer a hand like.'

An exhausted Ferguson felt like replying angrily, 'No ye cheeky booger, I've had enough hand as it is.' But he simply didn't have the strength.

Thus it was that they led him back to the boat through the growing darkness, the air full of the exotic scents of Arabic food and scents, walking in silence, each man wrapped up in a cocoon of his own thoughts. With difficulty they bundled CPO Ferguson on board and he staggered straight off to his little cabin, stared at by Dickie Bird and Smith. Finally the former broke the heavy brooding silence as the men began to disperse, 'I say, old chap, do you think our old Chiefie indulged? I mean I thought he'd be too old for that kind of thing. After all he did sail with Nelson on the *Victory,* didn't he?'

Together they burst out laughing. Then Smith pulled himself together and said, 'We'll allow them four hours' sleep, Dickie. We sail at midnight. Tricky in a port like this in darkness, but wiser, don't you think?'

'Exactly. Now what about a couple of pink gins and then we can get a bit of shut-eye too.'

'Well said, Dickie. Let's do that.' Together they went down below, watched as they did by yet another petty spy. But they did not know that. Two pink gins later, they were yawning their heads off and without too much further ado the two old friends stretched out on the leather couches which made up most of the furniture of the tiny wardroom and were fast asleep almost as soon as their heads touched the headrests...

A thousand miles away on the other side of the world, the lights still burned in the Cheka Headquarters in Petrograd's Technical Institute. Clerks in Red uniform strode up and down the echoing corridors purposefully. Behind frosted glass windows typewriters clattered and telephones rang. Down below in the cellars, fresh prisoners, reactionaries and White terrorists, for the most part, were being cross-examined to the accompaniment of slaps, kicks and blows from their interrogators' rubber clubs. All was purposeful activity and the huddled masses still trawling the frozen, snow-bound streets of Petrograd, now called Leningrad, told themselves the Red swine were working overtime again. But as they trudged by the hard-faced sentries guarding the building, they raised their clenched fists and said hollowly, as was expected of them, '*Mir boudit!*'

'Peace is coming, comrade,' the guards echoed the latest slogan routinely.

Up in his office in the second floor,

Aronson, tall, blond and muscular, waited impatiently. Marseilles had first alerted him on the Englishmen's arrival four hours before. During that time he and his operatives had got their voluminous files and agents' reports in a great hurry. By seven they had identified them. They were the same Englishmen whom they had failed to liquidate during the Russian-Polish War back in 1919 and one of them was, for certain, the swine who had sunk the *Spartak* at Kronstadt the years before.*

He had then called in his chief-agent for the Asia Minor area. Achmet Khan, dark, hairy with flashing black eyes, posed as a Soviet citizen from the south of the USSR. He spoke both Russian and several of the local southern dialects fluently. In fact, he was, as only Aronson knew, a British citizen, who had been educated at Oxford and there had been converted to the radical group of extremists devoted to freeing their native India from British rule by armed force.

In 1918 during one of his many trips abroad, which were used for recruiting agents, Aronson had won him over to the communist cause. He had been very useful in helping to foment anti-Government riots in London and among the British troops being sent to Russia to help the Whites

*See C. Whiting, *The Baltic Run* for further details.

fighting against the Reds. A year later Aronson had had him brought to Russia to take part in the campaign to create trouble in his native land and other parts of the British Empire in the Near East.

He had come in, raised his clenched fist and rattled off yet another of those obscure slogans the government in Moscow were always issuing, 'All power to the people, comrade!'

Aronson had looked up from his desk and smiled coldly. 'What power, comrade?'

Achmet Khan's dark face lit up. 'Yes, it is rather stupid, isn't it?'

Aronson had indicated the bottle of vodka and the glasses on the desk and said, 'Throw one of those down behind your collar stud and sit down.'

'You know my religion forbids me to touch alcohol,' Achmet Khan said. He poured himself a large glass, raised it, toasted Aronson with '*Nastrovya*' and downed it in one pleasurable gulp. '*Horoscho.* That certainly drives out your damned Russian cold.'

Aronson liked the Indian. At least he wasn't so scared and mealy-mouthed as most of his agents, frightened of their own shadows so that they didn't dare say anything that might be thought of as anti-party or anti-Russian.

'Well, Khan,' he had commenced, trying not to hear the rattle of musketry as they shot another bunch of traitors in the snowbound courtyard behind the building, 'those English I mentioned earlier have arrived in their boat in Marseilles. I am now awaiting news of their destination.'

'I am sure it will be Turkey,' the other man said eyeing the bottle. 'The British imperialists will want to stop this Turkish business if they can.'

'Yes, do have another drink. Yes I agree with you. Now we don't want it stopped. We want to set the whole area aflame. It will serve our aims to have the British Empire in disarray.'

'Mine, too,' Achmet Khan said simply, pouring himself another large drink. 'The British have carried the white man's burden for too long. I, for one, am eager to relieve them of it at once.' He smiled, showing a set of excellent white teeth.

'I'm sure you are. Now, comrade, this is what we are going to do as soon as we know the Englishmen's next port-of-call.' Rapidly he outlined his plan, ending with 'The code-name for the operation is "Accident on the High Seas". As soon as I give you it, you will go into action. And understand, comrade,' he had leaned forward and had looked at the other man with such penetrating force that Achmet Khan had felt a cold finger of fear trace its way down his spine, 'you must *not* fail.'

Khan had hidden his fear well. He said very confidently, 'I will not fail you, comrade.'

That had been two or so hours ago now. Impatiently Aronson waited for the next bit of information to be transmitted from Marseilles to the radio room deep in the cellars of the Cheka HQ. Finally it came in the shape of Ilona, who was his favourite messenger. Not only was she one of his current mistresses, but she was also his spy in the radio room.

Ilona, white-blonde with a splendid figure and exciting green eyes, thought he was some kind of reactionary, secretly plotting against the new Soviet state and she assisted him because she, too, was a reactionary, daughter of Czarist admiral who had been shot by his own sailors back in '18. And perhaps he was a reactionary of a kind, Aronson told himself, as she stood at attention in the doorway, message in her hand.

He loved 'Holy Mother Russia' fervently. In his lifetime Russia had been ruled by fools, even traitors: the German Empress besotted by that mad monk Rasputin, that weak-kneed liberal fool Kerensky and now this Mongol, Lenin, who had spent his life in exile, actively sabotaging their noble country. But Russia had survived them all in the past and it would survive Lenin, too, because there were men like him, who loved the black earth of Mother Russia and its ordinary people, drunken, ignorant and lazy as most of them were. Russia would survive because there were men like him, cunning but determined, who placed their country first and their private interests second: men who wanted no glory but only the welfare of Russia.

'Read it, comrade,' he commanded.

Da, da, tvarorishch.

She closed the door and relaxed. 'Their destination is Alexandria,' she said simply.

'Thank you, Ilona.' He clicked on the switch of the intercom. 'Comrade Khan,' he said.

'Yes?'

'Alexandria – put plan "Accident on the High Seas" into operation at once,' he ordered sternly.

He heard a sharp intake of breath at the other end, then Khan said, 'I depart this night.'

'Good and good luck, Comrade.' He switched off the intercom and looked at Ilona.

She knew immediately what he wanted. She turned and locked the door before slipping out of her skirt to reveal shapely thighs and the fact that she was wearing black silk knickers trimmed with real lace.

He affected surprise. 'Don't you know, comrade, that the new Soviet woman neither powders her face nor reddens her lips? Cotton is good enough for being next to her skin. Silk and lace are decadent and bourgeois.'

She laughed easily. 'But then I'm a reactionary,' she said and grinned naughtily. 'Now will you come and help me to remove this decadent and bourgeois under-garment?'

Now it was his turn to laugh. He rose saying, 'It would give me the greatest of pleasure...'

TWO

DEATH IN THE MED

'They call him the Grey Wolf. He is cunning, cruel, but a patriot. Such men are dangerous.'

Aronson, head of the Russian CHEKA on Kemal Ataturk, 1922

1

On the second day out, the weather in the Mediterranean started to change dramatically. They awoke that morning to find the sea a glassy pond. Above, the sun was a dull copper like a penny glimpsed at the bottom of a scummy pond. It was hot, oppressively hot, which was unusual for that time of the year. Indeed more than once as Smith stared at the empty sea all around him, he had patted the sweat on his forehead and Dickie Bird commented, 'I say, old bean, not nice at all – the weather I mean.'

As usual the cook had prepared the usual heavy stodge of porridge, followed by greasy sausage and chunks of fried bread, but even Billy Bennett, that notorious glutton, refused more than a sausage or two and hunks of fried bread. 'You can have my bangers, Billy,' Ginger offered. 'Seem to be off me grub this morning.' But Billy refused, munching at the hunk of bread slowly and without his usual appetite.

'It's the sirocco, I think, or perhaps the levante,' Smith opined. 'I remember they taught us all about those winds coming north from Africa to Europe, but I always forget which is which.'

Dickie breathed out and flapped his shirt back and forth – it was already black with sweat– 'All I know, Smithie, is that it is deucedly hot.'

Half an hour later there was the first faint stirring of wind. To the south the horizon flushed a faint pink and as the wind came closer the whole superstructure of the *Swordfish* started to turn the same colour as the wind coming straight from the Sahara deposited the desert sand upon it.

Dickie looked anxious. 'They say these winds can be stinkers,' he said as the horizon grew progressively darker. 'Do you think we should radio for met?'

Smith shook his head. 'I don't want to break wireless silence, Dickie and give our position away. We're somewhere off the Greek coast just below Salonica. According to Admiralty information there is a host of small fishing port down there. I can imagine they won't have much in the way of links with the outer world, just a handful of fishermen living in huts and what they catch in their caiques. At a pinch we can run for one of those places and shelter.' Suddenly he realized he was shouting, the wind was so loud.

All that morning it continued to rise in force. Waves buffeted the little craft. She was swung from side to side, as if punched by a great invisible fist. Down below the engines laboured mightily, as the *Swordfish* fought the current. More than once the vessel balanced on the crest of waves, her screws churning the air impotently. The galley fires went out. All that the harassed, angry cook could serve for the midday meal was a lukewarm mug of cocoa; and for those on deck most of that was slopped out of the mug, as the *Swordfish* lurched and yawped alarmingly.

Clinging to the stanchions in the little chart house, Dickie bellowed into Smith's ear, face crimson with the effort, 'Smithie, I think we ought to run for shelter. We're not making any headway and the bulkhead has begun to spring leaks in several places.'

Smith looked through the glass panel, streaming with seawater. Ahead the sea rose and fell alarmingly. Great grey-green vicious swells, capped with angry white water, which flung tons of water across the little craft's bows each time they struck here. 'Are the pumps working?' he yelled, capping his hands over his mouth.

'Not too well. One of them seems particularly duff, I'm afraid.'

'All right.' Smith made his decision. 'We'll run for the coast. Perhaps we won't even have to go into a port. We might be able to sit it out in the shelter of the shore.'

Billy Bennett was tied to a stout rope,

vomiting over the side when he saw it – or, at first, thought he had. He shook his big head, like a bull trying to rid itself of flies, and stared hard through the torrential rain. No, there was no mistaking it. There was a ship out there.

He strained his eyes, as the wind and the rain buffeted his face, blinking his eyes all the time to keep them clear. It was a big ship. Perhaps some sort of freighter, heavy with cargo, too. For it was wallowing deep in the water, the waves sweeping over its foredeck time and time again. But there was something strange about the one-funnelled freighter which he couldn't make out for a moment. Then it struck him. The vessel was without any kind of light, not even riding lights, and that in terrible weather like this when visibility was down to yards.

Billy Bennett overcame his sickness. He retreated backwards across the heaving, wet and treacherous deck, grateful for the stout rope which attached to the superstructure. He fought his way up the ladder to the little bridge, the wind howling all about him, threatening to snatch him from his precarious perch at any moment. With a grunt, he blundered his way into the bridgehouse where Lieutenant Bird himself was at the helm, eyes glued to his front, trying to peer through that howling streaming white-green gloom. 'Sir, sir,' he cried urgently, feeling

134

the nauseous stirrings of his guts once more. God, he hoped he wasn't going to be sick in the bridgehouse. God knows what CPO Ferguson would do to him if he were.

'What is it?' Smith roared, not taking his gaze off his front, 'and shut that bloody door.'

Bennett exerted all his strength, shoulder to the door and heaved it close. It was a little quieter inside now.

'Ship off the port bow, sir ... just saw her... And she's without lights.'

'What?'

'Without lights—' Billy Bennett's stomach heaved alarmingly. He flung open the door. Just in time. The hot vomit welled up in his throat uncontrollably, all thought of CPO Ferguson forgotten in his wretchedness.

Smith swung the wheel to port. He leaned forward, until his nose was almost touching the wet streaming glass, his eyes narrowed to slits, as he peered out.

Yes, there she was! An old coal-burning coastal freighter, very low in the water, trailing clouds of black smoke behind her from her stack, as she fought the gale. He looked hard. She didn't have a single light the length of her structure. Suddenly Smith felt a sensation of acute alarm – apprehension. What was the old tub doing running before a storm without lights on a day like this? There was something wrong. He made a swift decision. He swung the wheel to starboard. In the very same instant that whoever was on the bridge of the freighter spotted the *Swordfish*. And he knew instinctively they had been spotted. For the mystery ship had changed course and was bearing down upon them.

Groaning and creaking like a live thing crying out in protest, the *Swordfish* started to pull round. He exerted more pressure. She seemed to be turning with incredible slowness. *'Come on, damn you!'* he cursed the boat angrily though he loved the old *Swordfish* dearly, 'COME ON!' But that tremendous wind and furious waves conspired against them. The freighter with the wind behind her was moving at a much faster pace.

Smith flung a glance out of the front. She was almost upon them now. She towered above the *Swordfish* but peer as he may he could see no one on the bridge. Not even a light in the wheelhouse. His apprehension was replaced by a feeling of fear. There was something uncanny about this mysterious ship bearing down upon them like this. He remembered the *Marie Celeste,* discovered in the middle of the ocean in the late nineteenth century, with not a soul aboard her. Was this some latterday *Marie Celeste?*

'Damn fool,' he cursed himself and willed the *Swordfish* to come round in time, his shoulder muscles red hot with the pain of the effort.

Billy Bennett staggered back inside, wiping the vomit and rain off his fat face. 'She's doing it, sir,' he yelled. 'She's gonna do it–'

His cry was drowned by the great crash as the bow of the freighter swiped sideways against the bulkhead of the *Swordfish*. The *Swordfish* reeled crazily. Her wireless mast actually touched the surface of the raging sea. For one terrible moment Smith thought she might turn turtle. But she righted herself just in time, as the freighter swept on, leaving her wallowing there, already beginning to take in water. Moments later the freighter had disappeared into that crazy inferno – gone as mysteriously as it had appeared.

Now, with the water pouring in, her engines slowing down, the crippled *Swordfish* seemed at the mercy of that terrible sea. Anxiously Smith hung on to a suddenly sluggish wheel, waiting for the reports. They were bad. Dickie was first to appear. He had run below immediately on impact, flung a swift glance at the damage there and then done the same outside on deck, risking his life to hang over the side to do so. 'It's bad, I'm afraid, Smithie,' he roared above the frantic howl of the wind and the constant battering of the waves, 'devilishly bad. We're holed *above* the waterline, but in this weather it doesn't make much difference.' He shrugged helplessly.

He was followed moments later by CPO Ferguson. For the first time since he had known the old salt, Smith could see the former was afraid. 'Yon pump's still holding out. The water's coming in at a tremendous rate, sir,' he reported, licking his old wrinkled lips all the time as if he were parched. 'Once it gets to the engines we're finished, sir.'

'Never say die, Chiefie,' Dickie tried to cheer him up. 'We're not licked yet. We could–' the *Swordfish* lurched alarmingly and Smith at the wheel could feel the power going rapidly. He had to make a decision – and he had to make it fast. He did so. 'We're about five or six miles from land,' he shouted. 'We've got two boats – they're not damaged, Dickie?'

Dickie shook his head quickly.

'Well, we're going to lash them together and head for the land. With a bit of luck we can get to the lee of the coast and that should shelter us from the worst of the storm.'

'Abandon the *Swordfish* … abandon ship, sir?' Ferguson cried, horror replacing the fear in his old eyes. 'Ye no can do that, sir!' he objected.

'I'm afraid we're going to have to, Chiefie,'

Smith yelled above the howling wind. 'Come on now – smartish. *Abandon ship!*'

'Ay, ay, sir,' Ferguson snapped in his old style. 'I'll see to it.' He staggered along the sloping deck and with his hands clapped around his mouth, the wind whipping his clothes to his skinny body, he started shouting out his orders, while the two officers grabbed the weighted code books in the little canvas sack and whatever they thought was most needed.

The ratings needed no urging. They splashed their way through the knee-deep water below trying to keep their balance as the battered holed *Swordfish* began to list. With difficulty, heads bent against the wind and rain, they staggered up the decks to the boats.

Just as they reached them there was a loud rending noise. 'Christ,' Ginger cried in alarm, 'we're going down!'

'Don't be frigging stupid!' Billy roared and grabbed for the stanchion lines. 'The old *Swordfish* won't let us down – yet.'

Despite the terrific buffeting she was taking, the stout little craft still remained afloat, as they fumbled and tugged, trying to free the boats before it was too late. In the end someone found an axe and began hacking at the obstinate ropes, while the wind howled and the bitter raindrops lashed their ashen, tense faces.

The first boat slammed into the water. Smith breathed a sigh of relief. It had landed squarely on its keel and not over-turned. 'Come on ... come on,' he cried urgently. 'Over you go, the first crew.'

The men scrambled over the side, trying to judge the distance, as the crippled vessel bobbed up and down like a child's toy. Behind him Dickie Bird supervised the launching of the second craft, praying fervently that his boat was going to land the right way up. It did and Ginger who had recovered his nerve cried, 'All aboard the *Skylark*.' But the usual bantering, cheerful note had vanished from his voice. They all knew what this moment meant. They were leaving the *Swordfish* for good. For most of them it had been their home since Kron-stadt. Now they would soon see her no more.

Smith fought back his tears and he waited until Dickie had tied his boat to theirs with a stout rope. Then, sitting there wet and miserable, the little boats riding up and down the creamy white waves like cars on a rollercoaster, he saluted. A moment later, the *Swordfish* had disappeared and they were drifting and rowing into the un-known...

2

The Greek cavalry had changed from the 'walk' to the 'trot'. There were three lines of them well spread out. The thin winter sunshine glittered from their sabres which they held across their right shoulders. In front rode their officers, and their head-quarters group were tightly bunched around the blue and white flag held high aloft by the gigantic standard bearer. They made an impressive sight, as a thousand pairs of hooves sent up a cloud of grey dust.

In the Turkish lines there was no movement. The brown pits of earth, recently dug up by the Turkish infantry stalled by this sudden Greek defiance, seemed empty. Indeed there was no sign that they were occupied at all, save for the silver crescent of Turkey which fluttered from a flagpole in the centre of the Turkish line.

Now the Greek artillery thundered into action. 75mm cannon lobbed shells over the heads of the advancing cavalry, which slammed into the Turkish positions. Here and there were ripples of cherry red flame. But when the flame and the brown smoke cleared, there was still no sign of the

Turkish defenders.

On the hill overlooking the battlefield, the Grey Wolf nodded his approval. His *askaris*, peasants to the man, were showing just how tough they were. Those Anatolian peasants turned soldiers could survive all day on a bottle of water, a slab of unleavened bread and a handful of dates and sultanas. The Grey Wolf was proud of them; they were the best soldiers in the world.

The Grey Wolf, as the new dictator of Turkey Kemal Ataturk was named by his people, was happy so far with how the battle was progressing. The Greeks were still using the same suicidal tactics that their French instructors had taught them. The direct attack to the front *'à l'outrance'*. All to the good. It was the easiest way to kill as many of the Greek swine as possible. But if the Grey Wolf was pleased, nothing of that stern visage showed it. The gaunt face, the grim mouth and the washed eyes revealed nothing of his complex emotions. For all his face showed, he might well have been simply watching some pre-war tactical exercise.

Now the Greek cavalry had changed from the 'trot' to the 'canter'. The riders were moving up and down in the saddle. Here and there their horses swung their heads to one side, as they already knew what was soon to come and were afraid. But their riders held them to a tight rein. Swiftly the distance between them and the Turkish positions lessened. Soon the Greek bombardment of the enemy lines would cease and then the Greeks would charge. The Grey Wolf raised his glasses. All around him his staff, obviously all feeling uncomfortable in the new caps he had ordered them to wear instead of the traditional fez, raised theirs. Inwardly the Grey Wolf smiled. They were all time-servers and lick-spittlers, apeing his every move. He knew why, too. Only the last month he had sacked 200 officers, including 168 generals, of whom he didn't approve. They knew on which side their bread was buttered.

Suddenly, startlingly, the Greek bombardment ceased. Penetrating the loud echoing silence which followed came the silver notes of a Greek bugler, signalling the charge. The standard-bearer raised the flag of Greece high above his head. Next to him the regimental colonel rose in his stirrups and shouted something to the men behind him. He waved his sabre, the blade glinting in the sun.

A great roar rose from the ranks of the Greek riders. As one their sabres came down from their shoulders. Arms extended. Sabres came parallel with the sweating sides of their mounts.

'They charge!' one of the staff officers cried, unable to contain his excitement.

'*To their deaths,*' the Grey Wolf told himself. Aloud he said, a little harshly, but without raising his voice, 'Quiet please. I am concentrating.'

'Pardon, *Effendi,*' the staff officer whispered and dabbed his brow with a handkerchief that stank of cheap Turkish *eau de cologne*. He had incurred the Grey Wolf's displeasure. Rapidly he ran off a prayer to Allah, to whom it was officially forbidden to pray, that he wouldn't be dismissed from the army.

Now the Greek cavalry was riding all out. The horses' hooves kicked up a great cloud of dust, their manes flying in the sudden wind, as their riders lay along the length of the outstretched necks, sabres at the ready.

Still the Turkish lines lay silent and the Grey Wolf told himself what good soldiers his *askaris* were. He had fought in the Balkans, in North Africa, in Europe but he had never seen infantry so solid when faced with the awesome spectacle of a cavalry charge.

Suddenly a lone officer appeared on the parapet of one of the holes towards the centre of the Turkish positions. He smoked a cigar and the only weapon he carried was a fly whisk, which he held casually over his shoulder. The Grey Wolf gave a wintry smile. The officer, whoever he was, had style, *panache* as the French called it. He stared at the charging Greeks as if they were barely of interest.

Almost casually the unknown officer on the parapet dropped his cigar. He raised his fly whisk. Sharply he brought it down, lashing the thongs against his knee.

The Turkish line erupted in fire. At both ends and in the middle machine guns started to chatter like angry woodpeckers. Tracker sliced through the air.

The galloping men were galvanized into frenetic action like puppets controlled by a puppet-master suddenly gone crazy. Men fell screaming from their mounts. Others slumped in their saddles, while their panic-stricken horses galloped on, going all out to their death. Horses tossed their riders. They towered on their hind-legs, front hooves pawing the air furiously. Others turned, dragging screaming riders with them, caught up in the stirrups. Others went down on their knees, their white flanks flecked with scarlet blood, dying as they crouched there, whinnying piteously.

Still the Greek cavalry came in. There were great gaps in their ranks now, but they still charged, carried away by the wild, unreasoning blood lust of battle. Their colonel sprang across the first trench. An *askari* rose and tried to bayonet them. He missed. The colonel's sabre flashed. Through his binoculars Ataturk, the Grey Wolf, could see the look of absolute agony on the soldier's dark face as the sabre slashed into his neck. Next moment his head, complete with helmet, rolled to the ground, leaving the headless body to sag slowly after it.

Now more and more of the Greek riders were springing over the Turkish trenches. *Askaris* rose out of their holes to meet the challenge. Bayonets and sabres flashed and locked. Little groups of men and horses were locked in murderous combat on all sides. The Turkish commander went down under the flailing hooves of a Greek horse before he had a chance to draw his revolver. The Greek cavalryman leaned down low from his saddle and slashed his sabre to left and right of the wounded man's face. Through his glasses the Grey Wolf watched as the Turk's face slid down to his jaw like molten red wax.

To the rear another Greek regiment of cavalrymen came thundering across the plain. They cared nothing for their dead and dying comrades or the wounded horses struggling to rise again. They rode straight into them. They were wild with excitement. Even at that distance the Grey Wolf could hear them screaming and shrieking as they anchored their lances, pennants flying, in the leather cups below their saddles ready for the charge.

It was too much for the Turkish infantry.

In ones and twos at first and then in increasingly larger groups they started to pull back. At first they did so apparently reluctantly, backing off, turning to fire a shot or two before retreating again. But now as the lancers came riding at full gallop across the trenches, their great pointed spears gleaming in the weak winter sunshine, the withdrawal became a retreat.

Suddenly they were running, through the second line of defence, throwing away their rifles and helmets as they did so, the ones to the rear of the running men screaming shrilly, as the lances dug into their shoulders and transfixed them.

The Grey Wolf's face showed no emotion. He had seen it all often enough before. Those who lived would fight another day. They were not cowards. Turks were never cowards. But the impact of full-scale cavalry charges was just too much for them. He lowered his glasses and barked one word in a voice thickened by years of drinking cheap *raki* and smoking too many cigarettes. 'Artillery!'

Immediately the staff officers went into action. The field telephones whirred. Officers snapped orders. A signaller started wagging his flags. All was sudden hectic activity, while the Grey Wolf stood there, his arms folded, his dark face revealing nothing, as he watched the infantry run.

Minutes later the horizon behind him flooded a deep pink. Lights flickered, as if the doors to some huge furnace had been opened. A great boom. Moments afterwards there was a bansheelike screeching, as shells hurtled overhead, straight towards the charging Greek cavalry. Men and horses went down on all sides, as the shells ploughed huge brown-smoking holes in the fields like the work of gigantic moles. Then it was the turn of the Greeks. The survivors started to pull back, leaving behind the churned-up battlefield littered with bodies and dead horsemen.

The Grey Wolf shrugged to himself. There would be no further advance this day. In the Prophet's name, he cursed to himself, when would he get rid of those damned Greeks and set about his real task – the restoration of Turkey, no longer the sick man of Europe, but a new powerful modern state respected by the world and no longer looked down upon?

'*Effendi?*'

It was one of his staff officers. With him he had a European in civilian clothes, though from his ramrod-straight posture, the Grey Wolf could see he was an officer in mufti. He stared hard at the European. Then he remembered that hard face with the cruel-looking duelling scar running down one side of it. 'Major Willmer,' he said in French, 'you were with me at Suvla Bay in the Dardanelles in '15.'

'Yes sir,' the German answered in his harsh, clipped French and gave a stiff bow.

The Grey Wolf didn't offer to shake hands in the European fashion. He respected the Germans for being good fighters and organizers, but he didn't like them. Indeed he didn't like any foreigner. He had long determined ever since the Germans had taken over Turkish affairs during the war, brought in by the Sultan, that only Turks should run their country and find their own salvation. 'Are you here as *Schlachten-bummler*?' – he used the German word for a battlefield tourist.

'No, your excellency,' Willmer replied, still standing stiffly to attention. His eyes switched from left to right, as if he were checking who was listening to him. 'I have come at the behest of Captain Canaris, the head of our naval intelligence.'

The Grey Wolf actually smiled. 'I didn't know you still had one. You are very devious persons, you Germans. But pray what have I to do with your intelligence?'

The artillery had ceased thundering, now that the Greeks were in full retreat and the German major lowered his voice gratefully. He knew of old just how easily the Turks could be bought. He didn't want the secret he had brought with him all the way from

Berlin to go any further than its recipient.

'The English,' he said selecting his words carefully, 'know of your plans for the Greek civilians at Smyrna, Excellency.'

The Grey Wolf frowned. 'Hm,' he said, '*baksheesh*, I suppose. Or perhaps those Germans of yours who have been accompanying our troops during the campaign. Germans can be bought, too.'

The Major flushed. Once the Turks had been under German orders. Back in the war, he would have ordered the *bastido*, that terrible Turkish punishment of having the soles of the victim's feet lashed with canes, for anyone who had dared to insult the good name of the Fatherland. But those days were over. Germany was now weak, the loser, its great empire taken away from it by the Allied victors. So he kept his temper and said, 'I don't know how, Excellency. But they do and they are attempting to do something about it.'

'What?' the Grey Wolf demanded harshly.

'They will try to stop you,' Major Willmer hesitated.

'Go on!'

'Stop you with business of the civilians.'

'How?' the Grey Wolf had learned long ago not to waste words.

'Those two former enemy battleships, the *Implacable* and the French one – they intend to sabotage them.'

The Grey Wolf forced himself to smile. He needed the Germans after all. 'Major,' he said taking the other man's arm. 'You will dine with me and tell me more.' He said in guttural German. *'Meine Leute haben einen Esel geschlachtet.* You will enjoy the meat.'

Willmer's stomach churned at the thought. Donkey, he told himself revoltedly. 'My God.' Aloud he said, *'Danke sehr, Exzellenz. Es wird mir ein Vergnugen sein.'*

Down below the returning Turkish infantry was going from Greek to Greek, kicking them in the ribs to see if they were still alive. If they were, they slit their throats, looted the bodies and then as a kind of afterthought, ripped open their flies and sliced off their genitals...

3

The storm had passed. It left the sky and sea calm, but with a washed-out look, visibility down to a hundred yards or so. Smith and Dickie Bird could see the men were about exhausted. Fighting the storm had sapped most of their energy, even big Billy Bennett, strong as an ox, was about at the end of his tether. Still two young officers knew they had to keep the men going till they reached land. Who knew how the weather might change and another freak storm like the last one would finish them off? They wouldn't survive a second time, both of them knew that.

'Come on, lads,' Smith croaked, his lips cracked and parched from thirst, 'let's have a song. What about *"There's a long, long trail a-winding to the—"'* He stopped short. He saw it was no use. The men were about done. They looked up from their oars, with their hands red-raw and bleeding from the effort, their eyes blank and unseeing.

It was then he decided they'd have to chance it. More than anything the exhausted men needed rest – sleep. 'All right, lads,' he commanded, 'ship oars. Have some shut-eye.'

'Thank Christ for that,' Ginger Kerrigan sighed, pulled up his oar, bent his head and was fast asleep at once.

Ten yards behind, Dickie Bird signalled his agreement with the order and told his own men to do the same. A moment later, as he sat there, holding the rope to the rudder, his head sank to his chest and he, too, was fast asleep within seconds.

But despite his almost overwhelming weariness, Smith could not sleep. The events of the last hours kept flooding his mind – the great storm, the mysterious freighter, the ramming, for that was what it was, he was quite sure of that, the sinking of the poor old *Swordfish*. He was sure, of course, that they would reach land sooner or later and be rescued. But he hated to return to London, tail between his legs, defeated. He wasn't an emotional or sentimental man – he had seen too much action and sudden death in these last terrible years to be that – but he could visualize what was going to happen to those Greeks now. Those helpless civilians, men, women and children, would be massacred *en masse*.

He forced his eyes tightly shut. Still sleep wouldn't come. All around him his weary men snored, as the two boats drifted slowly to the north-east, lulled into the boon of a heavy sleep by the soft lap-lap of the wavelets on the hulls. Smith cursed to himself and opened his eyes. They felt as if someone had thrown a handful of grit at them. They were very sore and he imagined they were red-rimmed. He rubbed them, stared about and then rubbed them again hastily.

He looked hard, mouth gaping like some village idiot. It couldn't be! But it was. 'Lads,' he croaked, 'wake up... Now come on, show a leg! Wake up for Pete's sake!'

Dickie Bird opened his eyes and said, 'Smithie, old bean, must you be so loud?'

'Look to port for God's sake,' Smith yelled, hardly able to contain himself; his excitement was so great. *'To port!'*

Slowly, exceedingly slowly, as if his head were worked by rusty springs, Dickie Bird turned his head in that direction, face dull and ashen with exhaustion. Then he saw it. His face flooded with sudden animation. The light came back into his lacklustre eyes and colour flushed his skinny cheeks. 'Oh my sainted aunt!' he exclaimed happily. *'It's the dear old Swordfish!*...Wake up, chaps.' He shook the rating next to him roughly by the shoulder. 'See what the cat has just dragged in!'

Suddenly all their exhaustion was forgotten. Men cheered. Others slapped one another over the shoulder. Some rubbed their eyes as if they could not quite believe what they saw. But it was true. Limping towards them, quite deep in the water, carried by the slight currents in their direction was the battered old *Swordfish*.

'Come on, lads,' Smith cried, getting to his feet clumsily and raising his battered black merchant seaman's cap above his head. 'Three cheers for the old *Swordfish*... She's come and found us again. *Hip-hip!'*

A ragged hurrah rang out, echoing over the empty sea right across to the dirty smudge of land which was now appearing out of the haze and which was the coast of Greece.

As they rowed closer to the *Swordfish*, the sea was littered with objects which had escaped from the large slit in her side –

154

cork-lined life jackets, an airtight tin of *Woodbines,* which Ginger promptly grabbed, a bosun's chair and a couple of empty turps bottles from the engine room. But although so much stuff seemed to have escaped, the *Swordfish* was lying low but level in the water, with the damaged hull now above the waterline so that no more was pouring in.

Smith's heart leapt at the sight, as CPO Ferguson ordered 'ship oars' and let the two boats glide the rest of the way to the *Swordfish,* giving Smith his first opportunity to assess the amount of damage to the hull.

The hole was large, but could be padded he thought, and although the engines were obviously flooded, the pump was worked by petrol and worked independently of them. If they could get it started, which Smith was confident they could, it would take only a matter of a few hours to pump the *Swordfish* dry. That was just the minor problem.

He took his eyes off the *Swordfish* for a moment and started to tell the expectant ratings what he was going to do. 'We'll do a patch,' he announced. 'We'll make it of whatever wood, iron bolts and anything else we can find to plug the hole–'

Suddenly there was an obscene belch as a giant bubble of trapped air escaped the *Swordfish* and exploded on the surface. 'Did you just let one rip, Billy?' Ginger quipped and there was a burst of weary laughter from the rest of the men.

Smith smiled happily, knowing that he could rely upon them, despite their near exhaustion. It was all to the good, for what was in store for them over the next several hours was going to increase their weariness to almost dropping point. Now he spelled it out to them. 'I don't think we can board her yet, save for Lieutenant Bird, who'll start the pump – I hope? My thinking is that if we all go on board, we'll add to the weight and might just put that ruddy great hole down below the water line and then–' He didn't end the sentence. He didn't need to. All the men knew what would happen then. The *Swordfish* would sink and that would be that.

'So,' he said, raising his voice and trying to sound as if it were just a matter of routine, 'we row her to that piece of land over there. There we'll patch up the old *Swordfish* and start her up...'

His voice trailed away to nothing. He could see by the look in their weary eyes just how horrified they were at the thought of towing the waterlogged craft to the shore which looked a good couple of miles away.

CPO Ferguson was the first to react. 'Come on, you ratings. None of yer messing about. You're not a lot of old women, are ye?' He turned to Dickie. 'If ye'll be as kind as to get aboard the *Swordfish,* sir, we'll get cracking.'

Dickie Bird threw them all a mock Roman salute, crying, 'Those who are about to die, salute you.' Then he did a neat jump from the standing position on to the *Swordfish*'s littered deck.

Swiftly the two rowing boats separated to left and right of the craft's bows. Dickie grunted and hurled out a stout towing rope to the first boat. It was made fast swiftly. Then he did the same with the second boat.

Smith waited impatiently until the second boat was finished with the tow rope, then he commanded, 'All together now – take the strain.'

'Ay,' CPO Ferguson, manning an oar himself, said sternly, 'away with ye now. Put yer backs in it!'

They grunted. They heaved. Reluctantly, or so it seemed, the *Swordfish* started to move.

What followed next were hours of sheer merciless hell. They rowed fifteen minutes and rested five, heaving for all they were worth, their eyes bulging from their heads like those of men demented, their breath coming in harsh strangled gasps, their shoulder muscles ablaze with that awful strain. Each time Smith ordered 'Rest', they slumped over their oars, sobbing for breath, holding up their red-raw hands to the air in order to soothe them.

When he ordered 'Pull oars', they grasped

them with hands that trembled violently, dreading the next fifteen minutes of hell. Time crept by leadenly. No one spoke any more – they didn't have the energy. The only sound was the rusty squeak of the oars, the slap of the water being moved and their harsh strained breathing. And still the land seemed as far away as ever.

After two hours, with darkness sweeping across the sea like a giant black hawk, there was a sudden throbbing from the *Swordfish*. Without orders, the men ceased rowing and with infinite slowness, turned their heads in the direction of the battered craft. The first white trickle of water was emerging from the bows.

'The pump,' Smith croaked slowly, 'the pump.' He could hardly recognize his own voice, 'is … is working.'

'D'ye hear that, lads,' CPO Ferguson said, trying not to look at his red-raw bleeding palms. 'That'll lighten our load. Now come on, you bunch o' Mary Anns, take the strain!'

Now as the water started to pour in a steady stream from the *Swordfish* and she began to rise visibly, they set off again. It was the same back-breaking torture as before. But the men, their gazes set hypnotically on the land, willed themselves to keep going, knowing once they stopped this time they would never start again.

Smith knew it, too. Now he gave no more rests. He kept them rowing. Whenever one of the men seemed to falter, he'd croak angrily, 'Keep going there... No lead swinging... *Keep going, damn you!*'

Now in the growing darkness, they could see the shore pretty well. A barren stretch of coastland, rocky, with a fringe of yellow sand and to the left, almost hidden by a small wood of olive trees, a huddle of white-painted houses. To Smith it looked ideal – isolated and probably with no real communications with the outside world. As Ginger Kerrigan described it in between grunts and gasps, 'Looks like the arsehole of the world – worse even than Withernsea.'

'Nothing ... can be ... worse ... than Withernsea,' Billy Bennett grunted, his face crimson and running with sweat despite the cool evening breeze.

And then they were in the shallows, with a dog barking furiously somewhere in the little hamlet. Smith made one last effort. He rose groggily and tried to see the bottom of the darkening water, attempting to judge the depth. Finally he said, 'All right men, that's enough... Rest your oars!'

They collapsed as one, sobbing and gasping like small children who had suffered some irreparable hurt. Behind them the *Swordfish* drifted to a halt and Dickie Bird tossed the anchor over the side.

In a small voice, forcing himself to speak before he collapsed, Smith said shakily, 'Dickie. Use the wireless. Signal the Admiralty our position ... that we'll make emergency repairs... When we reach Alexandria, we'll need–' He keeled over and was asleep before his head hit the oar.

On the *Swordfish*, Dickie Bird, his usual silly, affected grin vanished, watched their bent, weary bodies like a fond mother watching over her sick children. 'Poor sods,' he said gently and turned. Over at the village, now plunged into darkness, a few yellow lights, probably petroleum lanterns, began to glow. There'd be hot food over there, he told himself, perhaps even wine. But he knew he couldn't take the chance of leaving the *Swordfish* and the sleeping men unguarded. Instead he went back below, made himself a greasy corned beef sandwich from two stale slices of French bread and a wad of the meat straight from the tin. Then he sat down next to the radio and still chewing the tasteless food started to tap out the message in Morse, using the only surviving code book. Outside all was silent, save for the soft lap of the little waves on the stony beach. The world, it appeared, had gone to sleep.

4

Dickie Bird's signal to C was faint but definite. Deep below the Cheka Headquarters in Petrograd, now named Leningrad, they had picked it up all right. 'The Prof', as they called him, went to work on it at once, chain-smoking as he did so, occasionally stroking the beard which he had grown in imitation of the great Lenin's.

Within the hour he had broken it down. It was an elementary three-letter code, which he had encountered before. Five minutes later he had typed it out neatly, handed the message to Ilona and settled down to consuming the rest of the pepper vodka, which he kept at his desk at all times.

'Hm,' Aronson sniffed as he read it. Outside it was snowing. Men and women, huddled in rusty black, were busy sawing branches off the skeletal trees for fuel. It was forbidden, but whenever a policeman came in sight they offered him a handful of worthless kopecks and he would go away.

Aronson sighed. One day they would cut out bribery in Russia and it would be a better country. Then he concentrated on the message, walking over to the huge map of

Europe on the wall opposite his desk. As Ilona watched in silence, he followed the map reference given in the radio message to London, tracing it with his nicotine-stained finger till it came to rest at the tip of the peninsula below Salonica in Greece. Again he sighed.

'Problems, comrade?' Ilona asked formally because there were others in the outer office.

'There are always problems, comrade, when one is furthering the revolution,' he pontificated and winked.

She winked back.

'Well, it looks as if Achmet Khan failed the first time. But if their boat is as damaged as the message says it is, it will take some time for them to repair it,' he mused thinking aloud. 'That should give Achmet Khan the chance he needs to summon up – hm,' he laughed shortly, 'religious guidance.'

'Religious guidance?' she echoed puzzled.

'Come here, and I'll show you,' he commanded.

She did so and with her back to the door to the outer office, she dropped her hand to his crotch.

'Ah,' he said, suddenly in a good humour, 'the helping hand. All hands to aid the revolution – it's the latest slogan from Moscow.'

She repressed her giggle with difficulty and stroked the sudden bulge a little harder.

He pointed to the map again. 'Here Salonica. And here, perhaps a hundred kilometres to the east, Mount Athos, the holy mountain. Have you heard of it?'

She shook her head, more interested in the bulge in his tight-fitting trousers than the Holy Mountain, whatever that was.

'Well, I shall tell you, comrade,' he said somewhat breathlessly now.

'For two centuries that mountain area has been a theocracy, a religious state, run by the monks and hermits who live in monasteries all over the mountains. They farm of course and grow wine to eat and drink, but that is not sufficient. They need money to–' He paused suddenly and said, 'Comrade Ilona, I think your clever hand has helped the revolution enough for the time being. Soon I'm afraid there could be an unseemly – er – eruption.'

She pouted her lips. 'I was enjoying it,' she said in a little girl's voice.

'Never fear, comrade,' he consoled her. 'You will probably stay behind late tonight and lend the revolution a hand once more.'

'Of course, gladly, comrade.' She brightened up immediately.

'*Horoscho.* Then let's get on. As I was saying. They need money to buy other supplies, cloth, seeds and the like. Where does that money come from?' He answered his own question. 'From devoted Greek

Orthodox co-religionists and in the case of the Russian monasteries – for there are several of them on Mount Athos – from followers of the now rightfully banned Russian Orthodox church.' He clenched his fist and looked severe. 'As Marx said – religion is the opium of the people.'

He winked at her and she repeated the Party formula although she still went to secret church service herself once a week.

'So where do the Russian monks get their funds from now? I shall tell you. From us.' He saw the look on her pretty face and said, 'You look surprised. But you ought not to be. It is an ideal way for us to keep an eye on the Greek scene and infiltrate the whole White Russian emigré scene. Whereas our agents are immediately shadowed everywhere in Europe once they have crossed the Polish heading westwards, Russian orthodox monks can travel freely anywhere without let or hindrance.'

She looked at him in naked admiration. 'How clever you are,' she breathed.

Suddenly Aronson was very serious. 'Ilona,' he said, 'this might sound to you all like some sort of silly game. But it is necessary. People like me have to consolidate their position, make our new leaders feel we are loyal, hard-working and necessary. That is till the time comes,' he lowered his voice to a mere whisper, 'when we get rid of them and their stupid political theories, dreamed up by a German Jew who lived off women and never did a stroke of real work in his whole life.'

Abruptly she was worried and not a little frightened. One dare hardly dream of such things. He was putting them into words. That was very dangerous.

He smiled suddenly, aware of just how worried she was by his words. 'Don't fear, Ilona,' he said softly. 'I shall not let my feelings slip through again like that. Now to Achmet Khan and–' he laughed '–divine intervention in the shape of the Russian Orthodox Church...'

On the other side of the world, far from a snowbound freezing Petrograd, C also pondered that message sent by Dickie Bird as he chewed away at his greasy corned beef sandwich. He sat at his desk in the fading light, his naval jacket slung over the chair behind him. For though long since retired, he still wore naval uniform and it could be, as the mood took him, any rank from sub-lieutenant to admiral. Face hard and concentrated he stared at the paper through his gold-rimmed monocle.

He had felt immediately he had read the words that the 'accident' was not an accident at all; it had been a deliberate attempt to ram the *Swordfish*. But he knew, too, from an immediate check with naval intelligence, that there were no German vessels within a hundred sea miles of the area where the *Swordfish* had been struck. He also knew from the Lyon's PCO at the British consulate there that von Horn had returned to Germany. 'So who in the devil's name,' he asked aloud, talking to himself as lonely men often do, 'tried to kill Common Smith, V.C. and his stout fellows?'

He stared out of the window at the rooftops of chimneys as if he might find the answer there. But no answer came. He frowned. Taking out his silver cigarette case, which had been personally presented to him by his majesty, the King-Emperor, George V, he lit one of the handmade cigarettes which he bought from a shop in Bond Street.

He leaned back in his chair and puffed out a stream of smoke, as he thought out the problem. Naturally the Empire had its internal troubles with the natives and the malcontents from Ireland to India. But there was also the problem caused by the collapse of the German and Russian Empires. Both of their collapses had caused constant trouble throughout Central Europe and Asia. Now the British Empire was desperately trying to keep some sort of order, stepping into the vacuum and attempting to stop a dozen different warring factions from killing each other.

But the secret plotters in Germany and

the official ones in Communist Russia wanted that chaos to continue, even to increase. It suited their purpose to keep Europe in disarray. So, he reasoned, stubbing out his expensive cigarette, if the Huns weren't behind this latest attempt to stop Smith's mission, it had to be the Reds. And unlike the Huns, the Russians had a naval fleet. The raid on Kronstadt had put paid to their northern fleet, but they still had a fleet of a kind in the Black Sea. Officially they were forbidden by treaty to send naval ships through the Dardanelles into the Aegean and Mediterranean. But C could hardly see the Turks, under present circumstances, attempting to stop them.

'What if they managed to get a small warship through?' he asked aloud, and tapped his wooden leg. 'What chance would poor young Smith stand then?'

His frown deepened.

Over the years the Admiralty had been very shirty about providing naval vessels for operations being carried out by the Secret Service. Their Lordships argued – quite rightly in C's opinion – that there were not enough ships to go round as it was. The massive cutbacks since the end of the war had meant that the Royal Navy was finding it exceedingly difficult to supply enough ships to fleets all over the Empire.

'But they'll damn well supply one on this

occasion,' he snorted fiercely at the wall. His mind made up, he took up his quill pen and dipped the nib in the inkwell which was filled with green ink – at the HQ of the Secret Intelligence Service only C, the chief, was allowed to use ink of that particular hue – and began to write to their Lordships of the Admiralty.

Young Smith was going to have the protection he needed while he crossed the Med to Alexandria in his battered vessel. And if their Lordships refused, 'I'll damn well take it up with the King-Emperor himself,' he declared, as he slashed the paper with great green strokes. 'Just see how he'll make them dance a deuced different tune!'

Across on the other side of Queen Anne's Gate, the man with the telescope hastily adjusted the lens. Once a long time ago he had served under C himself as a young sailor. But times had been hard since the war and his discharge from the Royal Navy without a pension. They had worked on his bitterness at the treatment he had received and his need for ready cash.

Now, with the telescope propped against the parapet, he started to take down the words the Secret Service chief was writing with his free hand just as he had once done as 'Bunts', chief yeoman of signals in the RN when he had been a young man, happy, patriotic – and loyal.

5

The interior of the *Swordfish* was a shambles. The water which had almost flooded and sunk her was down to ankle-deep level now thanks to the powerful pump which was still clattering away. Otherwise it was a mess of twisted metal, sand and seaweed which stank to high heaven, as well as a hundred and one things belonging to the crew.

But none of these things was of importance to Smith and CPO Ferguson as they made their first inspection below that morning. Their first concern was the engines. 'They're no damaged externally, sir,' the old Scot said after a few minutes of thoughtful perusal.

'Looks like it, Chiefie,' Smith agreed. 'I hope only that the force of that impact didn't bend the pistons inside.'

'Ay, we'll see yon when the time comes, sir. But the old *Swordfish* hasn't let us down yet.' He slapped the engine cowling with his horny old hand, showing rare affection for him, as if the *Swordfish* were a living creature.

Smith nodded and then said, 'Well, first things first. We'll make a patch. When we've got that in place, we attempt to start the engines.'

'Ay, ay, sir,' CPO Ferguson said briskly. 'I'll get on to it – right away.'

'We're all in on this show, Chiefie,' said Smith. 'Officers as well as men.'

Ferguson grunted something and looked black. He was a snob. He believed that there should be as little mixing as possible among the various ranks. But he said nothing.

Smith smiled softly. He knew Ferguson's views. He turned and spoke to the others crowding the entrance to the interior and staring at the mess. 'You've heard what we're about to do. While we're starting, I want you Ginger – you're the best scrounger in the *Swordfish* – to go across to that little hamlet on the other side of the wood and see what you can rustle up in the way of bread and something to drink – beer if you can find it. And Billy, you'd better go with him to give him a hand and watch his back – you never know.'

'Ay ay, sir,' the two of them said with alacrity, knowing what was soon to come.

'Jammy great boogers,' the others said enviously.

'All right, be off with you. Take a sack or something and ask Lieutenant Bird to give you two gold sovereigns each. They should do the trick, even if you don't speak the lingo.'

'Don't worry, sir,' Ginger said with a cheeky grin on his narrow face. 'Mrs Kerrigan's handsome son will bring home the bacon.' Then they were gone.

Now the back-breaking task of making the 'patch' commenced. It consisted of building a wooden patch across the gaping hole, forming plank by plank. Each plank seemed to take an eternity to fix while they stood in the freezing water, with in the background the pump thumping back and forth like a metallic heart. They were held in place with 'walking sticks' – lengths of iron rod, threaded at one end and bent at the other. It was all hard physical work, which required a lot of muscular power; for they had few tools to help them in their task and by the end of the first hour on the job all of them were filthy and lathered in sweat, despite the freezing water lapping around their ankles.

Another hour passed and when CRO Ferguson, who was on the deck at the time reported, 'Yon cheeky boogers, Bennett and Kerrigan, are coming up, sir,' Smith ordered, 'All right, lads, down tools for a few minutes. Let's see what they've brought back with them.'

'Let's hope it's whallop,' someone said urgently. 'My mouth feels like a harlot's armpit.' There was a round of weary laughter and they climbed up the ladder to the deck instantly, glad to leave that damned 'patch' behind for a little while.

'It's a sleepy hollow, sir,' Ginger explained, as he put the big bulging sack on the wet deck carefully and the expectant crew could hear the soft clatter of glass as he did so, 'a one horse town – when even the horse left years ago!'

Smith laughed and asked, 'How did you make out?'

'Easy, sir. Look at this.' Ginger reached in the sack and pulled out a big bottle. 'Gallop. Here you are, Chiefie, you have first go – cos you're old and you might not survive much longer.'

'Cheeky scouse booger,' CPO Ferguson grumbled but he took the bottle quickly enough, flipped back the pot-and-rubber cap and took a hefty swig, his Adam's apple racing up and down his skinny upturned throat like an express lift.

'Fishermen by the looks of them, the kids all barefoot, and a kind of wooden shed, which was the shop where I got this.' He pulled out a long loaf of bread and another bottle of beer.

'Yessir,' Bennett agreed. 'Too poor to have a pot to piss in.'

'Good. All right, Ginger, distribute the loot and then we'll reward you by letting you have a go at the "patch".'

Ginger crossed himself with mock solemnity. 'For what we are about to receive, may the Good Lord make us truly grateful.'

Smith laughed again and then he, too, was chewing huge chunks of fresh, still warm bread, washing them with fizzy weak Greek beer.

All that afternoon they laboured to complete the patch. By about four it was finished, but Smith did not let the men rest yet. 'Now we put in the "pudding",' he commanded.

The weary dirty men moaned and Dickie Bird, unrecognizable as his usual elegant self, said, 'Have a heart, Smithie.'

'I know ... I know,' the latter said, 'I sound like a second Captain Bligh, but I want to get the *Swordfish* watertight by darkness. At dawn I want to attempt to start the engines and get underway. The longer we are beached here at this Godforsaken place, the more dangerous it could become. After all,' he added, handsome young face suddenly stern and worried, 'somebody else might have picked up that signal you sent, Dickie.'

'Point taken,' Bird said and rose from the deck with a sigh. 'All right, chaps, back to the saltmines.'

The 'pudding' consisted of rolls of canvas. These were filled laboriously with packing – anything they could find that wasn't metallic – and then inserted to caulk the 'patch'. Again the same it was dark and they were exhausted by the time they had finished it.

Wearily they slumped on the damp sand around a huge crackling fire of bone-dry olive tree branches which Ginger and Bennett had collected during their break and lit. It was cool now and they were glad of the warmth, ignoring the turtles, which attracted by the fire, were now scurrying through the sand on all sides making a strange slithering, dragging sound.

'We could make turtle soup,' Dickie Bird suggested lazily, eating a piece of the bread which had been toasted on a stick over the fire and taking careful sips of his last bottle of precious beer.

'Well, catch your turtle,' Smith suggested, glad to rest his aching bones. 'You ought to–'

He stopped short. A small broad figure was trudging through the sand, carrying what looked like a basket on his head. '*Psari kalamari,*' he was calling in Greek, of which none of them understood one single word. But when he came into the circle of light flung by the flickering fire, they saw the basket he bore on his head contained what was obviously fresh fish, for the scales gleamed a bright silver in that ruddy hue and the squid the basket also contained were still wriggling.

'Cor ferk a duck,' Billy Bennett exclaimed at the sight. 'Them octopuses are still alive.

Wouldn't want to eat nuthin' like that.' He shuddered dramatically and his fat jowls wobbled.

'Come off it,' Ginger teased him, as they stood up and looked at the little Greek fisherman, 'you'd eat an old seaboot as long as there was enough relish to cover it!'

The Greek smiled proudly, as if he thought they were complimenting him on his wares.

'A fish fry, that's what we need,' Dickie Bird said with renewed energy. He took a half sovereign out of his pocket, held it up to the light to show that it was gold and pointed to the basket. 'We'll have the lot.'

The Greek grabbed the coin from Dickie's hand and, putting it between his stained-brown teeth, bit it hard. He nodded and placed the basket on the sand. For a moment he stood there simply looking round at their faces, his dark eyes hard and calculating. Then he touched his hand to his greasy forelock and was off, trudging back the way he had come, with Smith's gaze fixed suspiciously on his back until the Greek had disappeared into the darkness.

Half an hour later they were replete with the fish, mostly charred, lying on the sand, smoking a last cigarette or picking at their teeth with their nails, trying to dislodge some piece of half-cooked, half-burned fish still lodged.

'Penny for them?' Dickie Bird asked Smith idly, as he puffed at his cigarette watching the fire slowly die out. 'Your thoughts, I mean, old bean.'

Smith sniffed and stared as the fire flared up again for a moment in a sudden wind and threw their shadows gigantic and distorted on to the sand beyond. 'Don't know exactly,' he said slowly, almost reluctantly.

'Come on,' Dickie urged. 'Spit it out, Smithie.'

'Well that Greek...'

'What about him? Beware of Greeks bearing gifts, do you mean?'

'Oh shut up, you silly ass. No, it's this. Why was he the only one from the whole village to come over here and have a look at us?'

'How do you mean? You'll have to be clearer, Smithie.'

'Well, you'd think it'd be normal human behaviour in a lonely sort of place like that village, that at least the kids'd be across here, having a look at us. You know how nosey people in small places usually are. The locals might even have come across to beg and cadge as well. But they didn't. Why not?'

Dickie shrugged carelessly. 'Search me, old boy.'

'Because somehow they'd been ordered not to come over or perhaps they're scared to do so. But why should they be scared of us?' In the fading glare of the fire, Dickie could see that Smith's brow was wrinkled in a worried frown and he realized once again just how seriously the skipper took his responsibility for the lives and welfare of *Swordfish's* little crew. 'They've seen Ginger and Billy – and they're harmless enough. Well, most times they are. Then suddenly out of the blue up turns our lone fisherman, well after dark, offering us his wares and carefully – very carefully – surveying the scene. Did you notice that, Dickie?'

The other man nodded. 'Now you come to mention it, I did.' He drank the last of his beer and asked, 'what do you think their game is, Smithie?'

'Frankly I don't know. All I know is I wish now that I had pushed the men a little harder into starting up the motors. Well, it's too late for that now. That will have to be done at first light. But there's one thing we can do, Dickie.'

'What's that?'

'Shove the *Swordfish* out into a little deeper water. That'll ensure we'll hear any-one trying to wade through the shallows.'

'Jolly good idea, old bean. What then?'

Smith was silent for a moment, as the fire gave a last spurt and then died away altogether, leaving the beach in darkness. When he spoke again, his voice was very low and very serious. 'Break out the firearms to the men,' he said. 'Somehow, I have a feeling we shall need them this night.'

Dickie Bird shivered.

6

The soft grating of the surf on the shingle along the beach drowned any sound their paddles made as they came ever closer to the *Swordfish*. They spoke not a word. They didn't even grunt with the exertion. Why should they? They spoke little at the monasteries clinging to the steep sides of Mount Athos; and they were all physically very strong. They were used to hard work.

The Russian Orthodox monks which Achmet Khan had recruited for the task were not the skinny, bearded old men who painted their monasteries' famed icons or produced the wonderful illustrated books in Church Slavonic. They were peasant sons, barely literate, sold to the monasteries before the Revolution of 1917, to provide the muscle that the elderly, highly educated Russian monks – many of them minor aristocrats – needed. They tended the grapes in the vineyards that ran down the steep slopes hundreds of metres right to the sea. They provided the religious police, whose duty it was to ensure that nothing female, including all animals belonging to their farms, ever crossed the border into Mount Athos. And to a man they were all homosexual, despite their hairy appearance with dark bearded faces and great rippling muscles. There were no women on the mountains. So their sex had to be between themselves.

Now they paddled ever closer to the dark outline of the *Swordfish*, riding at anchor, just off the shore, in boats provided by the frightened local fishermen. They were armed with a variety of weapons – spears, home-made coshes, hunting rifle and in one case, a carved Turkish scimitar dating back to the Middle Ages. But they had been ordered by their Russian paymaster to 'avoid force, if you can. Take them by surprise. If you can capture them alive, it will make splendid trouble for the British. *Boshe moi*,' he had exclaimed which had caused some frowns at the mention of God in that holy place, which had been replaced by looks of delight, when he had added, 'There will be plentiful gold for all of you if you succeed!'

Dmitri, the biggest of the monks and their natural leader, for he was the powerful lover of at least six of the raiding party, whispered, 'We shall now go round the other side of the ship. You', he indicated the other two craft, 'stay at this side. Once you hear the signal, board – and board quickly. Understood?'

His listeners nodded their heads under their tall square hats and allowed their craft to drift towards the silent *Swordfish*, carried forward by the current; while Dmitri's crew rowed softly a little further out to sea with the intention of coming in on the lee side of the ship. Dmitri smiled his approval and fingered his black chest-length beard. All was going well. The communists were godless, but they did pay well. When they got back to the Mountain, he would buy *ouzo*, much *ouzo* from the villagers and then there would be an orgy. A fresh bunch of novices had arrived recently. There would be plenty of plump young pigeons to seduce. He smiled at the thought, and placed his hand between his sturdy thighs as if to reassure himself that his organ was still there. It was and erect to boot!

Billy Bennett was on watch. Huddled in a greatcoat he sat on the deck at the bows, trying to keep from dropping off. It had been a long, hard day and he longed desperately to crawl into the warm bunk of his relief and fall into a dead sleep, but that wouldn't be for another hour yet. So he forced himself to stay awake, raising his head to view the star-studded night sky, saying the names of the constellations to himself as he spotted them. *'The Plough ... the Milky Way...'* It was the old sailor's way of staying awake when on night watch and nothing was happening. *'The Great...'* He stopped suddenly. He sniffed the air suspiciously. Mixed with the odour of wild pine and thyme which came from the shore, a score or so yards away, there was another smell, which he couldn't quite identify. It was sweet and a little bit sickly. 'Like a woman's scent,' he told himself, slowly, for Billy Bennett's brain was sluggish, not accustomed to making quick decisions.

Abruptly he recognized the odour. 'Oil of violet!' he exclaimed startled, 'Hair oil!' Now he was suddenly wide awake and alert. He stood up and peered over the side. There were shapes out there, moving silently, and instinctively he knew whoever was in those rowing boats was up to no good. 'Bleeding hell!' he cursed. 'We're being attacked.'

He tugged the .38 revolver out of his pocket. In the darkness he fumbled with the safety catch just as Dmitri's boat nudged almost noiselessly against the far side of the *Swordfish* and out of his sight. *'Stand to,'* Billy bellowed at the top of his voice. *'Stand to – there's boarders!'* He pressed the trigger. Scarlet flame stabbed the silver darkness. Someone yelled out in pain. Next moment there was the crack of a rifle and a slug howled off a stanchion, only inches from

Billy Bennett's big head.

In an instant firing broke out on both sides of the *Swordfish* and the startled crew running up to discover what was happening had to drop to the deck to avoid the slugs peppering the superstructure of the little craft.

'Chiefie,' Smith called out urgently above the angry snap-and-crackle of the small arms fire, 'start her up… Start the–'

'Bloody hell,' Ginger next to Smith yelled, 'they've frigging well hit me.' He held out his hand. It was covered with red gore.

Dickie Bird clambered over him and dived on to the deck. He had an automatic in his right hand. Immediately he started blasting away, firing to left and right, hoping that his wild fire would hit someone. It did. He heard cries of pain and the sudden splash of a body going into the water.

Frantically Smith joined in the defence, while the men crouched behind him unable to get any further as the bullets slammed into the woodwork above them.

Below, CPO Ferguson, aided by one of the ratings, set to work on the engine. Almost instantly the old Scot knew it was going to be difficult, damned difficult. The Thorneycrofts had been thoroughly soaked by the seawater. Inside all would still be wet. Still he persisted, trying to coax the first tiny cough from the engines which would indicate that they were turning over, ears closed to the desperate battle for the *Swordfish* which came down from above, the sweat already beginning to drip from his brow.

Dmitri waved his big paw to left and right. His followers knew what to do. So far they had not been detected. With luck, Dmitri told himself they'd be able to get on deck before the alarm was sounded. According to the fisherman they had sent to sell fish to the English, they, the monks, outnumbered them by three to one. Dmitri knew there was a chance of being killed, but at heart he was still a simple fatalistic Russian peasant. So instead of thinking of death, he thought of the boys and the drink the communist gold would buy him.

Crouched low, steadying the boat with their feet, the big bearded monks hauled themselves aboard the *Swordfish* silently, any noise they made drowned by the noise of the battle going on overhead. Quietly for such big men, the skirts of their gowns tucked into their broad leather waistbelts, they stole forward clutching their makeshift weapons. '*Davoi*,' Dmitri hissed and pointed to the big shape of Billy Bennett sheltered behind a bollard, hurriedly re-loading his revolver.

Two of the monks rushed forward. The first raised his club and smashed it down on the fat rating's head. He slumped forward, unconscious before he hit the deck.

Dickie Bird heard the sound of the fall. He swung round, saw the two dark figures who seemed to be monks, of all things, crouching over Billy and fired instinctively. The bigger of the two screamed shrilly and pitched over the side into the water, while the other slumped dead or dying next to Billy.

'They're on deck!' Dickie yelled urgently and slapped another magazine into his automatic.

Smith heard the cry. 'Tell Chiefie to hurry with the damned engines!' he yelled behind him and darted forward. Slugs howled off stanchions and splintered the woodwork, showering him with chips of wood. There were angry cries in Greek. What looked like a home-made spear hissed through the air. It struck the wooden bulkhead and stood there, quivering furiously. But Smith bore a charmed life. Gasping for breath, he pelted up the iron steps to where the Lewis gun was mounted.

Other feet came running along the deck. A giant of a man, dressed as a monk, lashed out with his foot at Dickie. The latter yelped with pain and went flying, his automatic clattering to the deck. He lay still. Smith groaned. With fingers that felt like clumsy sausages, he tugged the canvas cover off. He slapped the round magazine on top of the ugly-looking machine gun. A whole bunch of their mysterious attackers were running forward now, some of them firing from the waist as they did so. Bullets howled off the rails all about him. Smith knew they were finished, if he didn't do something drastic soon. He pushed the hard metal butt into his shoulder and pressed the trigger.

The Lewis gun burst into frenetic life. Flame stabbed the darkness. Suddenly the air was full of the stench of burnt cordite. Swinging the gun from left to right, Smith poured a hail of fire at their attackers. The monks went down in a sudden confused heap. Screams rang out on all sides. In a flash that first wave of attackers had melted away, with a few survivors crouching behind the bulkhead or cowering behind the shattered bodies of their dead and dying fellows.

But more and more of them were pouring over the side. Smith could not see them because they were hidden from his sight by the superstructure. He wiped the sweat from his dripping forehead with the back of his arm. He waited for the next attack and prayed that Chiefie would start the engines soon. They had to escape this trap! He couldn't hold off their attackers for ever. One man armed with an ancient Lewis gun that might well pack up on him at any moment. Besides he had only the one magazine and he had probably used half of that in the first burst of fire.

Down below CPO Ferguson sweated, too. His face contorted with frustration, he tried yet again, head cocked to one side, ears tensed for the first tiny cough from the Thorneycrofts indicating that they were going to work. 'Come on,' he whispered urgently to himself.' Come on, ye deevils – *start … start!*'

Now the monks began to snipe Smith's position. But he dare not return their fire. He had to save the rest of the magazine for the moment when they charged him. Bullets struck the platform all around him. Something very hot and painful struck his left arm. It was as if he had been kicked by a mule. He staggered back with a sharp yell of pain and for a moment he lost control of the gun on its swivel mounting.

The attackers saw him stagger. They gave a great cry and darted forward. Somehow Smith grabbed the gun. The pain was intense. But he forgot it, as they charged forward, a great mass of big men in funny square hats, firing as they came. He tucked the butt into his good shoulder and squeezed the trigger. The Lewis gun chattered into life once more. White and red tracer hissed towards the running men like a flight of angry hornets. They went down on all sides. The first rank disappeared. The others skidded to a stop, crouching low, as if they wondered what to do next.

Click! The Lewis stopped firing with startling suddenness. Smith cursed angrily. He pressed the trigger again. Nothing. The magazine was empty! One of the Greeks cried something. The others hesitated, as if they were not quite sure that the gun was empty. The Greeks called something angrily. They began to move forward once more cautiously and hugging the bulkhead for cover.

Smith was at his wits' end. They didn't stand a chance now unless.

Abruptly there was an asthmatic cough. A groaning. An instant later a ripe belch. In sudden, ear-splitting fury, the Thorneycrofts burst into full, vibrating life. The attackers hesitated. Ginger, wounded as he was, didn't give them a second chance to make up their minds and act. He sprang into the wheelhouse. In a flash he was behind the wheel. The *Swordfish* surged forward, dragging its anchor behind it. Ginger couldn't achieve full power because of the anchor but he brought her up to at least 20mph, hurling the boat from side to side in violent, dangerous sweeps, sending the rest of the Greeks on their feet over the side, as the crew came tumbling out of the companionway on to the deck, ready for any further trouble. But there wasn't any. The monks had had enough. Those who had not already jumped over the side started to drop their weapons and raise their hands in surrender. Smith slumped weakly against the rail, all energy drained from his wounded body as if someone had opened a tap.

A mile out to sea, Achmet Khan gave a sly smile. He had heard the sudden roar of an engine and the abrupt stopping of the fire-fight. He could guess what had happened. But he wasn't too concerned. He told himself, the English had escaped from one trap only to walk into another one.

7

Achmet Khan had always liked the British, at least until he had left India to go to Oxford he had. His father had made him. Once when he was a small boy, just after they had arrived in Calcutta, his father had told him, 'Remember this, my son, when I was a boy in the north, I learned about Bengal that it was a low-lying country inhabited by *low, lying people!*' The old man had smiled in that world-weary, cynical manner of his. 'Learn now that in Calcutta, in the whole of Bengal, perhaps in all India, the only people you can trust will be the British. They do not have our silly castes. They don't slaughter each other on account of absurd religious differences. They don't take bribes – and the only god they worship is the good honest gold sovereign.'

It was the same god his father had worshipped, too. He had started his business career at Bombay's zoo, where he had bribed the keeper of the rhinos to provide him with buckets of rhino urine which many middle-aged Bengalis believed possessed unique aphrodisiac qualities. From the sale of this product to those 'addled-minded impotent babus', as his father had always sneered at his customers, he had made several thousand rupees. With this he had opened his first small cotton mill and had gone into real business. By the time it was 1914 and Achmet Khan was ready to go to Oxford – 'there you will become a real English gentleman, my son' – father had been making fortunes supplying cotton singlets to the rapidly increasing Indian Army.

All that had changed at Oxford. Instead of becoming a 'real English gentleman', as his father had hoped, he became a budding revolutionist. And again it was the British who taught him to become one. For the most part his teachers were weedy conscientious objectors who declared the war was a 'struggle between imperialist powers'. They taught him that the British Empire was the greatest imperial power of them all. It provided the British upper classes with the funds they needed to live their foolish decadent lives by the exploitation of the sweated labour of the great black and brown masses of that Empire. By the time he left Oxford in 1917 with a first-class honours degree, he had already decided he would dedicate his young life to the overthrow of the British Empire, in particular in India. But how?

He felt only contempt for the Indian Congress Party – 'a lot of blethering babus', as his father had always snorted, 'who jaw, jaw, jaw about the cause – and then do nothing'. By now, too, he had come to realize that his left-wing teachers in England were just the same. They were all talk and no action.

Aronson, or as he was called in 1917 Dr Abelmann, had been Achmet Khan's first mentor and guide. In that year he had been in England supposedly buying medical supplies for the new armies formed by the Provisional Government which had just overthrown the Czar. In reality, he had been recruiting agents and spies. As he told Achmet Khan at the time. 'Kerensky', he meant the head of the new government in Russia, 'won't last long. The communists will take over under Lenin. And you know what their aim will be?' He had looked at the young Indian in that hard-faced manner of his, and answered his own question –

'*World revolution!* They – I – will need trusted agents and agitators throughout the world, if we are to carry out the demands of our new masters-to-be.'

That autumn Achmet Khan had returned to Moscow for training. A year later he was in Iraq, helping to cause a mutiny among the Indian troops of the British Army fighting there. In 1919 it had been Egypt, where he was instrumental in instigating week-long rioting in Cairo. In 1920 it was India. It was he who had brought the mob on to the streets of Amritsar that ended with British troops opening fire on them and killing scores of people. Again the British were represented as a cruel Imperialist nation which could maintain control over its vast empire by brute force. And those English intellectuals whom he scorned even more now had more 'crimes' to add to their long list of those committed already by Britain and its empire.

Now as Achmet Khan stood in the conning tower of the Russian submarine which had brought him from the Black Sea and secretly through the Dardanelles to this remote Greek shore, he told himself that this was his biggest operation yet. Once he had dealt with this handful of Englishmen and their pathetic little vessel, the Turks could go ahead with their massacre of the Greeks. The result might be chaos, perhaps even war for the whole of this area. Who knows, he mused to himself as the sun appeared, hanging on the lip of the sea like a blood-red crescent, Bulgaria perhaps even the new Yugoslavia might become involved. Both countries had a sizeable Christian majority with a Moslem minority. It could be a repeat of the Balkan Wars of the turn of the century with their mass slaughter of minorities. Then the British Empire would be forced to step in – with disastrous results.

'*Davoi, tovarisch,*' the little captain broke into his musings and pointed.

A black speck had detached itself from the smudge which was the coastline of Greece and was pushing slowly into the still lime-green of the sea.

The captain raised his glasses. Achmet Khan did the same. A lean, streamlined craft swept into the bright circles of calibrated glass. Hastily Achmet Khan adjusted the focus. There were dark shapes on the deck, which he guessed were bodies, and the ship's wireless mast hung in shreds. He nodded his understanding. The monks had failed but they had done quite a bit of damage to the British craft. That was the reason she was proceeding so slowly, he told himself.

He lowered the binoculars and turned to the captain of the submarine, a massive bearded Russian from the Baltic who walked with a permanent stoop due to always having to move bent low in the narrow confines of the little sub. 'How will you do it, Comrade Captain?'

'On the surface,' he replied without hesitation. 'We can't match the Englishmen's speed if their craft was going full out. But it isn't – for some reason. My guess is that they are doing barely twelve knots. On the surface we can match them. In five minutes they'll be within accurate torpedo range. Then I shall repay them for this.' He slapped his good right hand against his wooden arm. 'Kronstadt,' he said, as if that were explanation enough, bearded face hard and set.

'*Horoscho,*' Achmet Khan said cheerfully. He pulled out his pocket flask of vodka and handed it open to the captain. '*Nastrovya,*' he called the toast.

'*Spasibo,*' the captain said gratefully. He took the flask, raised it in the direction of the approaching vessel and grunted, 'Death to the English.' Next instant he took a mighty swallow of the fiery spirits and grinned happily at a smiling, triumphant Achmet Khan...

'Well,' Dickie Bird said, 'what a performance.' He watched as two crewmen pushed the dead monks overboard. 'I've seen some things in my time, Smithie, but never anything like this. Attacked by armed monks. What next?'

Smithie nodded. The wound in his shoulder was hurting like hell. But nothing was broken. It was a clean entrance-and-exit gunshot wound. In Alexandria he'd have it looked at properly. For the time being, however, he had patched it up himself. 'How's Ginger Kerrigan?' he asked, as the last of the big monks was shoved over to splash into the water without any ceremony.

'Oh, you know Ginger. Give him a gasper and tell him he'll have pretty nurses looking after him once we reach Alex and he cheers up straight away.'

'Yes, I suppose. But at this speed, we're not going to reach Alex so soon, Dickie.'

'I know. But we daren't risk going flat out with that "patch". It just might blow inwards and that would be that.' He shrugged eloquently.

Smith nodded his understanding. 'All right, Dickie, get the chaps to clean up this shambles the best they can. I'll go below and have a word with Chiefie about the engines, then I'll look in on Ginger–' He stopped short. Dickie was no longer listening. He was staring to port, hand shading his eyes against the red glare of the rising sun. 'What's the matter, Dickie?' he asked.

'Look at that!'

Awkwardly Smith raised his binoculars with his one good hand. A dark shape lay low in the water, hardly moving to judge by her slight bow wave. 'A sub,' he said, searching for a flag to identify it with, but finding none. 'Do you think it's Greek or one of ours?'

For a moment Dickie who was surveying the vessel himself through the glasses did not answer. Suddenly he let the glasses drop to his chest. 'Russki,' he said.

'You certain?'

'Def. A T-class sub. laid down just before the Revolution. Intended for inland waters like the Baltic or the Black Sea. Three or four hundred tons, armed with six torpedoes and a quick firer. If I remember correctly, she can do twelve knots on the surface.'

Smith was impressed by Dickie Bird's knowledge. He could never remember the details of the recognition tables that they all had had to study during the war. But he had no time to compliment his fellow officer on his knowledge now. His mind was racing electrically. What was a communist sub doing off this remote place? Was it just chance that she had surfaced here? Or was there something purposeful behind her sudden appearance?

'Are you thinking what I am, Smithie?' Dickie asked urgently.

'I think so. What's she doing out there? Is she up to no good, Dickie?'

'Exactly!'

'God,' Smith groaned, pain stabbing his

wounded arm again, 'not again after what we've been through already. It's almost as if there's been a jinx on this operation right from–' He had just spotted the first flash of angry white as a torpedo slid into the water. 'Helmsman,' he shouted urgently, 'hard to port … hard to port!'

'Come on Smithie,' Dickie cried, as the man at the wheel swung it round hard, though the damaged *Swordfish* reacted only sluggishly, 'Let's get up on the bridge.'

Together they clattered up the iron ladder as the flurry of crazy bubbles exploding on the surface of the water indicated the path of the incoming torpedo. At a tremendous rate the torpedo hurtled just below the surface of the sea, heading straight for the *Swordfish,* which was coming round at what seemed an incredibly slow rate. 'Give it more elbow, man!' Dickie yelled urgently at the red-faced helmsman. *'Quick – for God's sake!'*

Smith flung a look over the side, willing the *Swordfish* to do it before it was too late.

Then she was round and the torpedo went whizzing by, only feet away, rushing towards the beach where it slithered to a stop on the sand, screw still turning, to explode a moment later.

But there was no time to concern themselves with the one that had missed. Already the Russian sub had fired a second torpedo, and men were running the length of her bow heading for the quick-firer there.

'Here, give me the wheel!' Dickie yelled, grabbing the wheel from the helmsman. Now it was a question of guessing right. Had the enemy torpedo-mate aimed for the same spot a second time, or had he picked a different bearing? A sweating anxious Bird knew he had only a second or two to decide which way to swing the *Swordfish* round. All their lives now depended upon his correct decision. He rammed the wheel round to starboard, in the same instant that the quick-fire began to bark, sending a stream of 20mm shells hurrying towards the crippled ship.

'Come on ... come on!' Dickie yelled in a frenzy of impatience, 'Come on! Turn *Swordfish ... for God's sake!*'

Slowly, very, very slowly, the *Swordfish* started to come round...

8

'By God,' Black Jack snorted, peering through the old fashioned brass telescope which he affected together with the high wing starched collar of pre-war design, 'It's them. For once their Lordships have got it right, Number One.'

His Number One, who privately thought that 'Black Jack' Manners was a throwback to the Stone Age who should have been beached years ago, said diplomatically, 'So it should appear.' He peered through his own modern binoculars at the far distance. Silhouetted a stark black against the rising sun, he could just make out what he took to be a Thorneycroft and to port of it the long black shape of a submarine deep in the water.

'Yes,' Black Jack said, mind made up. 'That's them all right.' He jumped involuntarily as another stream of white tracer shells hissed towards the Thorneycroft, peppering the water all around her. 'And our little friend is in serious trouble, it seems. Why the tarnation don't they make speed?'

The Number One didn't answer. He was wondering how His Majesty's destroyer *Black Swan*, known throughout the Mediterranean Fleet as the 'Mucky Duck' would fare when *she* had to make speed, which would be soon. After all she had been laid down just after the turn of the century and she had seen much hard service since. For that reason he had a sneaking suspicion that was why the *Black Swan* had been picked for this secret mission. Fleet HQ had probably thought if we are going to lose a ship doing the civvies work for them, let it be the *Black Swan*. We can afford to lose her.

Not that 'Black Jack' Manners – 'I ain't got no manners', he was wont to boast when he was in his cups, 'that's why they call me "Black Jack the Pirate"' – had had any such thoughts. As soon as they had huffed and puffed their way out of Alex harbour, creaking and groaning at every rusty plate, he had opened the sealed orders with fingers that had trembled badly.

'I say,' he had snorted, peering up at the tall trim Number One from beneath these ferocious black bushy eyebrows of his, 'we've got a show, Number One – a ruddy great show!'

'Have we, sir?' Number One had replied urbanely. It was one of his private dreams that 'Black Jack' would make such a mess of things one of these days that he would be dismissed from his ship and Number One would be given command, plus another half stripe.

'By George, yes! One of our ships – er – formerly *HMS Swordfish* is in trouble off the Greek coast.' He strode to the map in the wardroom and traced the latitude – 'Here! We're to escort her over to Alex. And my dear Number One,' he boomed – Black Jack tended to boom most of the time (privately Number One thought he was deaf) – 'there might be trouble!' He chuckled heartily at the thought and rubbed his horny old hands, hardened to tough slabs by years of immersion in seawater.

'May I enquire with whom, sir?' he had asked.

Black Jack had shrugged carelessly. 'Oh, I don't know, Number One. Who the devil cares?' He had beamed at the other officer. 'What's it matter – as long as there's a chance of a decent scrap, eh?'

Now it appeared to Black Jack as he surveyed the scene to his front that there was a chance of a 'decent scrap'. A foreign sub appeared to be attacking a British ship – that was enough for him. 'I'll think we'll sound "action stations" Number One,' he said briskly, as another burst of shells landed all around the slow-moving Thorneycroft, churning up angry fountains of white whirling water.

'But sir,' Number One protested mildly. 'We do not know where that sub is registered. It could be American, Greek, even Italian.'

'Lot of foreigners,' Black Jack snorted. 'Shouldn't mess around with one His Majesty's ships. Sound action stations!'

'Ay ay, sir!' The Number One, who knew there was no use protesting any further, turned and snapped to the waiting Royal Marine bugler. 'Bugler,' he commanded, 'sound action stations.'

The Royal Marine, resplendent in white solar topee and starched khaki, his boots and belts gleaming, stepped forward as if he were on the parade ground at Portsmouth. He placed his sparkling silver bugle close to the tannoy public address system and blew into it urgently.

At once, sailors in various stages of undress started tumbling out of their quarters pulling on helmets, tugging face masks over their heads if they were gunners, pelting along the decks to their posts, bumping into one another and cursing. It was all controlled chaos, as the bridge telegraphs clacked and jingled and the old ship groaned and puffed with the effort of raising steam, great clouds of black smoke pouring from her twin stacks. The old 'Mucky Duck' was going into action once again...

Achmet Khan cursed. The damned English seemed to be bearing a charmed life. Already two torpedoes had been fired and had missed. Now the gunners manning the 20mm quick-firer on the submarine's deck weren't having any better luck. Time and time again when it appeared they'd riddle the slow English craft with a volley, the helmsman swung his boat out of danger.

'Davoi, davoi!' he yelled at the captain, his dark brown face which rarely revealed anything, now showing anger for the first time.

'Da, da!' the one-armed captain yelled back over the mad clatter of the quick-firer. He knew the civilian was a creature of the

dreaded *Cheka*. It wouldn't do to get on the wrong side of him. He ducked below the edge of the conning tower and spoke rapidly to the men below. He rose grinning, showing his gold teeth of which he was so proud. Most of the crew who needed false teeth had them made of stainless steel; it was cheaper. He raised two fingers. 'Two fish,' he yelled, 'that should finish them off.'

Achmet Khan and the Captain waited anxiously. Then came the soft hiss in the voice tube. The skipper unplugged the cork, held the tube to his ear for a moment, then cried, *'Fire one … fire two!'*

There was the hiss of escaping compressed air. The little submarine shuddered once, twice. Achmet Khan leaned over the top of the conning tower, dark eyes gleaming. This would do it. The Russians, inefficient as they were, could miss at this range. This was the end for the British.

Dickie Bird thought otherwise. He saw the torpedoes plump out of the bows of the Russian sub and slap into the water. He knew, too, that the Russians had set the course on the two fish on the basis of the *Swordfish's* present speed. Now he decided to take a terrible chance. 'Smithie, I'm going to increase speed!' he yelled.

'Are you mad? You'll sink us.'

'We can sink one way or the other, old bean.' Not waiting for any further objections, he bent to the voice tube. 'Chiefie, give me full ahead. The works.'

'*What?*'

'You heard – *full ahead, both!*'

Down below CPO Ferguson opened the throttle. The *Swordfish*'s sharp prow rose out of the water almost immediately. Under his feet Dickie could feel the deck begin to shiver and tremble. The engines were all right, after all. They were delivering all they had. Now the *Swordfish* was slapping into each wave as if it were a brick wall. A huge wake rose to both sides of the craft's stern.

Smith prayed. Would the 'patch' hold? Would they dodge the torpedoes in time? His legs felt like rubber. His heart was beating like a crazy triphammer. Sweat poured down his taut, ashen face. Never had he been in a crazy situation like this before, when it seemed that either way they went would mean their destruction.

On the conning tower deck, Achmet Khan, himself now taut and biting his bottom lip with tension, willed the torpedoes to strike home before the English escaped. It was almost too much to bear. He found himself cursing in a mixture of Russian and his native tongue. Those damned English were as tricky as ever. Beneath their cultivated langeur and stiff glacial expressions he had seen so often in India, they were a cunning, devious people, who always kept pulling aces from beneath their sleeves.

The first one hissed behind the racing *Swordfish* and hurtled towards the shore impotently. Achmet Khan struck the steel conning tower in rage. 'Damn, damn, damn,' he cursed in English.

Next to him the one-armed skipper shook his fist at the craft and cried in Russian, 'I fuck your mother!'

Suddenly, startlingly, just as the second torpedo failed to strike home, the fleeing British ship stopped. Its sharp prow struck the surface of the sea. It heeled and rolled as the water started to pour in through the ruptured 'patch' and she lost speed immediately. *'We've got her ... we've got her,'* Achmet Khan yelled in sudden triumph. *'She's sinking!'*

'Boshe moi!' the submarine commander cursed. 'You're right, comrade. But we're going to make sure.' He bent over the voice tube. 'Both engines – full ahead,' he commanded. Then raising himself once more, he said, iron in his voice, 'She's not going to escape us this time with any of her tricks. We're closing with her, comrade. This time she's finished!'

'Start the pumps!' Dickie Bird yelled urgently, as Smith stood next to him on the bridge, feeling weak and exhausted, his wounded arm throbbing painfully. He didn't seem to care any more, even though the old *Swordfish* was sinking slowly. This was the end of the road. They'd had it once and for all.

Dickie Bird didn't think so. He was full of brisk energy. 'Chiefie,' he snapped down the voice tube. 'Get on to that patch! Every man you can find … at the double now.'

'Ginger,' he cried to the wounded rating, who had staggered from his bunk to help in any way he could, 'Find Billy Bennett... Man the Lewis gun. You can help with the pans.' Dickie meant the round magazines of ammunition for use on the machine gun.

'Ay ay, sir,' Ginger said stoutly and went off as quickly as he could.

Dickie now turned to Smith. 'Listen I know you must feel like something the dog just dragged in, old boy. But do you think you could manage the wheel? Just hold her steady and true. That's all. I think you might manage it with your one flipper.'

'I'll try, Dickie.'

'Stout fellow.' Dickie Bird didn't waste any more time. He handed the wounded skipper the wheel and clattered down the companionway to below.

The patch had been forced open just below the waterline. But already a red-faced, seemingly angry CPO Ferguson had a crew going, trying to force it back into place with iron bars and stanchions, while the pump worked flat out, pumping out the water which was knee-deep, Dickie nodded his approval. Knowing that Chiefie Ferguson had the situation well in hand, he doubled back up the ladder and on to the deck. The *Swordfish* was wallowing in the water now, listing slightly to port, going no more than five knots – and perhaps half a mile away the dark sinister shape of the enemy sub was closing on them fast. He was going to see the white bone she had in her teeth. She was going flat out and Dickie Bird told himself he didn't need a crystal ball to know why. She was coming in for the final kill!

'Damn,' he cursed and then moved swiftly to the Lewis gun where Billy Bennett crouched, assisted by a very pale Ginger, who had deep circles under his eyes ready for action. 'All right, Billy, I don't know what good it'll do, but you can open up. The devils are in range now.'

'Ay, ay, sir,' the fat rating replied, eager to do anything which would break the tension. 'I'll aim for the conning tower. Might get their skipper.'

'Good show,' Dickie said with faked enthusiasm, though inside him a hard little voice rasped. 'You haven't a cat's chance in hell, my fat friend!'

9

Black Jack took in the situation at once. 'Stand by to ram!' he yelled as the old destroyer shuddered and shivered as her engines thundered as if they might break loose from their moorings at any moment. To his Number One, he cried, 'Number One, stand by with a rescue party. That craft is settling down pretty fast. Get some towing ropes on her.'

'Ay, ay, sir,' the Number One reacted. He knew Black Jack. Whatever else he was, he was a first-rate seaman. He knew his craft. He doubled down from the bridge and started shouting out his own orders, as the immaculately scrubbed deck beneath his feet trembled like a live thing under the intense pressure.

Up on the bridge, Black Jack was enjoying himself. He knew he should have challenged the unknown sub first. That was what King's Regulations required in peacetime. But at this moment he didn't give a tinker's curse for King's Regulations; they could court-martial him if they wished. They'd soon be putting him out to grass on a pension, as it was. Now he felt the old thrill of going into action once more with the white ensign flying and the smoke pouring from the old 'Mucky Duck's' stacks. At the moment he was a seventeen-year-old midshipman again sweeping into his first action against Chink pirates off the China coast.

'Square up Turret B,' he ordered the forward gun crew. 'Stand by to open fire!'

Hastily the men in the turret below the bridge brought their twin 5-inch guns to bear. Now the long slim, dangerous-looking cannon pointing directly at the lean black shape of the sub. And still it hadn't spotted the racing destroyer, slicing through the water at a tremendous rate, a white bone of foam in her teeth.

Grating his ugly brown sawn-off teeth, his knuckles white as he gripped the bridge stanchion, Black Jack willed the old 'Mucky Duck' to hit the sub before she spotted her and attempted to submerge. But that wasn't to be. Suddenly the men manning the craft's conning tower were pointing in the direction of the racing destroyer.

'Open fire!' Black Jack yelled urgently into the tube.

The turret crew didn't hesitate. With an ear-splitting roar, the two 5-inch guns crashed into action. Two great shells hurtled towards the sub, which was already beginning to flood her tanks. Black Jack could see the bubbles exploding everywhere on the surface around the submarine, as the compressed air broke the surface. 'Dammit!' he cried, face purple with fury. 'You bugger – you're not going to escape the Mucky Duck!'

Suddenly the submarine reeled violently. A burst of cherry-red flame exploded at the base of the conning tower. The wireless mast came reeling, trailing angry blue sparks after it. Abruptly the submarine was listing heavily and men were flinging themselves over the side, as the second shell struck her in the hull. Plates groaned, buckled and burst. Black Jack reeled as the blast of an explosion struck him across the face like a flabby damp fist. Involuntarily he closed his eyes momentarily.

When he opened them again, he gasped. A gigantic blow torch of flame was searing the whole length of the crippled submarine, as more and more diesel escaped from the shattered oil tanks. Wildly the survivors were flinging themselves over the side and swimming away from the sub, furiously as if the Devil himself was after them. And he was, too, in the shape of that terrible, all-consuming flame.

Next to Achmet Khan, the Soviet captain was tearing at his burning wooden arm with a hand that was already ablaze itself. '*Help me,*' he screamed hysterically, '*Oh, please help me!*'

But Achmet Khan had no time to help

him. Besides the Russian was almost beyond help. Now he had stopped swimming altogether. Achmet Khan cast a swift glance behind him. A sailor was burning to death, his head turning before his eyes into a charred skull and the sea of flaming oil had already engulfed him and was swimming quickly in his direction.

He gasped panic-stricken and struck out. The *Swordfish* was low in the water and she was still moving out of the path of the burning oil. If he could make her, he'd be saved. He swam for all he was worth, swimming like he had never swum before since he was a kid and he used to race the others on the River Hooghly. Behind him the flaming oil roared like some primeval monster scenting its prey.

'There's one of the poor devils,' Billy Bennett spotted the lone man swimming desperately in front of the flaming oil. 'Let's toss him a rope, mate.'

'Let the sod burn,' Ginger said sourly, as they watched that terrible spectacle. The slowly sinking sub, the charred corpses reduced to the size of pygmies by that horrific flame, the men lying burning and screaming in the water, their black skeletal arms thrashing the flame impotently – and the lone swimmer, trying to outrace death, in its most terrible form.

They were safe, they knew it. The current

would carry the burning oil past them and they knew, too, that once they had been past, the destroyer which had appeared so startlingly to rescue them would probably take them in tow.

'Aw, come on, Ginger,' Billy Bennett, urged. 'After all he's just a poor old sailor bloke like us.'

'That poor old sailor bloke just tried to frigging well kill us,' Ginger snorted. Then he relented as he saw the terrified look, one of absolute horror, on the frantically swimming man's face. 'Here,' he handed the rope to Bennett. 'You toss, you silly git, and I'll try to give you a–'

He stopped short. Even as Billy Bennett whirled the thick rope like a fat clumsy cowboy, the flames reached the swimming man. He screamed in panic, as the hot burning oil started to swamp him.

'Catch it,' Billy shrieked frantically, as he sent the rope out hissing towards the struggling man, hoping he wouldn't let it drop into the flames. Then he'd be finished.

But Achmet Khan somehow caught it in mid-air – he had always been good at cricket. While the searing heat started to tear the flesh from his body in black shreds, his nostrils full of the stench of his own burning skin, he held on.

On the deck of the *Swordfish*, Billy Bennett, with a little help from the wounded

Ginger, hauled as he had never hauled before, fighting the flames, desperately trying to deprive them of their prey. Gibbering with terror, screaming with the agony of it all, Achmet Khan prayed they'd save him. Sweating, grunting, Billy Bennett, gasping as if he were running a great race hauled and hauled. And then the intended victim was free from the clutches of the flaming oil.

With one last great heave, the two of them pulled Achmet Khan over the side of the little craft, where he collapsed on the soaking, littered deck, writhing with pain, while the two of them stared down at him in absolute horror. 'Gawd Almighty,' Billy Bennett choked, 'He ain't … got no feet.'

Ginger turned swiftly, unable to stand the sight any longer. Where Achmet Khan's feet had once been there were now a set of bones, which glistened white like polished ivory against the blood-red, charred gore of his ankles!

Five minutes later, a triumphant Black Jack was bellowing through his megaphone, 'Ahoy, down there. Royal Navy here, chaps. Secure these ropes!' Suddenly ropes started to snake down to the sinking craft everywhere. Smith leaned weakly against the bulkhead, telling himself it was hardly possible. They had been saved yet once again.

Seeming to read his thoughts, an equally weary and very dirty Dickie Bird wiped the sweat off his face and said, 'You know, old bean, somebody sitting up there on a cloud and clad in his night shirt, playing his harp must really like the dear old *Swordfish*...'

Smith nodded his head and croaked, 'He really must...'

So they sailed slowly – very slowly – across a glass-clear Mediterranean, heading for Alexandria. The *Black Swan* towed the crippled *Swordfish* at a steady five knots an hour, while men from both ships attempted to replace the 'patch' and the medical attendants from the destroyer patched up the wounded. But there was little the senior medical rating could do for their prisoner. He had taken one look at those horrible skeletal feet, shuddered, said, 'Hell's teeth! How can he survive that?' and had plunged a needle full of morphia into Achmet Khan's arm: something he did repeatedly every three hours.

Now Achmet Khan lay on the deck, covered by a blood-stained blanket, dying reluctantly. Once Smith had tried to question him, but he could obtain little from the drugged prisoner, save that he spoke fluent English, before relapsing into a sort of whispered ranting in a language that Smith could not understand. CPO Ferguson could, however. He had strode past, busy with the hectic business of reinforcing the 'patch' and out of the side of his tight

Scots mouth he had rasped, 'Sir, yon chap's a darkie.'

'A darkie?' Smith had echoed puzzled.

'Ay, that's no doot about that. Ye ken I spent two years in India afore the war.'Then he was on his way again, leaving Smith to stare down at the dying man, wondering how an Indian came to be aboard a Russian sub.

Once Achmet Khan sat up and caused Ginger, who was tending him something of a shock as he chanted in perfect Oxonian English, *'Redshirts, blackshirts, everybody come!... Join the Oxford Labour Club ... and make yourselves at home... Bring your Marx and Engels and squat upon the floor... And we'll teach your economics as you never heard before.'* Then he collapsed back on the deck and sank into a deep coma once more.

As an amazed Ginger said to Billy Bennett afterwards, 'Cor, he could speak English just as good and you and me. I've never heard a foreigner – and a darkie as well – speak English like what we can.' Sorely puzzled, he scratched his ginger thatch and went back to his 'patient' as he was now calling Achmet Khan.

The end came when they were in sight of the Egyptian coast. Now Achmet Khan was very weak but lucid, the pain apparently vanished. In a feeble voice he said to Ginger, 'Fetch me your commanding officer, sailor.'

Ginger, who like all Englishmen of his type and time always maintained that 'one Englishman is better than ten of them foreigners', obeyed without question. For despite his being a foreigner and 'a darkie' to boot, Achmet Khan had an air of authority about him; as if he were a man who was used to giving orders and having them obeyed.

Minutes later Smith appeared. His arm had been dressed and he bore it in a sling now. But the pain was vanishing, and he felt his energy beginning to return. 'Well,' he snapped. 'You wish to speak to me.'

Achmet Khan's eyelids flickered open. He was panting and his breath was coming in shallow gasps. Smith had seen many men die in his young life. He recognized the signs. The 'darkie' as CPO Ferguson had called him – and it was the name that the rest of the crew knew him by, for he had refused to give them his true name – beckoned for Smith to bend down and come closer.

Reluctantly Smith did so.

'I have something to tell you,' Achmet Khan gasped. 'You have won... You British think you can always win... You have done so for centuries...'

'What is this nonsense?' Smith said sharply. He, too, was a product of his time and class. Anyone who said anything against the 'old country' as he always called it, was liable to 'get a punch in the nose'.

'You have won this time,' Achmet Khan continued weakly, as if he had not heard Smith's words. 'But you won't win for ever, you know... We shall bury you and your Empire in the end...'

'*We?*'

'The downtrodden, the underprivileged, people of the wrong colour–'

'What bolshy rubbish,' Smith interrupted him sharply. 'No one will ever be able to bring down the British Empire. Man, don't you know the sun never sets on it – *and it never damn well will!*'

Achmet Khan smiled weakly. His eyelids were fluttering very rapidly now and the tip of his nose seemed strangely pinched and white – sure signs that the end was near. 'You shall see, sir,' he said, voice very faint. 'The British Empire upon which the sun never sets–' Suddenly his eyes went very dull. His head lolled to one side, his mouth falling open stupidly.

'He's dead, sir,' Ginger said and gently he closed the dead man's eyes.

'Toss him over the side,' Smith said gruffly.

'Just as he is, sir?' Ginger asked in astonishment.

'Yes, just as he is.'

CPO Ferguson, still busy with his 'patch', strode by and barked, 'What d'ye want, Kerrigan? A bluidy burial service with a padre, white ensign and a ruddy firing squad?' He shook his grizzled head as if in wonder at the foolishness of modern sailors. 'He's only a bluidy darkie, ye ken.'

But the last words of Achmet Khan upset Smith. Walking slowly back to the bridge, he said to Dickie Bird, 'You know that chap had the damned cheek to say that the British Empire will come to an end one day. Imagine that!'

Dickie Bird smiled tolerantly. 'Now then, Smithie, don't let the poor chap get your dander up. There are thousands of young fellahs like us coming out of good schools every year and then buzzing off to the colonies and the dominions to run the show, you know. There always will be, as long as we have young chaps like that, a British Empire. Mark my words, your grand-children, if you ever succeed in finding some poor deluded woman to marry you' – he grinned– 'will be leaving Harrow-on-the-Hill in – say, sixty years time to go out and carry the white man's burden.'

Somewhat appeased, Smith said, 'I suppose you're right. When you look at what the men have been through these last two weeks since we set off from Withernsea and are still full of beans, I think you can safely say we'll keep the show going for a long time yet.'

'Of course we will. Now then, skipper,' Dickie Bird gave Smith an elaborate salute, 'we're coming into Alex. Got to have the old *Swordfish* all ship-shape and Bristol fashion, sir.'

Smith said a rude word and said, 'All right, Dickie, tell the chaps to form up on the deck.'

Thus they limped into the great naval harbour at Alexandria, a motley bunch of young sailors standing to attention in their scruffy civilian clothes to jeers and cries from the decks of the spick-and-span warships of *'Cor luv a duck, look what the old Mucky Duck's brung in now!'* But despite the catcalls and the ribald comments, the young men of the battered old *Swordfish* were proud of themselves. They had come through a lot, a kind of war in the shadows that those jeering matelots in their immaculate white uniforms would never know. They had foiled the Russians and the Germans. Now they were to take on the Turks. What they were going into would be desperately dangerous, but there wasn't a single one of them standing on the holed deck of the *Swordfish* that warm spring afternoon who wasn't absolutely confident that they'd pull it off...

THREE

INTO TURKISH WATERS

'We'd rather fuck than fight. But we allus end up fucking fighting.'

The motto of Leading Seaman
Ginger Kerrigan

1

Alexandria!

They had been in the great Egyptian port city for forty-eight hours now. Still they had not quite accustomed themselves to the heat, the dust, the noise, the teeming vibrant life of the streets. After the greyness of a winter in a post-war England, where everything seemed gloom and despair and the nation still sorrowing its million dead in the Great War, Alexandria was all light, spectacle, exciting. There were jugglers, snake charmers, colourful rogues of beggars with feigned diseases from blindness to falling-down fits, but with good steady hands when it came to accepting money. There were coffee peddlers, shouting their wares in curious high-pitched voices, jingling their little brass drinking cups as they wandered up and down the bustling streets. The outdoor cafés were full of plump men in red fezes, running their worry beads through their fat hands, or fanning themselves with round fans: men who never seemed to work, but managed to get far on it. As Billy Bennett commented sourly to Ginger, 'If we've been carrying the white man's burden

221

for all this bleeding time, them lot don't seem to have done too bad out of it!'

But while the crew of the *Swordfish* took their ease, seeing the sights, chasing the local *houris* in company with hordes of other eager Jack Tars, the naval dockyard artificers went to work on the battered craft at top speed. Indeed an astonished Smith, his wound dressed and comfortable now, had never seen such devoted hard work since the Great War. 'We're putting in three eight-hour shifts,' the smart chief-artificer in his immaculate white overall told Smith. 'That means the lads are working the whole twenty-four hours a day – in this heat!' He looked at the pale-faced young skipper with his arm in a sling with undisguised admiration. 'The lads all know you won the V.C. in that scrap at the end of the war. They all volunteered to come on this job. And there's the weekend coming up as well.'

Smith had been positively embarrassed. He knew the old Royal Navy refrain, 'Never volunteer for nothing in the Royal, matey 'cept for yer discharge.' He had mumbled something and had gone away, leaving them to the poor old battered *Swordfish*.

The volunteers had gone to work swiftly. They removed old Chiefie Ferguson's 'patch' and began sealing the jagged great hole with new plates. The radio mast was replaced and all the shrapnel holes and those made by the enemy bullets were filled in. After the artificers came the painters, great pots of red and green paint hanging from their belts, the inevitable half-smoked Woodbine tucked behind their right ears. The basic red coat was followed by the grey and as soon as that had dried, the painters went to work, adding a series of zig-zags in dull yellow to the grey surface.

Returning home from the Alexandria races, a little tight on free champagne, Dickie nudged Smith significantly when he saw what the painters were doing. 'Camouflage, old bean.'

Smith nodded. 'Exactly. They're getting us ready for the show.'

Dickie giggled a little drunkenly and said, 'We who are about to die, salute thee, O Great Ceasar.'

'Oh shut up, you silly ass,' Smith answered. 'Listen Dickie,' he said more urgently. 'We've got this far – against all kind of odds. For a while, I must admit, I thought we were for the chop. But we survived. Now I'm convinced we'll see this show through to the end.'

'Of course, we will, Smithie, old chap.' He linked his arm through Smith's. 'Come on, I'm parched. I haven't had a drink for at least thirty minutes. Let's see if there's any pink gin left in the wardroom.'

But Dickie's comment upset Smith a little.

As the two of them sat in the shade of the awning at the stern, watching the sun set and sipping their iced gins, Smith couldn't help thinking that they didn't really stand much of a chance of getting in and out of the Dardanelles without being spotted, especially as they now knew the Turks would be looking for them.

He frowned at the dockside, packed with hawkers, peasants herding long stragglers of tiny, overladen donkeys, a few raddled White Russian whores, who all claimed to have been countesses or princesses under the old Russian Imperial regime... 'If we could only come up with some kind of dodge for getting in and out of the Straits without attracting the attention of Johnny Turk, Dickie, then I wouldn't worry about the other part – sinking the Turkish battleships.'

Dickie shrugged. 'Pigs might fly, old chap. 'Fraid I haven't got a clue...'

On the third day the naval armourers took over from the artificers and painters. They, too, went to work with a will. A camouflaged two-pounder quick-firer was mounted on the foredecker. 'Latest model,' the gunnery officer in charge explained. 'Doesn't weigh more than fifteen hundredweight, so it'll only knock a couple of knots off your speed. But it's a damned good little gun. It gets off ten rounds a minute. And the shells are top-quality steel. If you'll forgive my French, gentlemen, but it'li go through that old Turkish armour – *like shit through a goose!*'

They had all laughed at that.

The gun was followed by two brand-new torpedoes of the latest type. 'Still on the secret list,' the gunnery officer had explained, handing them a clip board and his fountain pen, "Fraid you'll have to sign the Official Secrets Act for this one again, Lieutenant Smith.'

Smith had done so happily, knowing that the Mediterranean Squadron, strapped as it was for cash and supplies, was giving him the best it could afford. But all the time, while outwardly, he seemed calm and relaxed, Common Smith, V.C. worried how he was going to get the *Swordfish*, camouflaged or not, in and out of the damned Dardanelles...

On the fourth day he began to find out. Commander Doyle, the Squadron's chief-of-naval-intelligence, was a big, bluff Colonial, whose Australian accent was clearly apparent although it was now nearly ten years since he had transferred to the Royal Navy at the beginning of the war. 'It just came to me at the time – back in '15,' he added hastily, as Smith, sitting in the big office with the fan whirring overhead, noted the bulge in his pocket which indicated a pistol. 'Nasmith had gone through the

Dardanelles in his sub, the *E-II*, and blown up half the Turkish fleet. He'd hidden out in the Sea of Marmara – here – for a week or so putting the wind up old Johnny Turk before managing to get out and receive the well-deserved V.C. from the King-Emperor.' Doyle's one eye twinkled, for a pit where the other one had once been was now hidden by a jaunty, piratical patch. 'So I thought anything a Pommy can go do, an Aussie can do better. But how?'

Both Smith and Bird smiled, but sat up. This big smiling Australian had obviously gone the same route they were about to take and had lived to talk about it. 'Yes, how?' they asked as one.

'Now it was May '15,' he continued, 'and Johnny Turk and the Huns who were helping them knew we'd have another crack at getting into the Sea of Marmara. They'd ordered more troops into the area, plus mining the channel, and setting up more batteries on either side of the Narrows, where the passage is the toughest. They were waiting for us. So how was I going to do it?' He paused and let them wonder, obviously enjoying himself at their expense.

Outside, one of the skinny little donkeys the Egyptians used for transport had gone down on its front legs braying in protest at the huge load of firewood, it was being forced to carry. Its owner, dark and villainous, dressed in a dirty white robe, started to beat its back savagely. Other Egyptians passing took no notice. 'Egyptians,' Doyle said, as if that explained everything.

'You were saying, sir,' Smith urged, taking his eyes off the poor animal, its rump already a mass of red streaming flesh. 'About the Dardanelles.'

'Oh yes. So what did I do? Well, in those days if you wanted something – er, not quite kosher – you went to old Kahn Bey.' He winked. 'Otherwise known as Sammy Cohen. He was – is – a Levantine. He could have been a Jew, a Greek, even a Turkish Cypriot, perhaps it was a bit of all three. But by Hades, was Sammy Cohen smart!'

Smith shot Bird a look. It said, 'Where is all this leading?'

Dickie shrugged. He didn't know.

Outside the donkey was on all fours now, its driver beating it systematically and without passion. Now the poor animal was streaming with blood. The civilians passed it without a second look. It was part and parcel of their short and brutal lives. Most of them were dead by the time they were 35. What did a donkey matter?

'Dammit,' Doyle said, 'Sammy Cohen liked the Aussies. The Aussies spent a lot of money in Alex during the war and where there was money, there was old Sammy, grinning all over his moonface, rubbing his fat paws, as if he could already feel those nice juicy piaster notes. I can see him now as I started to tell him in a roundabout way that I was wanting to pass through the Dardanelles. But he was streets ahead of me already. He was like that – very smart. "So you want to go through the Straits," he said, "admiral?" I was a sub-lieutenant at the time.' Doyle grinned. 'But old Sammy Cohen was never slow in using the old flannel.'

'So what did this Cohen chap say?' Smith urged.

Outside the donkey lay flat on its side, obviously dying. Still its owner beat the animal relentlessly, as if a few more blows would bring it back on to its feet.

'Something simple. I should have thought of it myself, but I didn't. So I had to pay for it.'

'Go on.'

Doyle chuckled. 'Impatient, ain't we? "Oh, the sap of youth!"' He chuckled again and Smith felt himself go red. 'Sammy knew everything. All the obstacles. The batteries, the lookouts, the minefields and a new one that our Intelligence people knew nothing about. Old Johnny Turk had put down a steel net, which was stretched across the Narrows, going down to two hundred feet. This net was patrolled by Turkish motor-boats. They were loaded with bombs –

something like spiders waiting for their prey to appear on the web.'

'Oh my sainted aunt!' Dickie exclaimed. 'So you couldn't even go through the Narrows submerged.'

'Exactly.'

'So what *did* you do?' Smith asked in exasperation.

Outside the Egyptian had stopped beating the donkey. It was dead already, lying still in a pool of blood, the big greedy flies already buzzing around the carcass. The peasant stared down at the dead beast, as if he were wondering how it had happened.

'Why waste time?' came back Doyle's surprising answer. 'Why don't we go and hear it from the horse's mouth, Common Smith, V.C.?'

'*Go?*'

'Yes,' Doyle answered. 'Old Sammy's still very much in business. No doubt, if we behave ourselves, he'll duly provide us with three nubile dusky maidens from his stable as well.'

'Gosh,' Dickie exclaimed and arose with alacrity. 'Lead on McDuff – *at the double!*'

Outside the Egyptian shrugged and lifting the burden off the dead donkey's back, staggered away with the pile of firewood. A moment later the vultures sailed down from the roof opposite and began to pick out the dead beast's eyes...

2

Kemal Ataturk raised his glasses. Behind him his staff officers did the same. As always they waited for a signal from the new Turkish dictator before they moved. Down below the great port city of Smyrna sprawled in the hazy sunlight: a mass of brilliant white buildings set against the emerald backdrop of the Aegean Sea.

'See the harbour,' Ataturk commanded. 'They are collecting boats.' He adjusted his field glasses. A varied collection of boats swept into the gleaming calibrated circles of glass. They came in all sizes from fishing caiques to large modern transports, which he judged must displace some ten thousand tons. All of them, whatever their size, bore the hated Red Cross flag.

'Do they think – those Greek pigs – that the infidel cross flag will protect them?' Ataturk sneered. 'I spit on it!' He hawked and spat in the dried dust at his booted feet.

Obediently the elegant staff officers laughed. All of them knew it could be only a matter of days now before the two antiquated battleships left the repair yards at Istanbul and sailed for the Aegean. Once the Greeks began evacuating their last foothold on Turkish territory, they'd be waiting for their convoys just outside Turkish territorial waters.

As if reading his officers' minds, as Ataturk said, 'They will disappear to the bottom of the sea without trace. Man, woman and child, they must all die. We'll be rid of the greasy Greeks for good – and this time, comrades, there will be no photographs of Turkish atrocities. For there will be no witnesses.' He tugged at the bit of his white stallion harshly and forced the animal round.

His staff officers did the same, telling themselves that Ataturk had no feeling for his animals – or his fellow human beings for that matter. For him both species were there to perform a service for the greater glory of Turkey – and Kemal Ataturk, no more. 'We shall see what the Greeks do when they see our *askaris*,' Ataturk announced as they trotted towards the rear where the regiment waited. He thwacked the rump of his horse brutally with his crop.

The regiment of infantry was drawn up in three rough lines. The *askaris* were raw recruits straight from their Anatolian villages. They were dark and sturdy and all were trying to grow moustaches so that they would appear older than they were; for most of them were boys not more than sixteen.

But in their new, ill-fitting uniforms they looked solid and unafraid.

Ataturk tugged at the bit hard. The stallion reared into the air, flailing it with its forelegs. It was an impressive sight and Ataturk knew it impressed the young soldiers. He could hear them whispering his name from rank to rank, *Ataturk ... Ataturk ... the great Ataturk...*'

He smiled coldly. In years to come they would be telling their grandchildren that they had actually once seen the great man, 'Kemal Ataturk – the Father of the Turks' – those who survived this day.

He rose in his saddle. 'Soldiers, comrades, fellow Turks!' he shouted in that harsh strained voice of his, roughened by years of yelling orders at soldiers. 'You are young, but you are Turks. Today you are being given the honour to be the first of our Army to fight on this new front. To the West, we have driven the Greeks out of our beloved Turkey. Now with your help we shall do the same here on this new front. Then we shall be rid of the hated infidel for ever. Spare no one, man, woman or child. They must all die, remember that, soldiers!' He waved his crop, as if it were a sabre. *'Askaris* – to *the attack!'*

The officers shrilled their whistles. NCOs bellowed orders. The regimental standard was unfurled. A drummer began to beat the cadence. The *askaris* bayoneted rifles came down level with their hips. The steel flashed in the sun. Stolidly the lines of grey-clad infantry began to advance. Dust rose at once so that the *askaris* seemed to be moving through a white mist.

'*Saida,*' Kemal Ataturk whispered softly to himself for he knew what must happen soon. 'Farewell, brave *askaris!*'

At the outskirts of the great city, broken barns and outhouses, where the Greeks dried the huge yellow tobacco leaves with which the Greeks made their fortunes, a series of trenches had been dug. Now Ataturk swept them with his binoculars. He nodded his approval. His practised eye, schooled in the long wars in Europe and Africa, told him that they had been dug by amateurs. That was good. Now he would soon learn what kind of weapons the Greek civilians and the handful of soldiers manning those trenches possessed. That's why those boys were being sent into the first attack. He couldn't risk losing too many of his skilled veterans.

Now the ragged lines of young *askaris* were within two hundred metres of the Greek positions. Kemal Ataturk tensed. The firing had to start soon. It did. Suddenly – startlingly – a single flare hissed into the afternoon sky. It exploded in a burst of hissing, unnatural green light. Ataturk sucked in his cheeks. It was the signal for the Greek line to open fire.

Almost instantly the lethal chattering of the heavy machine guns commenced. To each end and in the centre of the Greek positions they opened up. Swiftly Ataturk counted their number. Not more than ten. Good, he told himself. But what else did the Greeks have up their sleeves?

Stolidly the *askaris* plodded on. Great gaps were being torn in their ranks. But the survivors simply climbed over the dead and dying, bayonets held at the ready. Behind them the fields seemed to be covered in a new grey carpet. Now only a few officers were left. Most of them were armed only with swagger canes. A few of the more flamboyant were smoking as they strode out at the head of their peasant boys. Kemal Ataturk smiled in admiration. 'What soldiers we Turks are,' he told himself proudly.

Now the attackers were only a hundred metres from the Greek positions. Up front the infantry colonel, capless and bleeding from a wound on his forehead, blew three shrill blasts on his whistle. Next moment he went down, dead before he hit the ground. Still his men obeyed the signal to charge. All their resentment, anger, frustration exploded in a wild bass yell. They stumbled forward at the run, their bayonets flashing in the sun.

This was it, Ataturk told himself. If the Greeks had artillery, heavy weapons, they would use them now to stop the charge. But no guns thundered. Instead the whole length of the enemy line erupted with rifle fire.

Again huge gaps appeared in the ranks of the charging *askaris*. Still they continued, carried away by the wild unreasoning blood-lust of battle. But their numbers were getting fewer by the instant. Here and there Turks flung themselves over the parapets of sandbags and bales of hay. Blades flashed. Greek and Turk locked in solitary combat. But the Turks had little chance. More and more Greeks, soldiers and civilians, swarmed out of their holes and attacked the lone Turks. They were cut down ruthlessly, the Greeks hacking, slashing, gouging without mercy.

Abruptly the steam went out of the Turkish attack. The survivors, many of them wounded, began to pull back. Withdrawing and then turning to fire once more at the triumphant, yelling Greeks, they stumbled over the bodies of their dead comrades: a handful of men left out of the thousand who had attacked only ten minutes before.

Kemal Ataturk sucked his front teeth for a moment, face dark and brooding. Those young boys had suffered terribly. But they had served their purpose. It was obvious that the Greek defenders of Smyrna had no heavy weapons; their arms were limited to machine guns and rifles. They would be no match for the Turkish Army when it really attacked.

He swung round in the saddle. 'Signals,' he snapped.

The handsome young signals officer who reeked of perfume and who, Kemal Ataturk suspected, used powder to lighten his dark complexion, trotted over hurriedly. *'Effendi?'* he queried, flashing his excellent teeth.

Kemal Ataturk forgot the carnage all around. He liked the boy. He had always been attracted to handsome boys. 'Send a signal,' he commanded.

The boy flushed as he always did when the Great Man spoke to him. Hurriedly he pulled out his pen and message pad.

'Signal this. "To the Ministry of War, Ankara. Will begin the offensive on the Southern front with four divisions within next forty-eight hours. Alert warships, Istanbul. Must be ready to sail by May 1st, 1922 at the latest. Signed and approved, Kemal Ataturk." Got it, young man?'

The signals officer fluttered his long eyelashes delightfully. 'Got it, *Effendi*,' he answered, colouring again.

'Cok gusel!' Then encode and send at once.' He reached out his hard hand and took the boy's soft one in his own. The signals officer shuddered slightly. His colour deepened even more. 'It is a very important message, my boy,' Kemal Ataturk said. 'Ensure that it

is not garbled. For it will have a place in modern Turkish history. It signals the end of the Greeks in Turkey after a thousand years. Please come to my tent later to confirm dispatch.' He licked his lips which were suddenly very dry. 'You shall drink a glass of *raki* with me this evening.'

'Thank you, *Effendi*. Yes, *Effendi*.' The signals officer, his face crimson, saluted, swung his horse round and trotted off to the signals tent. With some interest Kemal Ataturk watched as the officer's lean buttocks, clad in his tight breeches, rose and fell with the motion of his mount. Then he dismissed the handsome young officer from his mind and turned his attention to the city below once more.

Raising his binoculars he studied the port city's great sprawling layout. In his mind's eye he visualized how he would employ his four divisions of infantry in the assault soon to come. He decided he must not allow his infantry to become involved in street-to-street fighting. That would be too costly in Turkish life. Besides he would be unable to use his artillery.

No, he would commence the infantry attack with a massed artillery bombardment. That would cause the civilians to run heading for the harbour and the boats. In the resulting confusion he would send in his infantry, forcing the rattled defenders ever closer to the shore and the waiting rescue flotilla. For all he cared, let all the Greeks escape. Why waste precious Turkish lives attempting to kill them inside the city? Let the Greeks sail. Then his two battleships could deal with the unarmed Greek craft at their leisure.

Besides he wanted as much of the city as possible to fall in to Turkish hands undamaged. Those warehouses down there were crammed with valuable dried fruits and tobacco which would bring a fortune in hard currency on the world's markets. And his poor bankrupt country needed as much foreign currency to buy goods abroad as he could lay his hands on.

He lowered his binoculars, his mind made up. He turned to his waiting staff. 'Gentlemen,' he announced, 'we shall take the train back to Istanbul this night. I shall commence my offensive against Smyrna in forty-eight hours. Within the week there will be no single living Greek left on our holy Turkish soil!'

One of his staff colonels rose in his saddle. Dramatically he pulled out his glistening silver sabre. He waved it above his head. At the top of his voice, he yelled, *'Death to the Greeks, comrades!'*

'Death to the Greeks!' his comrades echoed as one, dark faces flushed, eyes gleaming with excitement.

Kemal Ataturk did not seem to hear. For his mind was already occupied by what he would buy for his beloved homeland with the goods he would take from the Greeks. Slumped in his saddle, he turned and began to canter to the railhead, followed by his suddenly puzzled staff officers. Why, they asked themselves, did the dictator show no joy at the imminent defeat of the Greeks? They didn't know, of course, that Kemal Ataturk had already forgotten the Greeks of Smyrna. For him they were already dead. Now he had other operations and plans on his restless mind.

Behind them in the city, the frightened citizens waited, and wondered. Were they really going to be saved when the Turks attacked? If the boats didn't take them off then, there would be one of the biggest massacres in the whole of human history. *What were they going to do?*

3

The *ghari,* its canvas roof decked in gay colours, the bells along it jingling merrily, clip-clopped down the avenue which led from Alexandria's European quarter into the seedy, rundown area inhabited by the natives. Here the population, although most of them wore some sort of European clothing, was basically brown or black. But there was a fair sprinting of what Commander Doyle called the 'Levantines', portly gentlemen, whose skin colour was olive brown and who exuded a cheerful, welcoming air, accompanied by a constant rubbing of fat palms, as if they were only too eager to shake hands with you – and take your money.

'Those are the chaps who made the Middle East,' Doyle commented cheerfully, as they passed a group of them seated in cane chairs outside a café, sipping tiny cups of Turkish coffee and idly whisking their fly catchers back and forth. 'They are invariably humble and polite, eager to do you any service you might require, legal or illegal. But they can buy and sell in half a dozen languages. Not just goods, mind you, but people too. Generals, politicians, judges, policemen. Oh yes,' he concluded with a wry grin, 'your Levantine knows the price of everything – *and everybody.*'

Smith and Dickie Bird seated opposite him in the open, horse-drawn carriage grinned. Old Doyle, they told themselves, was a bit of a world-weary cynic himself.

'So why is this Mr – er – Sammy Kahn prepared to help us, Commander?' Smith ventured.

Doyle made a gesture with his thumb and forefinger, as if he were counting banknotes. 'That's on the surface the reason why, Smith,' Doyle said. 'For all the gold you can afford to pay him. Of course if you asked him directly, he'd tell you something like this.' Doyle adopted a pose, head on one side, hands spread out, palms upwards, rolling his eyes expressively as he did so. 'A man has to live, Meester Smith,' he mimicked. 'As a friend, you understand, I would do this thing for nothing. But think of my many children, my aged mother, all my poor relatives in Palestine–' Doyle's voice resumed its normal robust Australian tone. 'But there's more to Sammy Kahn than that. Think of all those rich Greeks who will soon be fleeing Turkey. Where are they to go? Greece? *No*, that country's bankrupt already. It's ready for civil war and the rich Greeks are not going to put their gold in a place like that. Beside Greece is impoverished. Most Greeks don't have a pot to piss in! Nothing to be made there. But Egypt is another matter entirely. Here you can make heaps of money off the backs of the Egyptian peasants, who are born in debt to the money-lenders – and die that way, too. But how will the Greeks get passes, visas, work permits and all the rest of it? To obtain those sorts of necessary documents, someone has to use the squeeze–'

'And Mr Kahn is the gent who'll do it?' Dickie interjected quickly.

'Exactly. Kind-hearted old Sammy'll help to get them out, and once they're here, he'll squeeze them, too, till the pips squeak.'

Smith grinned. He told himself he was looking forward to meeting the old rogue as Doyle had portrayed the businessman. Suddenly his grin vanished. Out of the corner of his eye he caught a glimpse of an old Ford tourer speeding to catch up with the horse-drawn *ghari*. He frowned, as the car swerved and narrowly missed a donkey then came charging forward again, scattering a group of civilians. Why the hurry? he asked himself puzzled.

An instant later he found out. A dark villainous face appeared at the side of the speeding car as it came level with the *ghari*. In the man's hand he held a big automatic.

'*Duck!*' Smith yelled.

Next moment there was a burst of firing. The bullets slammed into the driver in front of them. He opened his mouth stupidly. A line of crimson-red holes had just been stitched the length of his robe. One second later he fell, slumping over the steaming rump of his horse.

The horse whinnied with sudden fear. It reared up in the traces, as the man in the speeding car fired again. The horse's side suddenly flushed scarlet. It went down on its forelegs, whinnying with pain, eyes frantic and wild.

Doyle reacted first. Although he was twice the age of the other two, he pushed Bird to one side, tugging out his pistol as he did so. *'Look out!'* he yelled urgently. Next moment he fired.

Three feet away the killer screamed with absolute agony. The second slug hit him in the face. Suddenly his features disappeared in a mess of red gore and shattered white-gleaming bone. The revolver dropped from abruptly nevertheless fingers and toppled to the road.

Doyle fired again. He missed. But the swarthy-faced driver of the Ford had had enough. Desperately he hit the brake and swerved at the same time. The Ford's tyres squealed in protest as he turned, the dead man still hanging out of the side of the car, dripping blood. For a moment the old Ford seemed to balance on two wheels. Then it hit the road with a metallic thud. The driver, his face contorted with fear, pressed the accelerator. The Ford started to pull away. But the driver hadn't reckoned with Doyle.

Coolly, as if he were back at the firing range, the big Australian stood up in the stalled *ghari,* one hand behind his back. He squinted along the barrel to where the sight dissected the fleeing Ford. The car was just about to disappear around the bend. Doyle pressed the trigger. The right rear tyre exploded.

Desperately the driver tried to keep the Ford under control. To no avail. A camel escaped being hit by shedding its load and fleeing out of the way. Shimmying crazily from side to side, while the frantic driver fought to avoid the pedestrians who were scattering on all sides. But he was out of luck. Next instant the Ford slammed into the side of the mosque where worshippers, their robes tucked up about their waist, were busy washing their private parts.

'Quick,' Doyle yelled. 'Let's nab the bugger!'

They sprang out of the wrecked *ghari*. They pelted towards the wrecked taxi, the air suddenly full of the cloying stench of escaping petrol. Women screamed at them. Men shook their fists. The three Britishers didn't care. They were intent on getting the driver before he escaped. They wanted to find out who had just attempted to murder them.

That wasn't to be. Suddenly there was a blinding flash. A burst of searing heat struck them in the face. They reeled back as the car went up in bright scarlet flame, against which the trapped driver was outlined a stark, screaming, struggling black.

'A bloody lash-up,' Doyle cursed, using the old naval slang. 'Damnation, I'd–' The rest of his words were drowned by the explosion as the Ford went up.

A few minutes later they were on their way again, reluctantly. Their faces were bitter with the knowledge that they had survived, but that there had been an attempt to kill them. It seemed that there would never be any let-up. From Britain to here in Egypt, it appeared, that every man's hand was against them. Doyle broke the heavy, menacing silence as he thrust his way through the natives who looked at them, their dark eyes full of hatred, with 'Come on, let's see what Sammy's got to say. He knows everything...'

Sammy Kahn, all glittering gold teeth, heavy paunch and permanently smiling face – though his dark eyes remained wary and guarded – said immediately, 'Could be Germans, Russians, Turks, even Egyptians. They are all interested in setting the Middle East aflame and are not particular in the methods they use.' He shrugged his fat shoulders, took another puff at the bubble pipe which squatted next to the spitoon at his right and said, 'So Doyle Pasha wants to return to the scene of his wartime triumphs, eh.' He changed the subject immediately.

'Hey, how the devil did you get hold of that?' Doyle protested.

Sammy dismissed the matter with an airy wave of his pudgy, beringed hand, 'It is of no consequence,' he said, still smiling. 'Tut,

tut, at your age, Doyle Pasha, I was more interested in women and the delights of the flesh than risking my fat neck. Still, gentlemen, let us discuss this tricky business of getting into the Dardanelles undetected.'

Smith and Bird leaned forward expectantly. Now at last they were going to hear of a way to dodge the Turks.

'You know the problem. On the right bank there is first the fort of KumKale and thereafter there are forts and batteries at regular intervals all along the seventy miles of waterway. In essence any craft is under observation all the way along and can, at the same time, be taken by artillery fire. There is little fog in that region so we can't hope for that means of dodging the Turks.'

'Well, we did it last time, Sammy,' Doyle urged, tugging at his eye patch, as if to remind himself that his successful penetration of the Dardanelles had also cost him an eye. 'Now the question is, can we get away with it once again, eh?'

Sammy Kahn laughed, a thick rumbling sound that seemed to come from the depths of his ample stomach. 'Of course, we can, Commander! The Turks might be brave, cruel, greedy, etc. Fortunately they are very stupid. They see only what they want to see. So we shall let them do just that.'

'What do you mean, Mr Kahn?' Smith asked hastily.

'They shall see one craft sailing down the Dardanelles – harmless sort of fishing vessel. But they will be unable to see the other one that will sail with it.'

Smith looked puzzled and Sammy laughed once more. 'It will cost a trifle,' he went, making that counting gesture with his fat thumb and forefinger with which Smith and Bird had become familiar by now.

'We've got the money, Mr Kahn,' Dickie reassured the other man. 'Oodles of it.'

'Excellent.' Kahn beamed, obviously well pleased by the response. 'So let me explain.' He took a quick draw at his waterpipe, making the liquid bubble and belch, then lowering his voice, as if afraid of being overheard, he began...

Ten minutes later he stopped speaking and sat back, plump hands resting on his belly, as if waiting to see their reaction to his scheme. Doyle waited, too, eyeing the two young officers in silence. From outside came the muted noise of the street traffic and somewhere in the big rambling Turkish-style villa, an old clock ticked away the seconds of their lives with metallic inexorability.

Finally Smith broke the heavy brooding silence. 'Well, Mr Kahn, it is a very ingenious scheme. But can I trust your man? After all he is a Turk, working against the interests of his own country by helping us.'

'I think so, Smith Pasha,' Khan replied easily. 'It will be dangerous for both parties, and he would get a reward if he turned you over to his own people. But the Turkish pound is worthless and he knows it. The Horsemen of St George are more important to him than Turkish patriotism, believe you me. I know him well.'

Smith nodded, his mind racing electrically. The scheme was daring, as Sammy Kahn had outlined it, but it had worked before for Doyle. With luck it would work for the *Swordfish* nearly a decade later.

Sammy Kahn nodded encouragingly, then his fat face grew serious. 'But let me advise you of one thing, Smith Pasha. You have seen yourself this afternoon that there are killers at work. Sooner or later they might well make another attempt on your lives – or something similar. So please accept this advice. Sail as soon as possible for your rendezvous. Each hour now that you spend in Alexandria increases the risk.' He took another suck of his pipe, and looked at Doyle a little expectantly.

Doyle got the message. He reached in his tunic and fetched out a small leather bag. 'A contribution from a grateful His Majesty's Government,' he said.

Sammy Kahn beamed. 'Ah, diamonds I see. Much more interesting than banknotes and not as easily traced. Thank you, Doyle

Pasha.' He palmed the little bag neatly, and raised his other hand in a final salute. 'God's blessing on you both, young gentlemen.'

Smith didn't know whether to laugh or to be serious. Kahn, he told himself, would be the last one he imagined to invoke the deity.

So they passed out into the hot Egyptian afternoon, minds full of what was soon to come. Soon they would start on the final leg of their long journey. Now everything depended upon an obscure Turk, whose name surprisingly enough was 'Abdul the Terrible'. Why, Sammy Kahn had not enlightened them.

Doyle hailed another *ghari* and they set off for naval headquarters, each man cocooned in his own thoughts, until finally Doyle broke the silence, with 'You sail on the night tide, Common Smith, V.C.'

Dickie Bird's face lit up. 'Damn fine show, Commander!' he said excitedly. 'But one thing, sir.'

'What?' Doyle asked.

'Don't give us your blessing, sir. I simply couldn't stand another one after old Sammy's.'

He laughed and the big Australian did the same. 'All right then, you shall go, unblessed by me.' His grin vanished. 'But remember this. Last time it cost me an eye. Right. Take care that this time around it doesn't cost you any more.' And with that he relapsed

into a sudden sombre silence. Thus it was –
in silence – that they made their way back to
naval HQ.

4

'Tenedos!' Dickie exclaimed, as the dark
shape of the little Turkish island came into
view, set in the purple nightscape of the
fragrant Aegean Sea.

All was quiet. There was no sound save the
gentle purr of the *Swordfish*'s engines as they
approached the island at five knots. On the
bridge, an anxious tense Smith raised his
night glasses. He swept the island, which
was mainly populated by Turkish fishermen,
so Doyle had told him. Here and there a few
yellow lights still burned. But there was no
lighthouse and as far as he knew no Turkish
garrison. All seemed to be going well.

He turned to a waiting Ginger Kerrigan,
'All right, Ginger,' he commanded, 'send
the signal.'

Ginger hesitated a fraction of a second. He
knew the danger they were all in. If there
were Turkish troops on the island just off
the coast of the mainland and they spotted
the signal, too, all hell would probably break
loose. Then he sent the signal on his Aldis

lamp. It was the Morse for 'SOS,' the only morse signal they thought an illiterate Turkish fisherman would recognize.

Nothing happened.

No light illuminated the darkness. Smith peered through the gloom. Next to him a worried Dickie said, 'Hell's teeth, do you think they're not–'

He stopped short suddenly. About a mile away a faint yellow light was flickering off and on slowly. 'Answer, sir,' Ginger said excitedly. 'It's them!'

'Keep it down to a dull roar, Ginger, *please*. They can probably hear you all the way to Istanbul.'

'Sorry, sir.' Ginger gave a quick flick of his Aldis lamp to acknowledge receipt. Then Smith ordered the engines stopped and so they waited, no sound heard but the soft lap-lap of the Aegean against *Swordfish*'s hull. Now they waited, with a double lookout posted and Billy Bennett tensed behind the Lewis gun. For they knew from Doyle that there had been increased patrolling of these coastal waters by Turkish gunboats and light craft. The Turks were on the lookout for any attempt by the Greeks to escape from Smyrna to the north of their present position.

'What did the Levantine say again?' Dickie asked in a low voice.

'Pay the Turk in instalments of twenty

Horsemen of St George at regular intervals during the passage up the Straits,' Smith replied. 'Twenty at KumKale. Twenty at Chanuk. Twenty when we're through the Narrows and so on.'

'Donkey and carrot sort of thing,' Dickie said.

'Exactly... I say, Dickie,' Smith's voice rose, 'there she is! To port. Can you see?'

Hurriedly Dickie turned in that direction. A dark shape was emerging from the purple-scented gloom and now the young officers could hear the soft chug-chug of an ancient engine. Together they raised their glasses. The low shape of a fishing caique slipped into the bright circle of glass. It was the Turks, all right, Smith told himself. Still he did not relax his guard. 'Stand by gun crew,' he ordered. 'Billy keep your eyes peeled.'

'Like tinned tomatoes,' Billy replied in the old Naval fashion, and tucked the butt into his shoulder – just in case.

But there was no need for him to use the Lewis gun. Five minutes later, the caique nudged against the side of the *Swordfish,* giving off a penetrating odour, composed of rotten fish, oil and perfumed Turkish tobacco.

'Abdul the Terrible,' a deep bass voice announced from the deck of the Turkish craft, 'feared from Montreal to Miami.' The voice was pure American-English. 'Never been beaten... Well,' the voice corrected itself, 'now and again, he has.'

Next moment the owner of the voice appeared over the side of the *Swordfish* and Ginger crossed himself in mock panic, exclaiming, 'Gawd Almighty. Heaven help a sailor on a night like this!'

Next to him Dickie Bird's mouth dropped open in sheer awe. The Turkish skipper was a huge mountain of a man. His head was clean-shaven, a gold earring glittered in his left ear and his broad mouth was full of gold teeth. With a hand like a small steam shovel he pulled himself over the side of the *Swordfish* and dropped to the deck with surprising agility for such a giant of a man. For a moment he poised there, knees bent and huge hands held out to his front, as if he were half-expecting a fight – or worse. Then he thrust out his right hand at Smith.

The latter took it gingerly. Next moment he wished he hadn't. The Turkish skipper gave it a squeeze, saying, 'I'm welcoming any friend of that Jewboy, Sammy Kahn.'

Smith's eyes nearly popped out of his head. In a strangled voice, he said, 'How do you do?'

'Doing very good,' the big Turk answered. 'But I was doing more good in the good ole US of A., God's own country.' For a moment he straightened up to the position of attention and looked very solemn. 'Then the bums gave me the old heave-ho in '17 when America entered the war. Sent me back here – to crappy Turkey. But Sammy, the Jewboy, has promised me a passport, visa, work permit – the whole shoot – if I help you limey gents.' He licked his thick lips. 'You got no English whisky like those limeys in skirts make?'

Five minutes later Abdul the Terrible was filling the tiny wardroom, drinking pink gin – 'we have no English whisky made by the limeys in skirts' – explaining how they were going to penetrate the Straits. The ex-wrestler, for that had been his profession in the United States, said, 'You see that Turkish jerk Kemal Ataturk hasn't got enough doughboys. All used up, fighting the goddam Greeks.' His big face lit up suddenly. 'I once had a bout with a Greek. Gussie the Gorgeous Greek, they called him. Big handsome guy. He wasn't very gorgeous when Abdul had finished with him.'

Smith flashed Dickie a look which said, 'I'm not surprised – with those paws of his.'

'Well, as I was saying. Ataturk hasn't got enough soldiers to garrison both sides of the Straits. So he is only defending the southern side. So I – and you – will sail the northern side, as far away from the troops as we can get.'

'But they'll still be able to spot us.'

'Not with my boat in between you and them and with my fishing net thrown over you. All the soldier boys will see is some poor jerk of a Turkish fisherman trawling for what he can find in the Dardanelles, perhaps for the Istanbul market. You got it?'

Smith nodded his head. 'Yes I've got it.'

Next to him squeezed against the bulkhead by the Turk's enormous girth, Dickie asked, 'When do we start?'

Abdul the Turk lowered his glass. 'Just before dawn when the sentries change, Admiral. That goddam Ataturk thinks he's smart. But his shit don't smell like ice-cream. Old Abdul the Terrible'll have him out in one round, yessir!' He drained the rest of the waterglass, and said, 'Say, could I have another one of them red gins. Tastes swell…'

It was just before dawn. Now the caique and the *Swordfish* were linked together by stout rope lines, with the superstructure of the British vessel covered by the caique's stinking fishing net. Up ahead Smith, peering through the mesh, could just see the dark smudge which was the entrance to the Dardanelles. Periodically a bright light parted the darkness and he told himself that would be the lighthouse at Arche Baba.

Next to him Dickie said, 'There's a lighthouse, too, according to the chart, at

KumKale. But it doesn't appear to be operating. Abdul must be right. The Turks are only manning one side of the Straits.'

'Let's hope so, Dickie. Because if they rumble us in that Straits, we're dead ducks.'

'*Very* dead ducks,' Dickie agreed.

Time passed slowly, as the *Swordfish* chugged along at five knots, the maximum speed of the ancient caique. Slowly the sun was beginning to rise, a blood-red ball to the east, colouring the still sea a dramatic crimson, so that it looked as if the water ran with blood.

At a snail's pace the two craft sailed into the Straits, with the Turkish crew of the caique going about their deck duties in their usual slow manner, while the crew of the *Swordfish* crouched under the netting, the sweat trickling down their tense, apprehensive faces, waiting for that challenge which would spell doom for them.

From his hiding place Smith could see the sheep and goats roaming the rugged cliffs on their side of the Straits, the waterway which divided Europe from Asia. Here and there there were series of trenches surrounded by rusting barbed wire, which Smith took to be the defences prepared by the Turks when the Allies had landed at the Dardanelles back in 1915. But stare as he might he could see no sign of modern Turkish soldiers, for which he was very grateful.

The hours passed. At the moment the Straits were four and a half miles wide. But soon the two craft would be approaching the Narrows, some fourteen miles upstream. There, the passage was reduced to just over a mile. There they would be at their most vulnerable.

But Abdul the Terrible, glimpsed occasionally through the netting, seemed unworried. He swaggered about his little craft, bellowing orders, sometimes cuffing one of the barefoot crew about the ears when he seemed to be too slow in reacting and occasionally winking in an exaggerated conspiratorial fashion in the direction of the *Swordfish*. It was something that Smith prayed he wouldn't do. Hadn't the big Turk ever heard of telescopes or binoculars? For Smith was sure their passage was now being observed from the opposite side of the Straits.

Another hour passed leadenly. Now the two vessels were fighting the strong current coming down the waterway from the Sea of Marmara so that they were moving barely over two knots an hour. But already the stretch of water was beginning to narrow as they started to approach the most dangerous section of the passage and now an anxious Smith could see the batteries and forts on the southern shore quite clearly.

Smith decided to order the crew to stand

to. Crouched low the men crept to their duty stations and at the wheel CPO Ferguson donned an ancient steel helmet, which he had found somewhere or other, as a clear indication that he was ready for anything. Smith shook his head and hoped it would never come to that.

At ten-thirty that long tense morning they were just beginning to pass the fort of Kilid Bahr, in the centre of the Narrows, when they were hailed by a man in uniform bearing a megaphone.

Smith chanced a look, wiping the sweat from his brow as he did so, noticing that his heart was beginning to pump excitedly.

A man was standing on a mound at the water's edge calling something in Turkish. Behind him there was a squad of heavily armed soldiers, one of them bearing the barrel of an ancient machine gun on his shoulder.

Abdul the Terrible took it all very calmly. Balancing on the rail of his caique, he cupped his mighty paws to his lips and shouted back.

Smith bit his bottom lip. What did the official want? Were they in trouble?

'Do you think they've twigged?' Dickie asked hastily in an excited whisper. 'Gosh we're for it then.'

But Dickie Bird was wrong. Abruptly the Turkish official lowered his megaphone and gave a wave of his hand, indicating that the caique should proceed.

'Phew,' Smith sighed and relaxed as Abdul the Terrible swaggered across the deck in apparent unconcern and whispered out of the side of his mouth. 'A bribe, he wanted. Typical Turk – always after the baksheehs.'

'Money?' Smith asked.

'Ner,' Abdul snorted. 'Turkish pound is no good. He wanted fish when we come back.'

'Fish,' the two young officers exclaimed as one.

'Yer, you heard it,' Abdul said and then swaggered off, leaving Smith and Dickie to stare at each other incredulously. They had bribed their way into the Sea of Marmara to torpedo two Turkish battleships at the price of a catch of wet fish!

5

As the darkness swept across the Sea of Marmara like a great black raven, the *Swordfish* cast off from the Turkish caique. Abdul the Terrible cupped his huge hands around his mouth and yelled in parting, 'Remember, Limey gents, I wait here twenty-four hours only. Good luck.'

'Thanks, Abdul,' Smith yelled back, 'I'll

remember.' He turned to CPO Ferguson at the wheel. 'All right, Chiefie,' he commanded, 'take her away.'

'Ay, ay, sir,' the ancient Scot answered. 'With the greatest of pleasure. Can't get away soon enough from yon muckie craft.' He eased the throttles forward and the *Swordfish* reacted at once, heading for the open sea. Within minutes the coast of the Dardanelles disappeared behind them in the darkness.

Half an hour later they were riding at anchor just off the great Turkish port of Istanbul. Before them lay the city, stretched out over seven hills, the golden domes of the many minarets gleaming in the light of the yellow gas lights. It was an impressive sight, but the two young officers had no eyes for the beauty of the city. They were searching for the Turkish naval repair yards just off the Golden Horn and at the same time keeping a wary lookout for Turkish patrol boats. But there seemed little activity off the port. Just a few small fishing boats, with hissing brilliant white carbide lights at their sterns as their owners looked for fish.

'To the left of the railway line to Uzum Keipri,' Dickie coached his friend, remembering the details from the chart below. 'Follow the line to Haider Pasha railway station. That's where they coal up their naval craft and–'

'Got it,' Smith interrupted him excitedly. 'Use your glasses. There! Do you see?'

'I see it,' Dickie said, equally excited, as the towering superstructures of two pre-war battleships were clearly outlined a stark black against the purple glare of welding torches. Obviously the dockers were still working on the two former Allied ships. 'That's the old tub. Remember seeing her before the war at the last Grand Fleet Review when we were still at Harrow.'

'Yes, the other one's got to be the French battleship. What's a name?'

'The *Bouvet*,' Dickie said. 'Gosh they're stuck in there like two fried ducks on a silver platter!'

'Not exactly, Dickie,' Smith corrected him. 'To starboard, do you see? There's a destroyer out there and a fairly modern one by the cut of its jib. According to Doyle the Turks have long range guns all along that stretch of coast – just beyond the heights.'

Dickie nodded his understanding and asked, 'What's the plan Smithie?'

'We go in at dawn. From the east – so that the enemy gunners will have the rising sun in their eyes. Might put them off their aim. I hope. We'll keep as clear as we can from that destroyer. We'll fire two fish each into each ship. If we don't sink them outright, then we'll make one hell of a mess of their engine rooms. That'll keep them out of commission for a goodly while.'

'And what then?'

'Well, Dickie, I'm sure they'll realize immediately that we did the dirty deed. After all they – and their allies – have followed us all the way here. So I suspect they'll think we've headed straight back for the Narrows tootsweet. And that's where they'll start their search. But we won't.'

'We won't what?'

'Head straightaway for the Narrows.'

'What will we do then?'

'Well, even with the help of Abdul the Terrible we wouldn't stand a chance in daylight. We'd be better off going through in the darkness. So we hide during the day and rendezvous with Abdul after dark.'

'But where do we hide, Smithie? After all the Marmara is an inland sea.'

'You've forgotten the Seven Sisters.'

'The what?'

'Those islands behind us. With a bit of luck we can lie up off the coast of one of the less inhabited islands, away from prying eyes and then head for the Narrows at top speed as soon as it's dark.' He looked at the glowing green dial of his wristwatch. 'All right, Dickie,' he announced with a note of finality. 'Let's–'

'*Circumcise our watches,*' Dickie beat him to it with the time-honoured naval phrase. They adjusted their watches and Dickie asked, 'When is dawn?'

'Two hours, old friend.'

'Then I suggest old friend, we'd better go and have a pink gin to prepare us for what is to come.'

Smith tut-tutted. 'Pink gin at three o'clock in the morning. You'll become an alcoholic.'

Dickie shrugged carelessly as they went below. 'I should live that long...'

The sky was beginning to flush a light pink. Over to port where Istanbul lay, grey streaks of coal smoke were beginning to ascend to the still sky. Slowly the city was awaking. And already the watchers could hear the steady tap-tap of riveting hammers as the workers commenced their work on the two ancient battleships. Now it would be only a matter of minutes before the sun came over the horizon in full force.

Smith spoke to Ferguson. The old Scot eased the throttles forward. The *Swordfish* started to move forward. Ferguson increased the speed. The sharp prow lifted out of the water. At their duty stations the seamen braced themselves. Suddenly the deck was heaving and trembling beneath their spread feet.

The revs on the machometers began to mount rapidly. A white wave swept up on either side of the bow. The noise grew. It would be only a matter of moments now, Smith told himself, before the Turks were alerted to the fact that they were being attacked. At an ever-increasing speed the little craft hurtled towards its target, spray lashing the men's tense faces.

Now the sun had risen fully over the lip of the sea. Its rays threw everything into sharp stark contrast. To the men in the hurrying craft everything was clearly visible: the two battleships, the dark figures scurrying about, a train pulling slowly into the coaling station, dragging a grey cloud of thick smoke behind.

Smith said a quick prayer, God, he told the sky, blind those gunners ... blind them for a little while...

The *Swordfish* was going all out now. It hit each wave, as if it were made of solid brick. Spray flew over the deck all the time, drenching the ratings. All fear vanished, the crew were transfixed, every sinew concentrated on the task ahead, eyes fixed hypnotically on the two battleships.

'*One thousand yards!*' Dickie sang out, voice wild with excitement.

At their posts the two torpedo men tensed next to the deadly fish.

'*Seven hundred and fifty!*'

Over at the docks a siren began to shrill its dire warning. The first burst of tracer came sailing lazily towards the hurtling craft.

'Take evasive action, Chiefie!' Smith yelled urgently.

As the tracer, all glowing white and lethal, sailed past them harmlessly, Ferguson swung the *Swordfish* violently from left to right.

Over at the docks there was a burst of cherry red flame. A puff of white. A huge shrill keening like a great sheet of canvas being torn apart. Next moment shells began to fall around the *Swordfish*, sending up huge gouts of water, thundering down on to the craft's deck. The wireless mast smashed. It tumbled down in a shower of angry blue spark.

'*Six hundred!*' Dickie shrieked, water streaming down his oilskin. '*Six hundred yards, Smithie!*'

Smith felt absolutely in charge. His nerves were steady. It was as if ice-water ran through his veins instead of warm blood. He ignored Dickie's cry.

Across the bay another Turkish battery had opened up. In a moment he knew the Turks would be coning him in a crossfire from the two batteries. '*Stand by tubes!*' he cried above the ear-splitting howl and roar of the Thorneycroft engines.

'*Five hundred,*' Dickie bellowed above the racket, as the whole waterfront now erupted in fire and on the battleships, the gunners spun the turrets of the great guns round slowly to meet this daring challenge right in their very own backyard.

Smith knew he could wait no longer. Shells were landing everywhere. The water erupted in angry white fountains all about the flying boat. Tracer zipped towards them from all sides. Their luck *had* to run out soon. He cupped his hands above his mouth. *'Fire,'* he shrieked, *'one ... and two!'*

The craft shuddered violently. There was a thick asthmatic cough. A flash of yellow smoke. The first deadly fish, packed with a ton of high explosive, slid from the gaping mouth of the torpedo tube. The next after it. On both sides. *'Splash ... splash ... splash ... splash...'*

'Running true, sir,' the torpedo men yelled as one, faces glistening with seawater and excitement.

Angrily the four torpedoes fanned. A ripple of bubbles. Like a shoal of vicious steel sharks they cut through the water towards their helpless targets. Already Smith could see panicked Turkish sailors diving over the sides or running frantically to the ladders connecting the ships with the quay. They knew what was coming.

As Chiefie Ferguson swung the *Swordfish* around in one wild sweep, nearly knocking Ginger off his perch on the m.g. tower behind the bridge, the four torpedoes exploded as one. The dawn was torn apart. A great white whirling mass of angry water shot high into the sky. It flashed above the towering superstructures of the battleships. It was followed an instant later by a blinding orange flash. The boiler of the ex-French ship had exploded.

Suddenly the air was full of great shards of flying metal. Abruptly the water all around boiled as the descending metal rain struck it. Next to the sinking ship, the ex-British battleship listed crazily to port, its shattered superstructure already aflame, with men diving off her tilting decks in panic before it was too late.

'Bring her round, Chiefie,' Smith cried above the tremendous racket – the racing engines, the explosions, the angry pounding of the Turkish artillery. 'We'll have one last go – for sure.' Smith knew he was mad. But he knew, too, that the lives of many thousands of innocent civilians depended upon their crippling the two battleships for good. What did it matter if *they* were killed?

'Well, we'll make handsome corpses,' Dickie chortled, as Ferguson, craggy face grim and set, yelled, 'Ay, ay sir,' and brought the *Swordfish* around once more.

They hurtled forward through what seemed a solid wall of shellfire. Time and time again, the daring little boat seemed to disappear in a huge gout of whirling water. But their luck held. They seemed to bear a charmed life.

Now Smith could see every detail of the

stricken battleships, clearly outlined in the mounting flames – the ever-increasing list to port, the great ghostly clouds of steam erupting to the sky, the panic-stricken efforts of the Turkish sailors to escape before it was too late and the boiling sea all around, littered with dinghies, rowing boats, life-rings – and dead bodies.

But he could feel no pity in his heart for the Turks. He remembered what they would have done to the Greek civilians. There was no time for compassion and remorse in this cruel secret war which was sweeping across Europe in all its savage fury since the 'war to end all wars' had failed to do just that. He raised his voice. *'Fire one and two'* – and then to Ferguson, *'Chiefie – now let's get the hell out of here!'*

'Ay ay to that, sir,' Ferguson sang out with unusual enthusiasm for that dour Scot. He ripped the wheel round and the *Swordfish* was on its way, racing for the open sea followed by the angry frustrated fire of the Turkish gunners. *They had done it!*

6

Kemal Ataturk swore savagely, his sallow, pockmarked face flushed with anger. He stared out at the Sea of Marmara from the tall windows of Istanbul's Pera Palace Hotel. Next to him the handsome young signals officer with the powdered face tensed. In moments of rage the Dictator was known to strike those around with his stick or riding crop.

But Ataturk didn't strike him. Instead he pulled himself together and said, 'Top priority message. Signal the Admiral commanding Istanbul Harbour. It is the English. They will attempt to escape through the Narrows. This shall not happen. They will be captured and brought to me. I, Kemal Ataturk, will deal with them personally.' His dark eyes blazed with barely contained fury. 'Then they shall learn what we Turks know of making criminals pay for their crimes.' He grunted. 'All right, make that signal – *quick!*'

'Yes, *Effendi*,' the signals officer said hastily and slipped out, glad to escape, telling himself that even Allah wouldn't help the Englishmen if they fell into Kemal

Ataturk's hands.

Alone, Kemal Ataturk continued to gaze through the window, ignoring the smoking, half-sunken wreckage of the two battleships to his right. Instead he concentrated his gaze on the Sea of Marmara, glistening in the light of the noon sun. He would force the Greeks out of Smyrna – there was no doubt about that. But there could be no massacre now. He could not risk slaughtering the damned infidels on land; there would be too much of an outcry internationally.

He had wanted to show the Turks and the world that the Turks were the masters of their own fate; that Turkey was no longer the Sick Man of Europe. The cold-blooded massacre of the Greeks at sea outside Turkish territorial waters would have shown that. Now that was quite impossible.

He turned and stared at his own reflection in the long mirror. He told himself he looked masterful, a man of destiny. It was something he had known all his life ever since he had been a barefoot poor boy in Turkish Greece. But how often had he despaired that he would ever be able to carry out the tasks he had set himself. Time and time again he had been frustrated by the Sultan, the Palace clique, the Germans during the war, by his fellow revolutionaries. How often had he placed his service revolver to his temple and pressed the trigger to put an end to it all! Always, however, he had been saved by some miracle or other. It seemed it was his destiny to survive and defeat his rivals and enemies.

He dismissed the past with an angry snap of his fingers. Now he concentrated on the present. The English bandits, out there somewhere in the Sea of Marmara, were unimportant in themselves. But they did represent the power of the British Lion. Now the tail of mangy lion had to be twisted – *and twisted hard!* The British would see just how he, Kemal Ataturk, would treat their jackals, once they had been captured. He turned and stared at the sea once more. Where were the damned English? They were out there somewhere, that he knew. But where...?

The crew of the *Swordfish* slumped at their posts, swearing in the noon heat. Now the little craft lay in the lee of a steep cliff, covered in the branches of the stunted olive trees which lined it. There was no beach on the side of the island in the middle of the Marmara and as a result no fishing village. 'It looks as safe as anything we can find in a hurry,' Smith had announced to the crew when they had spotted it. 'Of course, once the Turks wake up to what has happened, all hell with be let loose. But with a bit of luck we might dodge the ack-ack till nightfall.'

He had paused and added, 'Of course, they'll assume we're heading hell-for-leather for the Narrows. But if they've got enough naval craft to do so, they might well search the Marmara as well. After all they'll remember that Naismith and Doyle stuck it out among the islands here for days back in 1915.'

Thereupon, after they had camouflaged the *Swordfish* the best they could, Smith had ordered Ferguson to break out the precious case of Bass Light Ale which he had brought specially for this occasion from Alexandria. So they celebrated their victory, lolling in the sun, a group of happy young men, who had escaped death yet once, enjoying their simple pleasure – 'a gasper and a drop of ale' – in this brief time out of war.

But Smith, sipping the warm beer with the rest, was unable to dismiss the feeling that they were trapped; that there was no way out of the Marmara. Hot and tired as he was, he still couldn't relax like the rest of his weary men. Time and time again he scanned the brilliant yard blue sky and then the sea to the horizon, tensed for the first sign of an enemy craft.

Yet when the danger came, it did not come from the sea, but from the air. About two that afternoon, after the crew had wolfed down greasy corned-beef sandwiches, washed down with the last of the Bass Light

Ale, the heavy scented stillness around the island was disturbed by a faint drone which grew steadily louder.

The crew stirred lazily, the sweat trickling down their red hot faces. They searched the sea and then the sky for the source of that steady mechanical drone. 'There it is,' Ginger said suddenly. 'Port – over there!'

Smith shaded his eyes against the glare of the sun, as Dickie cried, 'Seaplane. Have you got it?'

'Got it,' Smith spotted the old-fashioned seaplane, a biplane with heavy floats. Flying just above stalling speed, it was heading around the cove straight for their hiding place. Smith felt himself burst out in sweat again. He knew well the biplane was searching for them, and it was very low. The cliff behind them echoed – and re-echoed with the sound of its engine.

'All right,' he snapped quickly, 'hide your faces. Keep beneath the branches. We'll make it as hard as possible for them.'

As they did so rapidly, all torpor vanished, Smith risked another look upwards. The plane was right above them now. He could see the leather-helmeted pilot quite clearly and the observer, leaning out of the open cockpit, surveying the terrain below through his binoculars.

Swiftly, just before he ducked his head again, he searched the plane's length for any sign of a wireless aerial. Nowadays, all British military planes carried wirelesses. But did the Turks? He could see no sign of one.

He made his decision. 'Ginger,' he snapped, 'knock her out of the sky.'

'Ay ay, sir,' Ginger said with an evil grin on his thin, sharp face.

He sprang behind the Lewis gun. In one and the same movement, he slammed the wooden butt into his skinny shoulder and cocked the machine gun. With a jerk of the muzzle he knocked the branches camouflaging the gun away. He tensed. The plane was flying straight into the ring sight. Ginger took first pressure, carefully controlling his breathing, and hissed to himself, 'All right, mateys, try this one on for size!' Next moment he pressed the trigger.

The butt slammed against his shoulder. Suddenly the air was full of the stink of burnt cordite. Tracer shot upwards in a lethal morse. The length of the plane's canvas was abruptly peppered with a series of smouldering holes. A strut snapped. The left wing drooped suddenly.

Laughing like a man demented, Ginger slapped on another drum of ammunition. Once more he pressed the trigger. Again the gun burst into frenetic chattering deadly life.

Desperately the pilot tried to keep his

battered plane in the air. Behind him the observer slumped dead or unconscious over the side of the cockpit as the first greedy little blue flames started to leap up around the engine cowling. Face contorted with fear, the pilot fought the controls. Suddenly the joystick went dead. Next moment the engine spluttered a couple of times and followed suit.

Suddenly, startling the crippled plane's nose dropped. The plane went into a steep dive. It passed over the heads of the *Swordfish's* crew, trailing black smoke from its silent engine. It disappeared behind the cliff. A few seconds later there was a tremendous crash. Slowly, very slowly, a dark pall of thick smoke started to rise above the island.

Hoarsely the crew broke the heavy silence with a cheer. But Smith didn't share their enthusiasm at their fresh victory. Face set and grim, he cried, 'All right, enough of that, lads. Stop that noise at once!'

A grinning Dickie said, 'What's up, old bean?'

'A lot's up,' Smith answered, handsome face set in a worried frown now. 'The plane didn't appear to have a wireless. But some-body'll spot that pall of smoke and put two and two together.'

'Which is?' Dickie's smile vanished.

'That we're the only ones to shoot at a

Turkish plane. Who else should in Turkish territorial waters?'

'Gosh, that's torn it.'

'It certainly has.'

'What's the drill?' Dickie asked after a moment's thought.

'We get underway at once. We might have an hour or two's respite before the smoke's spotted, reported to the appropriate HQ where they'll start adding up those damned twos and twos. But that's all.'

'But to try the Narrows in daylight–' Dickie began and then faltered to a stop. For he saw that Smith wasn't listening. Instead he was staring up at the top of the cliff.

Dickie followed the direction of his gaze.

Dark faces under outsize military caps were staring down at them suspiciously and Dickie told himself he didn't need a crystal ball to know why. The Turks had spotted them already.

'*Johnny Turk!*' Smith cried. 'Ginger, open up. Damn you, Chiefie, let's get underway … at the double now!'

Abruptly all was controlled chaos as a ragged volley of rifle fire broke out from the top of the cliff to be followed an instant later by the deeper hoarse chatter of Ginger's machine gun. Bullets howled through the air. Metal and wood splinters flew on all sides, as the *Swordfish*'s crew dragged away the branches and logs frantically and Ferguson on the bridge started up the engines.

A stick grenade came sailing over the top of the cliff. A thunderous roar. Gleaming metal shards flew everywhere. Billy Bennett clutched his shoulder, blood seeping through his fingers. 'Bugger this for a tale—' he began and pitched face-forward to the deck.

With a thunderous roar the engines burst into full throbbing life. Ferguson didn't hesitate, although he could hardly see for tree branches. He thrust home the twin throttles. The *Swordfish* surged forward. Above them angry flares of red and green were sailing into the afternoon sky. The Turks were signalling the mainland. Smith cursed. Everything was going wrong now. Their luck had finally vanished. Then he concentrated on getting the *Swordfish* out of the little cove without any further losses, his mind in a turmoil.

'What course, sir?' Ferguson cried as a bullet struck the wheelhouse and shattered the glass into a gleaming spider's web of shards.

Smith rammed his elbow against it and cleared a hole for the old Scot to see through to steer the boat. 'What course?' he echoed a little helplessly. 'God, Chiefie, I don't … know…'

7

They had taken Abdul the Terrible one hour before. The caique hadn't had a chance. Suddenly a Turkish destroyer, belching black smoke from its two stacks had come sailing round the edge of the cove, its three gun turrets levelled threateningly at the little fishing vessel. Minutes later, ratings armed to the teeth with rifles, pistols and old-fashioned cutlasses had come swarming down the sides of the stationary destroyer dropping on to the untidy, littered deck of Abdul's caique.

Of course, the burly wrestler had tried to bluff it out. He was only 'a humble fisherman, *Effendi*', working hard to make a meagre living. Naturally he was a loyal Turk. He would give his right arm for his beloved Turkey and his 'dear leader, the great and good Kemal Ataturk'.

But even as he grovelled and whined, the ex-wrestler could see the destroyer's officers, in their starched white uniforms, and didn't believe him. They watched his enormous bulk with suspicious eyes, obviously telling themselves that their captor looked like no fishing skipper they had ever encountered. They were usually skinny, undernourished toothless peasants who looked as if they didn't have the strength to haul in a net. This man looked as if he could tackle a whole army – with one enormous pay tied behind his back.

But Abdul the Terrible had realized the game was up when one of the search party had come running up from below deck, clutching an open purse – his – and crying 'Gold, Captain Bey... *Ingilizi* ... gold!'

The tall hook-nosed officer in charge had seized the purse and shot a look at its contents. All around the ragged crew went on their skinny knees and began wailing for mercy, for they, too, realized they had been found out. 'It was him, the skipper ... he dealt with the English infidel... We are loyal Turks ... he forced us to help them... Let Allah be our witness,' they wailed, flailing their arms around and rolling their eyes in terror.

The officer with the big beak of a nose ignored the crewmen. Instead he looked hard at the big ex-wrestler with his dark, cruel eyes and said slowly. 'English gold, eh... The celebrated Horsemen of St George. Where does a *poor* fisherman,' he sneered over the word, 'get English sovereigns from, eh?'

Without waiting for an answer, he smashed his fist into Abdul's impassive face and gave a stifled whimper of pain. It felt as if he had just struck a slab of chiselled granite.

Abdul looked down at him in obvious contempt. All the same he was afraid. He knew his fellow countrymen. They were a cruel people. For five hundred years they had dominated southern Europe and the Middle East with their barbaric cruelty. He knew what they were capable of. Yet the price of his silence was high. A passport to the United States and a fresh start in that wonderful country away from the mess that was Europe and Asia. So he pressed his thick lips together stubbornly and said nothing, as all around him the crew wailed and cried.

The hook-nosed officer looked at him hard. 'Just tell me this,' he hissed, 'and you'd better if you don't want to suffer, when will the English arrive here?'

Abdul shook his head. 'I know nothing, *Effendi*,' he said, trying to keep calm.

The officer's sallow complexion flushed angrily. 'I warn you,' he snapped. 'I tolerate no delay. Kemal Ataturk himself is in charge of this bad business. He wants answers and he wants them quick. You are a creature of no importance,' he snapped his manicured fingers contemptuously, 'a big pig who deserves to die. Speak and you will die quickly. Don't and you will die very slowly –

and very painfully!' His dark eyes bored into the big ex-wrestler.

Abdul the Terrible remained silent, eyes fixed on the horizon, his broad face revealing nothing.

'Speak!' the officer demanded threateningly.

Abdul continued to gaze in the distance.

The officer lost patience. 'Seize him!' he ordered.

Immediately four or five of the white-uniformed sailors leapt upon the giant. Abdul did not attempt to defend himself, although he could have dealt with puny sailors easily. How often back in the beloved United States of America had he invited all comers to tackle him in the ring, taking on as many as a dozen country hicks at a time! But now instead of beating the sailors off, he concentrated on what he should do.

'Bastinado!' the hook-nosed officer cried, quivering with rage now.

The crew of the caique stopped their wailings and protestations.

'But that is forbidden, *Effendi,'* one of the junior officers protested. 'It has been prohibited ever since the Sultan fled. You cannot–'

'Bastinado!' the officer shrieked and made as if he were to strike the naval officer who had protested.

The other man jumped back, as the sailors

turned Abdul on his back, tying his hands to the railing. Two of them sat on his legs while a third tugged off his battered old sandals.

Hastily rods of bamboo were brought from the destroyer while the hook-nosed officer towered over the prostrate Abdul and demanded yet once again, 'What is the plan with English? Speak now, pig, or you will regret it. Well?'

Abdul said nothing, keeping his head low so that the officer could not see the look in his eyes.

The officer shrugged. 'Very well.' He turned to the burly bosun, who had cropped over the side of the destroyer with the rods, 'Carry on bosun.'

Hastily the petty officer stripped off his shirt to reveal his burly hairy torso, well covered with tattoos. He spat on the palms of his horny hands and took up the first rod. He raised it high and then with an evil grin brought it down with all the force he could muster on the soles of Abdul's feet. The impact was so great that Abdul's head slapped against the side of the caique. But he uttered not a sound. Across the soles of his naked feet a great welt erupted immediately.

The pain was electric. It felt as if red-hot pokers had been driven deep inside his feet. Abdul gritted his teeth. As a young boy he had seen a criminal suffer the *bastinado*. The poor wretch had ended up a cripple, the flesh ripped cruelly from his feet until the bones had shown below in a bright white against the red gore. If he didn't talk, he'd end up as a cripple. If he did, he'd never see that beloved America again.

The rod slammed into his feet once more. The horny skin burst under that tremendous impact. Blood spurted out from the soles in a bright red arc. Abdul bit right through his bottom lip to prevent himself from crying out in agony.

Above him the hook-nosed officer looked down, a cruel smirk on his thin lips. 'You are enjoying it, I see, pig!' He crunched his boot into Abdul's ribs. 'I think the Bosun here has to use a little more force.' He spun round on the panting petty officer. 'Play with the pig no longer. Really hurt him now, man, if you know what's good for you!'

'Yes, *Effendi.*' The Bosun licked his lips, spat on his big paws once more and raised the cane above his head. With all his strength he brought it down on the soles of Abdul's bleeding feet. Abdul shrieked, unable to suppress the sheer agony any longer.

The officer clapped his hands in delight. 'More ... give the obstinate pig more!' he demanded.

The Bosun, his face glazed with sweat as if greased with vaseline, his brawny chest heaving with the effort, raised the cane once more. Now the captured crew of the caique had ceased their own protestations of innocence. Instead they gaped at the skipper, his feet already in bloody rags of flesh, in awe. How could a man take so much punishment and not talk? There seemed something superhuman about their former skipper.

'*Now,*' the hook-nosed officer commanded.

Abdul acted. With a mighty grunt, he snapped the bonds which held him to the rail. Another grunt. He raised his massive, muscular legs. The two ratings holding them flew to one side. Next instant Abdul sprang to his feet, grabbed the hook-nosed officer from behind with one hand, while with the other he drew his pistol from the open leather holster. His face set in a hard tough grin, he pulled the trigger. The bosun's face seemed to explode in a welter of red gore and ivorylike bone splinters. He screamed, the screams being choked in his own blood, and fell to the deck.

With one mighty paw Abdul shoved the officer into the others standing on the deck of the caique. They stumbled back in surprise. A moment later Abdul did a neat backroll over the side of the little craft and slammed into the water. Even before the hook-nosed officer could shriek, '*Fire at him, you dolts!'*, Abdul had dived deep below the water and with his great strength was swimming furiously for the land, the scattered, ragged shots hitting the surface above his head harmlessly...

'It doesn't matter,' the hook-nosed officer said thickly, patting his swollen nose with a blood-stained handkerchief gently. 'Let the big pig escape. He won't get out of Turkey. Our people will pick him up.'

The junior officers nodded their agreement, still staring at the dead bosun with his horribly mutilated face.

The senior officer took his handkerchief away and tested. His battered nose had stopped bleeding, but it was already beginning to swell and was turning an odd shade of green. 'We know now that the English will rendezvous with these pirates.' He indicated the crestfallen crew with a sweep of his hand. 'It is obvious that they were to guide the English through the Narrows in return for the gold they had paid them.'

'But, *Effendi*,' one of the junior officers objected gently, for he knew his superior's uncertain temper. He would box a rating's ears at the slightest pretext. 'The English might have guessed that we have captured these renegades. They must know there is a national alarm in progress. Perhaps they might attempt to get through the Dardanelles without their help.'

The hook-nosed officer shrugged carelessly. 'Perhaps? But what chance do they stand, even during the hours of darkness? Every fort, every gun battery, every single *askari,* absolutely everybody, has been put on maximum alert. They are trapped. It is as simple as that. As a great French marshal once said in a battle for their city of Sedan, *"We are caught in a chamberpot, gentlemen, now the Germans are going to shit on us!"'* He laughed at the crudity and the others joined in politely. It would be unwise not to do so.

'However,' the officer went on, 'I am hoping that we shall have the honour of apprehending them. They tell me that Kemal Ataturk can be very generous when he feels he is well served. There could be orders, decorations, perhaps gifts of money.' He licked his thin cruel lips as if in anticipation. 'We must pray to Allah, that it will be our luck—'

'Effendi,' the shout from the deck of the destroyer broke into his words.

He looked up a little angrily.

A bareheaded radio signaller was leaning over the gleaming brass rail, hands cupped around his mouth.

'What is it, man?' he cried.

'A radio signal, *Effendi.* From Airship R88—'

'Oh, get on with it!' he snorted. 'I don't

want the pig's number.'

'Well, *Effendi*, they have spotted the English from the air.'

The hook-nosed officer slapped his hands together like a child in sheer delight. 'And on what bearing?'

The signaller shouted it down to him, leaning so far over the rail that it looked as if he might fall overboard at any moment.

'They're heading straight for us, gentlemen,' the hook-nosed officer exclaimed.

He dismissed the signaller with a wave of his hand, 'There is no time to waste,' he said hurriedly. 'We shall leave a small boarding party on the caique to watch over these dogs. They will go about their business as if nothing has happened.' He swung a quick glance at the coast behind him. 'We shall sail the destroyer to that covered inlet over there. The trees should give us the cover we require. Once the English come within range, we open fire. Bracket them and force them to surrender.' He gave an evil smile. 'I am looking forward to escorting them personally to Kemal Ataturk as my prisoners. The reward will be great. Gentlemen, the bait has been laid, the trap set. Now,' he slapped his hands together, 'it is our task to make that trap snap. *Hurry!*'

8

'*Damn, damn, damn,*' Smith cursed as the little airship continued to dog them, just staying out of reach of Ginger's Lewis gun, which frustrated the Skinny Liverpudlian no end. It was an observation ship of the kind the Royal Navy had used a lot during the recent war and it was obviously not armed. For it had not attempted to bomb the *Swordfish*. Smith knew the airship had one purpose and one purpose only. As he told an anxious Dickie, 'That aerial swine is signalling back our position and course to the Turkish HQ. That's its task.'

Dickie nodded his agreement, squinting his eyes against the sinking late afternoon sun and spotting the radio aerials without too much difficulty. 'And alerting the Dardanelles defences that we are coming as well, no doubt.'

Smith sucked his teeth morosely and nodded, too. 'That's about it, Dickie.'

'What we going to do, old chum?'

Slowly Smith shrugged his shoulders, his thin handsome face slightly hopeless. 'I don't rightly know, Dickie. But it does seem a damned shame,' he exclaimed in a sudden burst of resentment, 'to have come all this way and then get pipped at the post!'

'We could use smoke and make a bolt for it under cover of smoke?'

'Don't think that'd be much use. We've only got a limited number of smoke dischargers and at the height they're flying, they'd spot us immediately we emerge from the smoke. No, 'fraid that's not the way, Dickie.'

The two of them relapsed into a moody silence, as the *Swordfish* ploughed through the sea steadily forward, heading for the dark smudge which was the entrance to the Narrows.

Suddenly Dickie clicked his fingers together noisily.

Smith jumped. 'What's that in aid of it?' he snapped.

'This, Smithie. We've got to settle that gasbag's hash for it, haven't we?'

'Yes, naturally.'

'But at the moment it's just out of range of Ginger's peashooter?'

'Yes,' Smith said again, puzzled. 'You're not telling me anything startlingly new, Dickie.'

'Then let's put the gasbag in range and get rid of her for starters.'

Smith leapt up with new hope. 'Come on, spit it out,' he demanded urgently. *'How?'*

'Like this...'

The *Swordfish* had been carefully decreasing her speed for five or ten minutes now and the airship was catching up with her slowly, but the latter was still out of range. Watching her intently through their binoculars, Smith and Bird could see that the airship's skipper had not yet cottoned on to the fact that the *Swordfish* was slowing down. But he would soon fall back a little to keep out of the range of Ginger's Lewis gun behind them.

Now everything depended upon split-second timing. Smith turned to Ferguson at the controls, his battered white cap set on the back of his shaven, grizzled head, 'Are you game, Chiefie?' he asked.

'Ay, sir. I'm sick to deeth o' yon blimp. He's givin' me a reet sore head.'

Smith grinned a little tensely. 'All right, then Chiefie. *Now!*'

Ferguson acted with surprising speed for such an oldish man. In a flash, he swung the *Swordfish* round and thrust the throttles forward with all his strength.

The *Swordfish* shot forward. Her rakish prow lifted from the water. The decks vibrated under their feet. Suddenly, startlingly, the *Swordfish* was speeding at forty knots an hour, cleaving the water into two mighty brilliant white bow waves.

Through their glasses, the two young officers could see the shock in the control room slung beneath the airship. Leather-helmeted Turks ran back and forth. Orders were issued. To the rear the propellers started to slow down. Too late!

Now the *Swordfish* was directly below the airship. Ginger didn't hesitate. He'd never had such a big, slow target in all his fighting days. He sucked in the wooden butt of the Lewis, aimed at the fat shining grey belly of the airship and pressed the trigger.

Tracer streamed upwards. It ripped the length of the belly. Canvas came sailing down. Gas began to escape at once. Through their binoculars Dickie and Smith could see the looks of absolute, over-whelming panic on the faces of the officers as they felt the bullets strike the fabric. They had no parachutes. If the airship exploded, they'd burn to death. If it didn't they'd fall and suffer the same fate.

Ginger fired another fast burst. Fresh holes. Gas was escaping everywhere. The watchers could see it coming out in grey bursts. If only they had some explosive bullets, Smith told himself and it would be all over in seconds. But he need not have feared. Little spurts of blue flame were beginning to erupt from the holes. The blimp was beginning to sag as more and more gas started to escape. In the control room they had slid back the big windows. Panicked officers were staring down at the sea below, as if they were contemplating jumping now. But that wasn't to be.

Abruptly the airship went limp. It folded in the middle. Fire seared its length in an angry frightening flash. In an instant it started to break up. Burning torches which were men, screaming as they fell tumbled out of the dying ship and fell to their deaths in the sea below.

'Poor boogers,' Ferguson at the controls whispered, 'even if they are foreigners. Yon's no a guid way o' croaking it!'

It was almost over now. The deflated canopy, burning fiercely, came tumbling down to the sea. It struck the surface with a great hiss. Steam rose in the thick cloud. When it had cleared there was nothing more to be seen of the Turkish airship save a mass of floating debris and the still burning corpses of its crew.

Ferguson didn't wait for an order. He swung the *Swordfish* round in a great white arc, as if only too eager to leave that scene of death and destruction as soon as possible, while up on the deck the crew cheered and Ginger slumped over his gun in seeming exhaustion.

'Now listen, Dickie – and listen hard,' Smith said swiftly as the land grew larger and larger.

'I'm all ears, Smithie.'

'Well, for a while they're out of contact

with us. But from the gasbag's last signal they'll know roughly where we are and where we're heading. It won't be long before they attempt to put another tail on us or stop us.'

'Agreed. So?'

'This. We've been letting them do our thinking for us.'

Dickie looked at him sharply, as the *Swordfish* raced for the land. 'What's that supposed to mean?'

'Well, all the time we've concentrated on getting out of the Sea of Marmara through the Dardanelles, and they've known it. Hence the measures they are taking now to stop us getting through.'

'Exactly, but what other way is there of getting out? We can't fly you know. The old *Swordfish* isn't equipped with wings, you know.'

'Don't be a silly ass,' Smith snorted. 'I know that. But look at that chart.' He indicated at the small chart of the area pinned up in the wheelhouse.

'I don't need to look at it, Smithie,' Dickie protested. 'There's only one way out, through Dardanelles. Unless you want us to sail the *Swordfish* back up the Marmara and into the Black Sea. I'm sure the Reds in communist Russia would welcome us with open arms especially as that nasty business at Kronstadt.'

'Who made any mention of *sailing* the *Swordfish?*' Smith answered enigmatically.

Dickie looked at his old friend as if he had suddenly gone mad. 'What did you say?'

Smith repeated his words.

'But I don't understand,' the other officer stuttered.

'Then let me explain,' Smith said with a tense little smile. 'See the chart. Look where Adrianople is. Got it?'

'Yes.'

'Well, that marks the border of Greece and Turkey and now, according to Doyle, it's firmly back in Greek hands and the Turks have no intention of advancing any further. The fighting there has died down.'

'So?' Dickie was completely puzzled now.

'At this moment we are some fifty miles from that border as the crow flies.'

'But there is no access to it by water,' Dickie objected.

'I know. But we wouldn't be going by water.'

'*What?*'

'You heard.'

'But you're not going to abandon the old *Swordfish* surely?' Dickie said bitterly. 'Damnit all, Smithie, we've grown up with the *Swordfish.*'

'I know, but our lives and those of the men are more important than the fate of the *Swordfish*. If as they say, ships have souls, then she'll know she's helped us to save us.'

'All right,' Dickie, reconciled to the idea a little now, said. 'What are you going to do?'

Smith flashed a quick look at the sky. 'It'll be pretty dark in a couple of hours. I intend to take her up the coast on the Istanbul side, land on any bit of isolated coast we can find and then set off on a forced march. I reckon it'll take us two days – with a bit of luck – to reach the Greek frontier. We march at night, lie up by day.'

Dickie whistled softly. 'Chancey. The place will be swarming with Turkish troops.'

'A chance we'll have to take. Desperate times require desperate measures. Besides I have an idea which might just well take off the pressure – at least for a day.'

'Go on,' Dickie leaned forward, face full of interest.

'They're expecting the *Swordfish* to approach the Narrows. Perhaps they've already cottoned on where we are supposed to rendezvous with that rogue Abdul the Terrible.' He shrugged. 'I don't know. What I do know is that *Swordfish* will turn up as expected. But without us.'

'You mean you'd set a course and lash the wheels so that the old dear keeps approximately on that course?'

'Exactly, Dickie.'

'But what happens when they discover she's a second *Marie Celeste* with no crew aboard? They'll see the birds have flown the coop and start searching for us at once. That won't give us the day you suggested we might gain.'

Smith smiled at him, and Dickie snorted, 'For God's sake, Smithie, don't look so smug and superior. Spit it out. What have you got up your sleeve?'

'Just that they'll see the old *Swordfish*, but just as they are preparing to board her, she'll be gone for good and they'll never know we weren't aboard. Indeed I half fancy they'll think we've gone to the bottom of the sea right into Davy Jones' locker – and that would be exceedingly good.'

Dickie looked at his old friend completely mystified now. 'But how ... how are you going to do that, old chap?'

But Smith had no time to explain now. 'Later, Dickie ... later, Dickie. All will be explained.' He turned to Ferguson who had been listening with one ear, his craggy face as puzzled as that of Dickie Bird's. 'Full speed ahead, Chiefie ... step on the horses now... We've got no time to waste.'

CPO Ferguson thrust home both throttles to their full extent, telling himself he'd always known officers and gentlemen were mad. But he hadn't realized till now just how barmy they were. Thus the *Swordfish* shot forward in the growing darkness, heading for the last voyage of her long career...

9

'*The searchlight ... quick, the searchlight!*' the hook-nosed officer snapped urgently, as the deep, steady chug-chug of a powerful motorboat came ever closer in the darkness. 'It has to be them!'

Behind him in the gun turret, the already alerted gunners swung their twin cannon round to meet the intruders.

The searchlight snapped on with dramatic suddenness. The brilliant white glare started to comb the darkness, swinging from left to right across the cove, while the hook-nosed Turkish officer peered along the beam, eager to catch the first glimpse of the English pigs; for he knew instinctively it had to be them. Who else would be abroad at this time of night; and Turkish fishermen did not possess boats powered by engines as powerful as those.

'There she is, *Effendi!*' the searchlight operator said excitedly. 'Bearing red three o!' The searchlight stopped its movement, flickering only slightly to left and right, as the operator struggled to keep his beam on the little craft.

The hook-nosed officer caught his breath.

It was the English all right. There was no mistaking that cursed white ensign of the English Navy fluttering proudly at the craft's stern. It was a deliberate, provocative challenge, as if the English pigs didn't care that they were sailing in Turkish waters, risking sudden death. He cursed and turned to the young midshipman next to him. 'All right,' he snapped, 'show what you learned at that American college of yours in Istanbul. Challenge them. Tell them to heave to!'

Nervously the boy picked up the megaphone, his throat suddenly dry and hoarse. 'This is the Turkish Navy,' he said through it. 'You are ordered to heave to at once. Otherwise we shall be forced to fire upon you. Do you hear? *Heave to!*'

There was no reaction. The English ploughed on through the still water, heading straight for the caique. It was as if they had not yet seen the Turkish destroyer waiting for them.

'Allah's curse upon them,' the hook-nosed officer shouted angrily. 'I know all the English are mad. But are they deaf as well? Challenge them again. Tell them we shall not hesitate to fire if they don't obey.'

The midshipman looked worried. There was something very strange about the English ship. He could see no one on the deck and the bright beam of the searchlight showed no one on the bridge. Was this some kind of ghost ship? What was going on?

'Hurry up, son of a camel,' the officer broke into his frightened reverie. 'Don't take all night. Tell them to heave to.'

Hurriedly the midshipman repeated the hook-nosed officer's order to the megaphone.

It had no effect. The long, lean vessel continued to sail on, though by now it was obvious that her crew must have seen the big destroyer lying in wait for her.

'What is it, sir?' The midshipman asked. 'I can't understand. I—'

The rest of his frightened question was drowned by a tremendous explosion, followed by a blinding flash of scarlet light. The English craft disintegrated before their eyes, as they shielded their faces against the glare and blast, opening their mouths instinctively to prevent their eardrums being burst by the great roar.

The hook-nosed officer staggered back, as shocked as the rest by this sudden mass suicide by the English, who had obviously seen that they had been tricked into a trap. But he recovered faster than his fellow officers who continued to stare open-mouthed like dumb peasants at the spot where the English craft had just been and where the surface of the heaving sea was littered with pathetic bits and pieces of wreckage.

The English were generally brave, he knew that from the last war. But they were not as brave as a Turkish officer who would sooner commit suicide than surrender. The English milords, he thought a little contemptuously, his brain racing electrically, thought too much of their precious hides for that.

Suddenly he made up his mind. 'Get a boat away immediately,' he ordered, breaking the stunned silence on the deck all around him. 'I want survivors picked up – immediately. Come on now, hurry it up!'

'But what is it, *Effendi*?' the nervous midshipman asked. 'There can be no survivors from that explosion–'

'Don't ask fool questions, boy,' the hook-nosed officer interrupted angrily. 'Get in the boat with a crew and see what you can find, even if it is only one of the pig's legs.' Then he crossed his arms across his chest and waited, his mind full of doubts and suspicions...

Abdul the Terrible, still damp, but unharmed, though very hungry, heard that tremendous explosion some two miles away and knew immediately that it had not been caused by gunfire. It was the English boat, he realized that instinctively, just about where it should have rendezvoused with his ciaque. But if the explosion had not been caused by gunfire, what had caused it?

Suddenly his broad battered dark face lit

up. 'Holy mackerel!' he exclaimed happily, 'I get it. Them limeys sure do wrestle smart. That's why they own a third of the world.' He spat into the bushes which had formed his hiding place till darkness and then stared at the star-patched velvet sky.

Abdul the Terrible was totally illiterate, but he knew his stars. Quickly he found the Plough and then the North Star, a plan already forming in his mind. He had already guessed the trick the limeys had pulled on his former captors. Now there was only one thing they could do if they were going to escape the trap. He'd find them and help them. 'Brother,' he exclaimed in sudden enthusiasm, 'Uncle Sam here I come!' A moment later he set off striding through the darkness heading north...

The little party, well strung out, revolvers and rifles at the ready, with the wounded Billy Bennett safely tucked away in the middle, was also heading north now, as fast as their legs could take them. It was half an hour ago now since they had heard the great explosion and seen the horizon to their rear flash a brilliant scarlet for a brief second. No one had said a word. But they all knew what that explosion meant. The old *Swordfish* had met her end at last after all those years when she had come through battle after battle. It was only five minutes later when Chiefie Ferguson broke the silence with a gruff, 'Ay, well yon was a fine old tub,' that her final epitaph was uttered.

Now they concentrated on covering as many miles as possible before first light when they would go into hiding. In the lead, Smith, a glowing compass strapped to his wrist, set a cracking pace, so much so that Ginger groaned, 'Cor ferk a duck, a matelot's plates o' meat ain't meant for all this sodding hiking,' to which Chiefie Ferguson replied, 'Hold ye wish man. You no made o' sugar!'

But by the end of the second hour of marching across that barren plain, with no sign of habitation or life so that they might well have been the last men alive on the planet, even tough old CPO Ferguson was too weary to speak.

At three that morning, Smith ordered a rest. The men were too tired even to take a sip of their waterbottles, although Smith had just allowed them to do so. Instead they slumped against the stunted olive trees which were their hiding place like dead men, the only sign that they were still alive, their heaving chests.

Smith allowed himself a sip of the tepid water (he was observing strict water discipline for he didn't want them to be trapped looking for water near one of the villages) and said to Dickie, 'Well, we've done well so far. My guess is we'll start coming to the Turkish Army positions just after dawn. If we can lie up behind them for the day, taking a gander at the set-up, we'll be in a good position to tackle them tomorrow night.'

'Suppose so,' Dickie answered without too much enthusiasm; he was too weary. 'How many miles do you think we'll have to cover before dawn, Smithie?'

'At least ten.'

'Oh, my sainted aunt! Ten miles in – say – two and a half hours. Have a heart, old bean.'

'There's no other way,' Smith said firmly, thin, drawn unshaven face set and very intent. 'Old Johnny Turk is no fool. Sooner or later they'll discover the trick we played upon them. As soon as it's light they'll examine the wreckage, what's left of the poor old *Swordfish*.' There was a sudden crack in his voice momentarily as he mentioned their old ship. 'And they'll find no corpses. Then they'll tumble to the fact we've pulled a fast one on them, tying down the wheel on a course which would take the boat to them, a time-fuse on the high explosive next to the torpedoes, the whole thing. Then they'll realize we're still alive and they'll come looking for us.'

'I suppose you're right,' Dickie agreed. 'But my dear fellow, do hold your horses again when we set off. My feet are damned worn down to my kneecaps, I swear.'

But Smith could not afford to waste time by 'holding horses'. Time, precious time, was slipping away too quickly. The air was already becoming warmer, a sure sign that dawn was on its way, and he could see in the distance faint puffs of smoke, a lighter grey against the purple darkness which could indicate human habitations or activities. Time and time again, he urged his men to keep on going. Seemingly tireless himself, he rounded up stragglers, carrying their rifles for them, giving them sips from his own waterbottle when theirs was empty, chivving, bullying, threatening, cajoling, he had to keep them going. He knew that.

About five with the stars vanished and the sky beginning to turn the dirty white of a false dawn, he spotted a group of ruined buildings to his left, perhaps a mile away. Behind it there was a fairly steep cliff face which he knew his exhausted men would be unable to tackle in their present state; and from beyond the cliff there came the streaks of smoke that meant people and probably danger.

Cautiously, leaving the men to rest on the stony ground, he and CPO Ferguson, revolvers clutched in their hands, approached the cluster of ruins, huddled around a wrecked little church. Obviously it had been one of the Greek Orthodox villages on the Turkish side which had been shelled and virtually destroyed during the winter's fighting. There were bullet holes and shell scars everywhere on the battered walls and the timbers were broken and charred, as if what had been left of the hamlet had been set on fire after it had been captured.

'You take the left flank... I'll take the right,' Smith whispered to the old CPO. 'Be careful. We want no trouble. There's somebody over the side of that cliff.'

Silently Ferguson nodded his understanding and they parted. Crouched, revolver held tightly in his hand, Smith crept forward into the ruins which still smelled of soot and ash. He assumed that because of it that the area had only recently been cleared of Greek troops. That heartened him. They were closer to the Greek border than he had thought. All the same, that meant the smoke they had seen might well mark the positions of the frontline Turkish troops.

He crossed the littered cobbles of a tiny alley and came up to the place's church: a small structure, which had once been painted white, with its domed roof holed by shells, and the cross which had once adorned it lying shattered on the cobbles. Everywhere on the walls, the red crescent had been adorned and there were crude caricatures of men in Turkish fezes killing men in the skirts of the Greek *evizones*. He stopped and looked at the door of the church.

It had been smashed open and hung creaking now from rusty hinges. He had a strange feeling of apprehension suddenly. The small hairs at the back of his head stood erect. A cold finger of fear traced its way slowly down his spine. Mingled with the dead smell of soot and ashes, there was a fresher one: the sweet, cloying odour of Turkish – or Greek – tobacco. *There was someone inside the abandoned church!*

He clicked off the safety on his revolver. His heart beating furiously he entered on tiptoe, weapon at the ready.

A solitary candle, probably stolen from the nearby churchyard, flickered on top of an empty wine bottle, casting an enormous shadow on the wall opposite. It was huge, virtually filling the whole wall, wavering and trembling in the flickering light of the candle stump.

Smith swung round, ready for action, knuckle white as he clutched the trigger of his revolver. Then he gasped. Standing up to greet him, a tremendous smile on his broad face, gold teeth glinting in the light was no other than Abdul the Terrible. 'What the devil–' he began.

But Abdul beat him to it, crushing Smith's

hand in his own enormous one, he chortled, 'I have been waiting for you, Limey gentleman...'

10

'Sorry, Limey gent,' Abdul the Terrible said regretfully, whipping the sweat off his ugly face, 'we can't get through there.' He stared at the crew of the *Swordfish*, gradually waking up in the dark, cool interior of the ruined church.

'Why? What's the problem?' Smith asked, running his fingers through his sleep-tousled hair. It was early afternoon now and most of them had slept away their exhaustion of the night before.

'Horse soldiers. Turks have got a lotta horse soldiers out there. I guess they're patrolling the frontier.' He stepped forward a pace and drew a line in the dust on the floor of the church with the toe of his boot. 'Here's the flat ground, leading to the frontier.' He drew rough X's at each end of the line. 'Here – and here – the Turks have their camps. In between they patrol regularly with their horse soldiers. Don't think you'd get through there – even at night.'

Smith cursed softly to himself. He knew the men were only fit enough to make one more effort this night. They were in no state for any further long marches. Besides, he reasoned, the Turks would be starting their search for the missing Englishmen this day. It was tonight or never. He spoke. 'What's beyond there?' He indicated the right 'X'. 'Is that stretch of the frontier patrolled by their cavalry?'

Abdul the Terrible squatted on his haunches in the Turkish fashion and shook his head. 'Doubt it. Well, not by their horse soldiers. It's too rugged. Just like the cliff behind us. Hills and forests.' He shrugged his massive shoulders. 'Perhaps they have a few guys on foot up there. No more.' He looked at Smith.

Smith took his time. Earlier he had gone outside to urinate and while he had done so he had stared at the cliff in the moonlight. It had seemed a formidable obstacle. The start was easy enough: a low incline, well covered in stunted pine and camel thorn. But further on, glistening in the cold spectral light of the moon the face had appeared almost sheer. Beyond he could see the woods which, as Abdul the Terrible now explained, stretched to the Greek frontier. They would be ideal cover, but first they would have to get up that steep incline.

He broke his silence with, 'What do you

think of our chances, Abdul, of clearing that forest in one night and reaching the Greek lines?'

'Boss, that could be done. The guys would have to move it though.' Abdul sucked his thick lips, as if thinking hard. 'But first you'd have to get up that mountain.' He indicated the cliff with a jerk of his thumb over his shoulder.

'Heights jolly well make me dizzy,' Dickie said out of the blue.

Smith ignored him. Instead he said quietly and apparently confidently, 'I think it could be done, if we gave ourselves enough time.'

Abdul shrugged in a non-committal fashion. 'Don't know, boss. But we can try. I'd help.'

Smith smiled suddenly. 'With your strength, Abdul, I should think you could carry the lot of us up to the top without even losing breath. All right, you chaps, pay attention now. This is what we are going to do...'

Night was beginning to fall. Dark shadows were racing across the plains where the Turkish cavalry were. A faint wind was blowing and with it it brought snatches of talk, the clatter of equipment and once the high-pitched tone of a mullah calling to prayer, though officially Kemal Ataturk had banned religion in Turkey.

Smith looked around at the faces of his

309

men in the growing darkness. They looked rested and resolute. All of them had shaved in the water they had found in an abandoned well, while Abdul the Terrible had stared at them incredulously, muttering to himself in Turkish, and all of them had cleaned their weapons. Now they were in their allotted positions. In the lead was Ferguson. In his youth in his native Highlands he had climbed a lot. He would lead the way. Bennett was again in the centre together with Dickie, who was, it turned out, genuinely afraid of heights. In the rear came Smith and Abdul, who would help any stragglers or those in difficulties.

'All right, chaps,' Smith said softly, feeling a genuine affection for these men who had followed him so loyally and for so long and whose lives depended upon him. 'We're going to do it this night. At dawn you'll be drinking Greek coffee, I'll be bound and be sleeping in warm snug Greek beds–'

'Ay, with warm snug Greek tarts no doubt,' Ginger interrupted him cheekily.

Ferguson shot the Liverpudlian a menacing glance, but Smith said cheerfully, 'And that, too, if you can find one. But remember this,' his voice hardened now, 'we've got to do it *this* night. We won't get a second chance. So you'll have to pull out all the stops, make one last effort. Got it, chaps?'

There was a murmur of assent and Smith

said, 'All right McDuff, lead on.'

Ferguson mumbled something under his breath, then he commenced the climb, with the others strung out at one yard intervals behind him, each man wrapped in a cocoon of his thoughts and fears.

At first it was relatively easy. It was steep enough but there were plenty of scrub bushes and the like to hang on to and Ferguson, proving he had not lost the skills of his youth, was adept in finding the easiest bits for them.

They cleared the first stretch in little more than a quarter of an hour and Smith allowed his panting men a little rest while Ferguson surveyed the rock wall above them, muttering to himself as he tried to work out the best route. After a few minutes' study, he turned to Smith and said, 'I mind the best way is to stick to the scrub, sir. Yon's camel thorn and it'll tear the hands off ye, but at least it'll give us some sort o' hold.'

Smith nodded his agreement, his ears suddenly becoming aware of the soft silver jingle of horse's harness. Instinctively he reacted with 'Down everybody! Not a word!'

They crouched on the ledge just as the first of the riders came round the bend in the track that led to the ruined hamlet, his blazing torch held aloft and flickering in the slight breeze, progressively magnifying and diminishing his shadow on the rock face.

'Turkish cavalry,' Smith hissed, 'and I bet they're looking for us.'

Hardly daring to breathe, the men of the *Swordfish* watched as more and more of the riders appeared to dismount at the edge of the hamlet. With a torch in one hand and a drawn sabre in the other they started to comb the place systematically, looking obviously for the fugitives.

Smith said a silent prayer of gratitude. He had made his men clean up the evidence of their presence in the ruined church before they had left. He personally had filed out last, covering their footprints with dust so there would be no trace that they had ever been there. Now he waited tensely to see whether the searchers would find anything.

The Turkish cavalry took their time, while their officer still seated on his mount smoked, his cigarette a red glow in the growing darkness. But finally they backed off from the shattered cottages and a soldier on foot, perhaps an NCO, reported something to the mounted officer. 'He say nothing,' Abdul the Terrible whispered into Smith's ear. 'They go now,' he translated, as the officer tossed away his glowing cigarette and gave an order.

The riders re-mounted. Another order was given. They formed up in a column and trotted away, still bearing their lighted torches, obviously intent on searching elsewhere.

Smith waited until they had disappeared around the bend in the trail before saying, 'Well, chaps, it looks as if they are on to us. But we've been lucky and,' he forced a note of confidence into his voice, though inwardly he was very worried, 'we are going to stay lucky. All right, off we go! Chiefie, lead on.'

The next hour was hell, sheer hell. With their knees dug into the almost sheer wall, searching feverishly for handholds, their faces ripped and torn by the cruel thorns, they fought their way ever upwards. More than once, men slipped and were caught in a slither of rubble just before they went down for good. Once Smith, losing his grip, grabbed desperately for a hold, the harsh rock ripping away his nails cruelly, sending an electric wave of sheer agony coursing through his body.

All of them were hard men, toughened by the harsh training of the pre-war sailing rigs and the long years of the Great War, but none of them had ever experienced such sheer torture as this. By now their faces were glazed with sweat. Their breath came in great sobs. The strain on their arm and leg muscles was almost unbearable; it was as if someone was thrusting red-hot pokers into them. Still they pressed on, each one of them knowing that this was their last chance.

Even Abdul, that giant, was feeling the strain now. The climb had opened the wounds on the soles of his feet. Now as he moved, he could feel the warm sticky blood slosh around in his boots and his bottom lip was ragged and bloody where he had bitten it in his efforts to stifle his cries of pain.

In the middle of the team, Dickie, feeling sick and faint, the sour bile constantly welling up in his throat, willed himself not to look down. If he did, he knew, with the certainty of a vision that he would loose hold and plunge straight to his death. He fought on.

The minutes passed in leaden agony. Peering upwards, Smith thought the cliff seemed to go on for ever. Was there no damned end to it? Now the tips of his fingers hurt so badly that he had to make a conscious effort of willpower to thrust them into the next handhold. He was sick with pain. But he knew he could not let up. *'There's no other way,'* the harsh little voice at the back of his mind commanded brutally. *'Don't be soft. Keep on, man!'*

Then, when it seemed there would be no end to this murderous torture, Ferguson's soft whisper came running down the column, 'Almost there... Just a little chimney ... perhaps thirty feet at the most ... pass it on...'

'*Chimney?*' Abdul queried puzzled. 'What is this chimney? There is no house here.'

For a moment Smith, his chest heaving frantically, was too numb with fatigue to answer. Then he made an effort, trying to control his breathing and failing badly. 'A hole in the rock,' he gasped. 'Climbers put ... their back on one side ... their feet on the other ... work their way up ... bit by bit like that...' He choked and could say no more.

Inwardly Abdul groaned. His feet seemed to be on fire. He had never felt so much pain, even in the worse of his bouts. Aloud, however, he said, 'Let's get to this chimney. Get it damn well over with.'

Ferguson had never tackled a chimney personally. 'I'm a climber, no bluidy mountaineer,' he had once snorted in his youth, when one of those fancy young climbers from Edinburgh University had offered the sturdy youth the chance of one. 'I'm a ragged-arsed wean whose mother'd skin him alive if she kenned how he was ruining his best boots.' But he did know the technique.

Now he levered himself into the narrow chimney. He crawled up a foot or two, thrust his shoulders against the hard surface of the rock and then did the same with his feet. He grunted and using his feet as a support, levered himself up another foot or so, feeling the cold rock tear at his jacket and the skin below. He gritted his false teeth and tried to take no notice. Grimly, doggedly he started to work his way up the fissure, telling himself as he did so that the others would not be able to do this. Once he had reached the top he would have to find some way of lifting them up. Billy Bennett's shoulder wound wouldn't stand the strain and he didn't think Mr Bird capable of doing it either. But for the time being he concentrated on the task on hand.

Five minutes later, bruised and aching all over, he had made it crawling out of the chimney to collapse for a moment on the cropped grass of the summit, his lungs creaking like a cracked leathern bellows. But the old Scot knew there was no time to lose. Every minute was precious if they were going to get across the border this night.

He pulled himself together and leaning over the mouth of the chimney, he called down to Ginger who was going to make the next attempt. 'Get a belt from every man below, including the officers.'

'*What?*'

'You heard. And get a move on!'

Five minutes later, panting just as furiously as the much older man Ginger reached the top, a good dozen stout leather naval belts tied over his shoulder. 'Hey you are Chiefie, haven't trouble with yer trousers or–'

'Shut yer blether,' Ferguson interrupted him fiercely, 'give me a hand to tie those yon things together.'

Half an hour later they were on their way again, each man having been hauled up the chimney by the improvised rope made of the belts (though they had almost despaired of ever hauling Abdul to the top. In the end it had taken the combined efforts of half a dozen men to do so.) Again Smith took the lead with his compass, heading straight for the trees, which would be their cover, and praying desperately that they had seen the end of the Turks.

11

About three that morning, the heat of the previous day started to give way to sudden cold. With the cold, as the two fronts met, fog began to drift in. At first it was a gentle milky white mist, trickling in and out of the trees like soft-footed cats. But as time passed, the white mist became a solid wall of fog. By 3.30 visibility was down to perhaps ten yards.

The fog was received with mixed feelings.

They knew it provided them with excellent cover. All the same, the escapers told themselves, as they plodded ever further to the west, it slowed their pace and, as Dickie Bird expressed it, 'In a peasouper like this, the whole of Johnny Turk's army might be out there and you wouldn't damn well see.' To which Smith nodded his agreement, but said nothing. He was too busy concentrating on the green glowing needle of the compass strapped to his wrist. For now the stars had vanished, he had to rely totally on the little magnetic compass.

By four he judged they were well past the positions of the Turkish cavalry down below in the valley. Soon they would reach the frontier and he wondered what kind of controls the Turks – and the Greeks for that matter – maintained along the frontier. The countries were still at war so he guessed the frontier would be guarded by soldiers and not customs officials. But were they in dug-in positions, something like the continuous trenchline of the last show? Or did the two sides have isolated posts, especially in this rugged mountainous area? He decided he would take no chances, just in case they bumped into a Turkish post. He whispered, 'Pass it down the line, Dickie. Send up Abdul the Terrible.' In case they did blunder into the Turks in this fog, it would be useful to have the Turkish-speaking ex-wrestler up front. They might just be able to bluff their way through.

Another hour passed. Now even in the heights they started to stumble into traces of the recent fighting. Here and there the forest trails were blocked with hurdles, rusting barbed wire stretched between them. There were trenches, too, some of them still containing damp bundles of rags which had once been men. Once in the middle of a trail they came across the decomposed body of a man in what appeared to be a skirt. He had been staked out by his arms and legs and hideously mutilated. They averted their eyes as they filed by the corpse in the fog, all save Abdul who said grimly, 'Turks are a cruel people.' But they didn't need to be told that.

At four, Smith allowed them a ten-minute break. Crouched in an abandoned trench, fortunately empty of rotting corpses, they slumped against the earth wall, as Smith briefed them in a low voice. 'It is my guess, chaps, that we're in a mile or two of the frontier by now. So far we have been lucky. But we could bump into either the Turks – or the Greeks. And you know the brown jobs – they're always so damned quick on the draw.'

The men laughed softly at his mention of the 'brown jobs', or soldiers.

'In either case, we've got to act first. It's

either bluff 'em or,' – his voice hardened, *'shoot 'em!'*

The men's laughter died. Again they realized the danger of their position, with seemingly every man's hand against them.

'All right then,' he continued, 'click off the safety on your weapons. We've got about two hours before dawn. By first light we want to be through. On your feet then. Here we go.'

Dickie Bird clapped his old friend on the shoulder encouragingly. 'We'll do it, old bean,' he said with strained cheerfulness. 'A couple of weeks' time we'll be strolling down Shaftesbury Ave, full of champers and kippers, pocket full of filthy lucre, out on the old razzle.'

'Of course, of course,' Smith knew that Dickie was only trying to cheer him up. He forced a smile. 'And I'll buy the first bottle of bubbly. Now off we go!'

They were working their way through a wood of fog-shrouded mountain pine, the cold damp air heavy with the scent of pine. But unconsciously Smith's nostrils were also picking up a less charming fragrance. For a few moments, tired and numb as he was from their long march across the heights, he couldn't identify the smell. Then he had it. It was the odour of unwashed bodies and that sweet-smelling stink of the Oriental tobacco which both Greeks and

Turks smoked. In the very instant that he raised his hand to stay the others behind him, Abdul grunted, 'Somebody there!'

They stopped dead. Suddenly they were very wide-awake, hearts beating furiously, alert to every sensation. Smith, for his part began to sweat despite the cold. He knew why. It was the prospect of violent action.

There were horses up there, too, tethered somewhere in the fog. The sailors couldn't see them, but the horses obviously sensed the presence of strangers. For now they were fretting, jerking at their hobbles, making low, nervous whinnying sounds.

Smith bit his bottom lip. He narrowed his eyes to slits and tried to penetrate the rolling white fog. Where the devil were they? Who were – Turk or Greek?

'Well, Smithie, there's only one way to find out,' Dickie Bird whispered, breaking the sudden tension, stating the other officer's thoughts aloud. 'We'll have to go and have a look-see.'

'Exactly.' Smith turned to the old Scot. 'Chiefie, you take charge here. Abdul and you, Dickie, come with me. And not a sound.' He drew his revolver. 'Come on.'

Like three silent ghosts the two officers and the giant Turk slipped through the wet, swirling fog, any sound they might have made drowned by the mist. The smell of the Oriental tobacco grew ever stronger. The horses, too, continued to make their nervous pawing noises.

'To the left,' Dickie hissed urgently. 'A fire.'

'Got it!' Now Smith could see the flickering faint pink flame of a fire, glimpsed every now and again through the fog. Around it he could also spot the dark shapes of soldiers, warming their hands against the flames.

'Turks,' Abdul whispered. 'And look there are more of them over there.' He pointed to the right. 'This is their line. This is the frontier.'

'You're right,' Smith agreed and the three of them crouched down on their haunches and studied what they could see of the Turkish positions through the grey swirling banks of fog.

The Turks were in a fairly continuous line, with about fifteen yards between each position, all of them marked by the burning fires. The soldiers on duty weren't patrolling, but grouped round the blazes trying to keep warm; while their off-duty comrades were presumably sleeping in the little tents grouped around the fires.

'Sloppy farmers, the Turks,' Abdul commented softly. 'Farmboys. No idea about discipline. But awake. They knew the punishment if they were caught sleeping.'

Smith nodded, wondering whether they

could manage to slip through between the various positions without being spotted. After a few moments he decided it wouldn't be possible. Somebody would surely wander off to get more wood or to have a leak and spot them. Then all hell would be let loose.

'Out flank them?' Dickie suggested, as if reading Smith's thoughts.

'Where?' he asked softly.

'Up there – to the right. On that hill or whatever it is – can't see it clearly enough in this damned pea-souper. But I can't see a fire burning up there. I'm guessing they don't have an outpost on it.'

Smith considered for a moment, feeling his bones becoming ever more chilled by the wet penetrating mist. Finally he said, 'There's no other way. Let's try it. Gosh Almighty – anything to get the blood circulating again!'

It was another terrible climb, not because the ascent was steep, but because the hillside was covered in camel thorn. For six yards or so they had to crawl on their hands and knees through the stuff, the cruel barbs pricking at their flesh and clothes. Once Smith's trousers were caught on the barbs and he worked himself into a lather in his attempts to free himself. For time was running out rapidly. As he struggled desperately he could feel the temperature beginning to rise and the mist starting to disperse. The sun would be up soon. The fog would disappear altogether and they would be completely exposed right in the middle of the Turkish front line positions. They had to reach the top *soon!*

Ten minutes later they had done it, sweating, cursing under their breath, all of them ragged and bleeding from a myriad of tiny wounds. But their ordeal wasn't over yet. They had begun to hobble over the uneven plateau at the top of the hill, with the fog vanishing rapidly now, when Abdul the Terrible thrust out his huge arms and hissed urgently, *'Stop!'*

'What's up?' Dickie asked, blundering to a stop.

'Look!' Abdul answered, pointing to a rusty length of barbed wire to their front. On it hung a sign in Turkish which Dickie couldn't read, but he understood the significance of the black skull-and-crossbones beneath the ancient Turkish calligraphy. 'Oh, my sainted aunt,' he exclaimed in utter dismay, 'mines!'

'What did you say?' Smith called.

'Mines!' Dickie repeated his dread warning.

Smith bit his lip. 'Damn,' he cursed. 'That, too.' He flung a wild angry look to left and right. There was no obvious track which might be safe. No wonder the Turks kept no outpost up here. They had simply mined the whole area. His brain raced. Then he came up with his idea. 'Chiefie,' he snapped, 'cut a branch from that tree. At the double now!'

'Ay, ay, sir,' the old Scot answered and sped away to the rear to carry out the order. Hastily he began hacking at a fair-sized branch while Smith fumbled in his pocket for his own knife and the length of twine he always kept handy: a sailor's old habit which he had picked up as a young cadet.

Moments later a panting Ferguson was back with a branch, fairly straight and about six foot in length.

Smith seized it from him. The mist had virtually disappeared now and the sky was already beginning to flush with the first signs of dawn. With fingers that felt like clumsy sausages, panting as if he had just run a race, Smith bound the blade of his knife to the branch with the twine. 'All right,' he announced, the job completed, 'everyone follow me, each man putting a hand on the chap in front's waist. Like a school crocodile.'

Ginger put his hand on Bennett's ample waist and cooed in what he supposed to be a female falsetto, 'Do you love me, Billy darling?'

'Stop that,' Smith snapped. 'No time for fooling now. We've only got minutes left before the sun comes up.' He turned and started forward, followed by his awkward crocodile of limping men. He passed the sign. His eyes intent on the ground, he took a step forward and prodded the damp turf to his front, to his left and then to his right. Nothing! He moved on. Again he stopped and repeated the process. Again nothing.

The fog had gone now. The horizon was beginning to flush red. It was going to be another hot day. Down in the valley he could hear the musseen calling the soldiers to pray. The Turks were beginning to stir. Desperately the absurd-looking group of sailors, with their awkward waddle, pushed on.

They were halfway across when it happened. Suddenly there was the harsh rasping grating of metal striking metal which Smith had feared all along. *'Mine!'* he exclaimed.

They stopped as one.

Smith released himself from Dickie's grip. 'Turn your heads to one side!' he commanded.

He waited until they had done so, hoping that in this manner he'd take the full blast of the mine, if he failed to lift it, and they would be saved. He could already see the headline in the 'Old Thunderer' now. *'Common Smith, V.C. Gives His Life To Save His Crew!'* He swallowed hard. It was a nasty thought.

He knew it was no use attempting to find

a way around the damned thing. The Turks had laid a line of them here. That was obvious. There'd be others to left and right. He bent. Cautiously he started to scrape away the damp earth with his hands. Two deadly little prongs were revealed. He felt the sweat begin to trickle unpleasantly down the small of his back.

With an effort of sheer naked willpower, he forced himself to continue. He knew that if he merely brushed against the two prongs while the mine was still armed, it would blow his face off. But the job had to be done. Hardly daring to breathe, he found the detonator cap. With hands that trembled, he tried to turn it. But the damned thing wouldn't move!

He almost panicked. He forced himself to be calm. Shaking his head to knock away the beads of sweat which were running down into his eyes, he grunted, exerted all his strength and tried once more. This time the rusty cap turned. He breathed a sigh of relief. He started to unscrew the cap.

From below there came the sound of horses' hooves. Not looking, Smith told himself it was a Turkish cavalry patrol. Ferguson confirmed it a second later, 'Turks coming this way, sir,' he hissed urgently.

Smith nodded, but had no time to look. Now he had got the cap off. Using his two front fingers like a pair of pincers, he inserted them into the well of the mine. Gingerly, knowing that the devilish thing was still armed and very deadly, until he had completed the task, he started to draw the detonator out slowly.

From below someone shouted in a voice which was hoarse and angry.

'They've seen us. They ask who we are,' Abdul cried.

With a last gasp, Smith pulled out the detonator and flung it to his right. It hit another mine. The mine went up in a blast of angry red, splattering them with clods of earth and pebbles. From below came the first angry stutter of a machine gun.

Smith waited no longer. *'Run for it, chaps!'* he yelled. *'After me. RUN!'*

All exhaustion vanished, they ran for their lives, as if the Devil himself were after them...

ENVOI

Merrily the ship's band played a selection from Ivor Novello's latest show. American tourists in bright tweed knickerbockers and dark glasses threw streamers at the dock. Porters and stewards cursed and puffed red-faced, as they lugged heavy ship's trunks below. Pursers pushed their way through the excited, shouting throng, engrossed in their checkboards. Elderly women were crying and dabbing their eyes with their hand-kerchiefs, then laughing merrily the next moment. All was busy, self-important happiness and excitement as the tugs attached their lines to the great liner to tow her out into the Thames where she would begin her long voyage to New York.

The liner's siren blew three shrill blasts. Stewards with gongs began hurrying through the throng, beating their gongs and crying above the racket, *'All aboard who's going aboard!'* Digging in their heels, the cloth-capped dockers took the weight of the gangplanks as they were detached from the ship. On the upper deck the brass band ceased Ivor Novello and began to play *'Auld Lang Syne'*. Slowly the great liner headed into the current.

On the third class deck, clutching his

precious bottle of whisky 'made by them limeys in skirts' and dressed in a bright red suit from Burton's 'the thirty shillings tailors', Abdul the Terrible cried. 'Goodbye Limey gents. Thanks. I had a swell time in London... I'll write when I learn to.' He grinned and showed that mouthful of gold teeth of which he was so proud. 'And don't take no wooden nickels.'

Smith and Dickie Bird grinned, though they had not the slightest idea what the huge Turkish wrestler meant. C had pulled out all the stops for the three of them during their stay in the capital. For Abdul it had been mountains of beef, washed down with gallons of whisky, a new suit, money, and most important, that faked American passport which Sammy had promised him in Alex. For them it had been night clubs, willing young flappers who had shed their inhibitions with their corsets, and 'beaucoup bubbly', as Dickie had expressed it.

Now hollow-eyed and a little wan, they waved as the great liner drew ever closer to the middle of the river and the crowd on deck started to wander below in search of new pleasure and excitement. Next to them C, dressed as an admiral today, clicked to attention. They could hear the joints of his wooden leg quite clearly. He raised his hand to his cap in salute and said out of the side of his mouth. 'Some of those Johnny Turk fellahs are not so bad after all. Perhaps we can use your Abdul fellah one of these days, you never know.'

He dismissed the wrestler who was still waving frantically from the liner, as the music stopped and the ship's siren howled indicating that the tugs should cast off; the pilot would take over now. C turned and with the two of them started limping back to the waiting Rolls Royce, his face set and thoughtful.

He ushered them inside and announced completely out of the blue. '*Swordfish Two* is already under construction just up the road from here.'

'*What?*' they exclaimed as one, faces suddenly excited.

C said the words again, pleased with their excited enthusiasm. He told himself it was young chaps like these who made the Empire what it was. 'You see I've got another show for you,' he went on.

'*A show?*'

'Yes – and I wish you wouldn't repeat everything I say like a double echo. Yes, a show. I don't suppose you have ever heard of a German called Hitler?… No, I thought not. Well, this is the story…'

The publishers hope that this book has given you enjoyable reading. Large Print Books are especially designed to be as easy to see and hold as possible. If you wish a complete list of our books please ask at your local library or write directly to:

Magna Large Print Books
Magna House, Long Preston,
Skipton, North Yorkshire.
BD23 4ND

This Large Print Book, for people
who cannot read normal print,
is published under the auspices of

THE ULVERSCROFT FOUNDATION

L.